BLOW THE MAN DOWN
Pirates of New Earth
Book 4

SARAH BRANSON

SOONER STARTED PRESS

Praise for Blow the Man Down

"*Blow the Man Down* caps Sarah Branson's wonderful, exciting *Pirates of New Earth* series perfectly. The deeply dimensioned characters leap off the page, the action is nonstop, and the thrilling ending more than satisfies. A real crowd-pleaser. I'm sorry the series had to end!"

— Andrea Vanryken, author and editor

"Don't mess with Kat Wallace! *Blow the Man Down* is the thrilling fourth installment in the *Pirates of New Earth* series. This action-packed novel will keep you on the edge of your seat with suspense and adventure as Kat strikes back when her family is threatened. Branson's writing is engaging and concise, making *Blow the Man Down* a fast and captivating read. You won't be able to put this book down until the very last page. It is a must-read for fans of action, adventure, and romance."

— Brittany Coffman, Kat aficionado and midwife, Aglow Midwifery

"Sweet New Earth—the Pirates series culminates in spectacular fashion! Rob Abernathy is one of the most hateable villains in modern literature, and now he seeks the flesh of Kat's precious loved ones. Even if you're a peace-loving pacifist, you will pray for Abernathy to suffer ultimate pain when…or if…Kat gets her vengeful hands on him. This story is more riveting than anything you can watch on Netflix tonight."

— David Aretha, award-winning author

"Kat Wallace has come a long way since the day she climbed as a stowaway into Teddy Bosch's vessel. But the shadow of her past is always looming. Strap yourself in for a rip-roaring, riveting ride through New Earth as Kat, Matty and the Bosch Pirate Force charge through the skies with vengeance in their hearts."

— Sally Altass, The Indie Book Nook and author of *The Witch Laws*

"*Blow The Man Down* dishes out the divine retribution and karmic justice that we've been patiently waiting for. Accentuated with signature Branson shock value, it's impossible to step away from this book once the first pages are opened. The only remaining question is 'what does Kat do next?'"

— Iris Hermann, wordsmithing farmer

"Kat Wallace, Bosch pirate, is at it again, swashbuckling her way through an art heist and doing her bit to stymie those trading in slaves and freeing those in bondage. Mum of three kids, she can instantly switch from doting mother to knife wielding, gun toting pirate who doesn't hesitate to wallop those who seek to profit from human suffering. Come on board for a roller-coaster, page-turning ride! Kat Wallace, you have done the Bosch pirate guild proud, and I will certainly miss you."

— Steven Savanna, author of the *Hotel Exotica* future crime series

"[In] *Blow the Man Down*, Sarah Branson builds a story that centers not just on Kat's strength, but the emotional currents and forces that buffet those around her. As Kat begins to realize the real impact of past, present, and future decisions, readers absorb a powerful crescendo of events that challenge her and solidify her life purpose. Sarah Branson creates just the right special blend of action and discovery that keeps Kat growing, evolving, and challenged to do and be more.

Women who look for characters that can serve as role models for adaptation and courage will find Kat's dilemmas emotionally compelling. Libraries that choose *Blow the Man Down* should consider the series as a whole. Each book builds another piece of Kat's character and world. Together, the books create a world both realistic and thoroughly absorbing. Book clubs will find many discussion points sparked by the series."

— D. Donovan, Senior Reviewer, *Midwest Book Review*

"This is the ending we've been waiting for! The first book in the *Pirates of New Earth* series starts off with a breathtaking chase and the last book ends up with another one. In between we watch Kat Wallace struggle with her past as a thrall and her burning passion for preventing others from the same fate. And of course, she wants to make the man who imprisoned her pay—with his life.

Kat goes through loves, losses, and redemption, and matures from a young woman to a mother with three children. Three children that her former owner decides are now his. I hate to see this series end because I've enjoyed all four books so much. Branson's creative mind dreams up details, settings, characters, and challenges that vividly bring this series to life. It's been five stars from me all the way."

— Jacqueline Boulden, author of *Her Past Can't Wait*

Praise for Pirates of New Earth

A Merry Life

"The author's Kat Wallace is one of the best heroines you'll find in contemporary sci-fi. We recognize Kat's flaws but admire her emotional depth and strength of character as well as her burning desire to do what's right — even if it means breaking conventional rules. Her passion is palpable."

— David Aretha, award-winning author & book editor

"A fantastically fast-paced page-turner, with a dark streak. Sarah Branson plunges readers into the action and doesn't let us catch our breath until the very last page. You won't be able to put it down!"

— Debby Applegate, author of *Madam: The Biography of Polly Adler, Icon of the Jazz Age*

"*A Merry Life* starts as an adventure tale but quickly becomes something richer — Kat Wallace gains far more than her freedom when she flees to the New Earth pirate nation Bosch. Branson shines at depicting the nuanced familial bonds which form the heart of this story. Watching Kat develop from hot-headed revenge seeker to a competent, mature, powerful woman is deeply satisfying."

— R. L. Olvitt, author of *The Feathered Serpent*

"Sarah Branson's novel, *A Merry Life*, is a rousing page-turner. Her tough-as-nails heroine is relatable and genuine, and the plot is action-packed from start to end. Great for any reader ready to buckle in for a lightning fast ride of a book!"

— Andrea Vanryken, author

"Swashbuckling, vengeance and heart - all wrapped up in one heck of a strong woman."

— Sally Altass, author of *The Witch Laws* and Reedsy.com reviewer

∼

Navigating the Storm

"As good as I thought the first book was, this is so much better. I absolutely loved the character growth we got from Kat. She is still one of my favorite heroines. We were introduced to her awesome (and diverse!) new unit. I hope we get more from all of them in the next book! And no saga with Kat would be complete without some huge plot twists and emotional destruction. I was angry, I laughed, I cried. I cried a lot.

Without a doubt, this series (and this book) is one of my favorite reads of the year. If you like pirates and sci-fi, Sarah Branson has masterfully combined the two, and you should absolutely check this series out."

–Melissa Loringer, bookstagramer
@heretotheplottwist

"Readers who enjoy a rollicking adventure firmly rooted in family interactions...will find that *Navigating the Storm* comes steeped in a battle between love and loyalty in which Kat reconsiders her ultimate goals."

–Diane Donovan, Sr. Reviewer, *Midwest Book Review*

"I absolutely adored *A Merry Life*.... If possible, *Navigating the Storm* is even better than the first instalment in Kat's tale. Branson isn't afraid to rip your heart out or to make you laugh."

–Sally Altass, author of *The Witch Laws* and
Reedsy.com reviewer

"This is an incredibly impactful, emotional, entertaining, funny, heart-tugging book."

–Martha Bullen, book publishing coach and owner
Bullen Publishing Services

"*Navigating the Storm* is not your typical pirate book. Rather, it is a blend of science fiction with steampunk and cyberpunk interlaced with realistic human emotions and experiences set in the twenty-fourth century. Action is high paced and riveting. Kat matures as the book progresses; hitting rock-bottom makes her stronger and savvier, and puts her on firmer ground to face whatever lies in the future."

—Cindy Vallar, editor, *Pirates & Privateers*

∽

Burn the Ship

"*Burn the Ship* is as action-packed and entertaining as the first two books in the series, but in the third novel we see Kat growing as a person, actually feeling her feelings—yikes—and this deepens her personality and increases the stakes in her relationships. *The Pirates of New Earth* novels are fast-paced, engaging, other world creative, and leave you cheering for Kat at every turn."

— Jacqueline Boulden, author of *Her Past Can't Wait*

"As with every installment of Sarah Branson's *Pirates of New Earth*, readers need to buckle up before blasting off with pirate-protagonist Kat Wallace. *Burn the Ship* is no different In the series' third book, we watch as Kat comes into her own as a leader and a woman.

Kat's sizable village of supporters continues to grow as she takes on new responsibilities that demand teamwork. Guided by her therapist, Kat works to tame her famous temper as she takes the first steps in her lifelong mission to end human trafficking. Threats from within Bosch and the BPF itself threaten to derail Kat's plans just as she gets started.

At its core, *Burn the Ship* is a pirate story, so that means lots of swagger, swashbuckling and narrow escapes. With Branson at the helm, it also means glimpses inside the home and family Kat has lovingly built – and will go to any lengths to defend."

–Mary Ann Sabo, owner and ringmaster, Sabo PR

"This is Kat's third outing, and each book has gotten better and better. Branson writes her heart and soul into these astonishing novels, bringing the reader joy and heartbreak in equal measure. [Kat is] the most imperfect heroine that I've ever had the pleasure to read, and it's what makes her so compelling. It's a brilliant narrative on how you can never really know who someone is behind closed doors. I only hope Kat's story is to continue. The snippets that were revealed about her past life were so heart wrenching – and with enough left unsaid that leaves you thirsting for more. Bravo, Sarah."

–Sally Altass, The Indie Book Nook and author of *The Witch Laws*

**Pirates of New Earth:
Book 4: Blow the Man Down**

Copyright © 2023 Sarah Branson

All rights reserved. No part of this publication may be reproduced, stored, or transmitted in any form or by any means without written permission of the publisher or author, except in the case of brief quotations embodied in critical articles and reviews.

Blow the Man Down is a work of fiction. Other than any actual historical events, people, and places referred to, all names, characters, and incidents are from the author's imagination. Any resemblances to persons, living or dead, are coincidental, and no reference to any real person is intended.

SOONER STARTED PRESS

Published by Sooner Started Press
For more information, visit www.sarahbranson.com

Cover design by The Book Designers:
Ian Koviak and Alan Dino Hebel
Edited by Andrea Vanryken and David Aretha

ISBN (print): 978-1-957774-10-7
ISBN (ebook): 978-1-957774-09-1

Printed in the United States of America

For Rick, who is always ready to co-pilot with me to any heist or adventure.

"Beware; for I am fearless, and therefore powerful."

Mary Shelley

Prologue

Thursday, June 2, 2366. Truevale, Eternia. 7:20 p.m.

"Arrange for a pilot and airship to pick the four up outside Kiharu. I want them delivered to the Karuk Estate near Haida. No, not an FA one, one from Abernathy Enterprises. The pilot will remain at the Haida hangar quarters until I indicate." The voice that came from the room was deep and commanded attention. The words were carefully enunciated and spoken in standard Federal Alliance speech, but the erudite inflection indicated its elite education and class. Farris Abernathy pushed a limp lock of her straight, light-brown hair back from where it hung in her face as she stood just outside of her father's office while listening in.

She had come up to the vice president's office in the Truevale house to ask for his permission to have her friends over to celebrate the end of her first year of university. He was the one she had to ask now. Her mother hadn't been around for several months, having departed, or rather sent, not long after the vice president was inaugurated, to attend Camp Serenity, "Where you are guaranteed to find peace." Farris knew the camp was code for "vodka dry-out clinic," and while she wished her mother well, she doubted it would take this time any more than it had the half-dozen other times Mother had been at one "camp" or the other.

She slipped into the room without a knock or a word and stood near the wall. She knew better than to disturb her father's comm. As she waited for him to notice her, she regarded him. He was tall and broad-shouldered, and his blond hair was, as always, perfectly coiffed. Even while on a comm, he moved with the self-assurance of a man used to power. News reporters always described him as handsome and charming. She didn't listen much to the news, preferring to game with her friends, but it was at times unavoidable.

She knew, because he mentioned it often, he was "constantly dismayed and disappointed" in her. While she suspected that disappointment extended to many aspects of her, it was her particular failure to not have inherited anything even slightly resembling good looks or even good taste. She tugged at her orange tank dress. It had ridden up in a series of wrinkles over her belly and bottom. It had flowed more loosely when she first bought it two years earlier, but it was still her favorite.

She looked down at herself to determine just what would be criticized in the upcoming conversation. She picked a few cracker crumbs off her front and wiped ineffectively at a faded stain from some errant iced cream dessert. She glanced back at the VP. He was, of course, dressed impeccably. His summer-gray pants, paired with a crisp, white, collared shirt, were finished with a navy jacket emblazoned with the emblem of his office on the lapel. Next to it was a small loop of blue ribbon that represented his alliance with the Chosen of New

Earth, often referred to as the Bluest, or by their nickname, Bluies.

His comm sat on its assigned stand on his large antique desk. He viewed pressing the devices to the side of one's face as "Graceless, Farris. Something you are all too familiar with." Instead, he used a small, silver ear device to listen and speak, allowing him to move about the room. He was currently surveying the spring gardens through the window, likely planning their overhaul. Farris loved the lavish wildness of the gardens, even though her father referred to them disdainfully as "overgrown and disordered." She was glad that the VP had not yet been able to have them restrained and bound into tidy rows.

The business comm went on and on, so Farris waited, staring at a small, brown splotch staining the elegant woven rug that covered the shining wooden floor. It reminded her of a similar stain in the old study of the New Detroit house. A stab of guilt ran through her at the thought, and she picked at a rough spot on the cuticle of her left thumb with its gnawed nail until it bled, and she had to suck on it and tried to imagine she lived anywhere but here.

Rob Abernathy continued to murmur. "Have Susan prepare the villa for the three children. They will provide the enticement my Mary will require to bring her pirates there. Prepare my private security force. And speak to DeLeon. I want enough of his soldiers—be sure to remind him who underwrites them—to crush them. And I want them mobilized, though without attracting any Haida attention, as soon as the ambassador and the children arrive from Edo." Farris generally avoided listening to anything her father said when he was conducting business, mostly because it was boring, but now the word *pirates* caught her ear, and she considered what she heard.

She decided to speak up. "Excuse me, Father." Farris kept her voice low and did not look directly at the vice president's expressionless eyes when he flicked them toward her at the sound of her voice. She had learned as his child to find just the right balance of confidence and deference to decrease the chance of being dealt a blow. He frowned at her and held up a hand indicating she must wait, so she quieted—but no, she also listened.

He returned to gazing out the window that was slightly open, blowing a warm June breeze in. "Yes. We will take care of all three issues at once. The fronts need to be coordinated." She heard him pause. "Well, that's what I pay you for and will continue to unless you disappoint me." Another pause as he listened. "All forces should be fully staffed and armed and in position by mid-June. The attacks will commence once we have drawn the defense away." He paused a third time. "That is of little concern to me. Find the markers necessary and make sure there are no mistakes."

He removed his silvery earphones and looked at his daughter. She saw him take in her plain round face and heard him sigh as his eyes flicked over her soft, rounded body. Her last boyfriend had referred to her as pleasingly plump and told her that her green eyes were pretty. Now Farris felt the familiar, vague sense of dismay emanating from her father when he looked her over.

"What do you want, Farris?" While the words held no malice, his tone told her to make her request and be gone.

"I wanted to ask if I could have some friends over tomorrow?" There, request submitted. She paused to hear him offer his boon of consent. As she waited, her curiosity overshadowed her better judgment and she heard herself ask, "What pirates?" She kicked herself inwardly. *Never listen in* was the rule. Though she and her brother, Ashton, had decided the rule actually was *Don't acknowledge you heard anything*. Either way, she had broken it.

The vice president's expression sharpened, and his eyes narrowed, and for a moment, Farris shrank, certain this blunder would earn her a hard slap. To her surprise, his face shifted into a smile, and when he spoke, his tone was genial. "The Bosch pirates, of course. They are well known to be criminals, and they want to destroy me and the FA."

Farris recalled learning something about the Bosch in school. Now she thought, *good for them*, but to her father, she simply nodded. "Oh. All right. Thank you, sir." She stood for a moment more, still awaiting his answer to her first question. The moment passed and her father sat down. From his desk, he drew out his custom pen and began to jot notes on the document he now focused on. This was not a good sign. She cleared her throat slightly. "Father, about my friends tomorrow?"

The vice president looked up, and this time, his face held a cruelness to it. "Oh, no. You must learn, Farris, that people who listen in on others' conversations cannot be trusted and so will not be socializing. At all. All summer. Go to your room and stay there. Occasional meals will be provided, and…" He gave a sigh and curled his upper lip the smallest amount. "…I will be sending in a coach. Look at you: fat, dirty, stupid, and lazy. You disgust me. Let's try once more to see if you can become something…better."

Farris flushed, initially with embarrassment but then with a growing sense of anger. She stammered, "But…but… I didn't… I'm not…" She saw her father's eyes go blank. There was no point in arguing. It would only result in bruises and more humiliation. She nodded, pressed her lips together, and said, "Yes, sir." At his wave of dismissal, she turned and walked out the door.

She ambled through the hallway, hands drooping at her sides. She wished she had the nerve to stomp, envisioning herself pulling the expensive artwork off the walls and defacing the deep, dark wood paneling. Confined to her room all summer. Damn him. It had happened before when she was younger and had angered him. She hated it. She hated the vice president. He ruined everything. She just wanted to be somewhere else and do whatever she wanted. *Stupid and lazy.* His voice echoed in her mind. Then, *the Bosch...they want to destroy me.* She stopped in the middle of the hallway, an idea forming in her head. She started to walk more quickly down the hall as the idea coalesced.

Upon arriving in her room, she closed the door behind her. She opened the device that sat on her desk, calling up maps and timetables and pausing at a decade-plus-old article about her father's trial, a trial she had overheard him say was the result of some evil woman who wanted to destroy him but failed. The Bosch were mentioned in the article. She printed it to read more carefully later as she traveled. Then she went to her closet and took her old secondary school backpack out.

With a glance at the door, she filled it with a few clothes, her wallet that held several markers, some of the most expensive jewelry she had been given but never wore, her dog-eared copy of the Old Days book, *milk and honey*, and several large chocolate bars from the drawer next to her elaborate lace- and pillow-covered bed. Each item she stowed seemed to affirm her decision.

She slipped on her shoes and pulled the backpack onto her back. Her hand on her doorknob, she paused at the family picture on the wall from last Winter Holiday. Her father and her brother smiled out from it, while she had a blank expression and her mother looked decidedly like she was floating on her vodka cloud. Farris pulled it off the wall and stuffed it into her bag. She pulled the door open a few centimeters and looked in both directions. No minder had been sent in to watch her—yet. She headed downstairs and directly out the front door.

She was happy to have taken the photo. It would be her inspiration as she made her way to Bosch and begged them to make her a pirate. Her father wasn't completely wrong. She was lazy. She had never before felt like she needed to accomplish anything. Now, though, she had a mission to commit her life to. If the Bosch wanted to destroy the vice president, she was certainly going to be on the front lines to be sure it happened.

Part I

ONE

Hey, I'm Fun!

Monday, June 6, 2366. Somewhere in the New Caribbean.
About ten bells.

We are running full tilt, weapons in hand, and over my heavy breath, I hear an ammo round zing past me. The mansion hall is long and wide and lined on both sides with what must be full floor-to-ceiling windows as well as some impressive statuary. Unfortunately, we cannot see out of the windows to figure out an escape path as they are covered with heavy drapes made from a deep blue velvet. Fortunately for us, this means the hall is poorly lit, impairing our pursuers' aim. Another round buzzes past me, and it hits the statue just off my left shoulder, causing a bit of the marble to splinter and split.

"Shit. That's too close," I pant. "Where the fuck are the stairs?"

Matty's deep voice answers from behind me, "Who the fuck knows." His big hand is on my shoulder, turning me to the left. "In here." We dodge into the first open doorway we have come to in the hallway. Reflexively, each of us takes a position on either side, and we begin to alternately return fire, causing our pursuers to halt and take defensive positions.

In between shots, I squint and look at Matty. Sweat, from the June humidity and our dash through this huge manor, has beaded attractively on his skin and drips from the hairline of his tightly curled black hair. He leans his big, muscular body back after firing his shot and glances at me. He grins, flashing his white smile. "Are you feeling like you are fun again, Kat Wallace?" His eyes are wild with adrenaline. As are mine.

I lick the sweat off of my upper lip and take a half-second to consider the question, running my hands through my short, light-brown curls. "Hell, yes. But if I didn't have your ass slowing me down, I'd have been out of here by now." I grin saucily back, turn, and fire four rounds out the door from one of my Glocks.

He chuckles quietly as he puts a new magazine in his Scorpion 1260. "Oh, is that so? Well, my ass isn't the one who turned right when she should've turned left." He runs several rounds of his own toward our adversaries, who wisely are keeping their distance.

"And you…" I fire twice. "…are far too hung up on details like directions."

He snorts. "Is that so? Then, pocket that little toy you have and figure a way out of here. I'll use my real gun." He tosses the long cylinder that holds our plunder from its place under his arm across the doorway to me.

I catch it with my free hand, which is starting to brown from the early summer sun but is still remarkably pale compared to Matty's. "Fine. But my Glocks are perfect for this kind of thing. You boys just think bigger is better." I slip my pistol into its holster.

He gives a dirty laugh in response and switches his Scorp

to automatic, pulling the door almost closed to act as a shield, as I try to evaluate the room. *Aha, a window!* I head to it, passing a row of two glassed-in display tables that likely are filled with intriguing treasure, though I can't see inside of them in the dim light.

As I work on exfil, I consider how we have found ourselves here on the third floor of a mansion on some tiny island in the New Caribbean, pinned down by hostile fire.

My Monday morning had started in the usual fashion. I had extracted myself from the children in my bed. This morning, it happened to be only Mac and Kik. Grey was not coming in during the night as much as she had just after Takai and I split. I guessed that was good, but I sort of missed waking up to her long, brown hair in my face.

I had gotten myself coffee and started breakfast for the kids, rousting them awake and cajoling them to get ready for school. Riki, the kids' nanny, who was the size of a bear and likely could best one in a wrestling match, had appeared and chatted with me for a bit, happily accepting the breakfast sandwich I made him before he had walked all three children to school. I was in the midst of buttoning up my general's vest when a knock sounded on my blue door.

A smile lit up my face as I opened the door and saw Major Matthieu Warner.

"C'mon, we have work to do." Matty stood wearing black, sleeveless coveralls and a grin that definitely held something more behind it.

I got lost for a moment looking at his tattoo-covered, muscular arms but then shrugged. "I always have work to do. The papers on my desk breed over the weekend, and now I have to get a meeting with Miles and Cal and get a call into Phil to see what progress he has made since Friday with the Abernathy situation."

My handsome friend-who-might-become-more, if only my kids and my job would give us a break, leaned on the door jamb. "Doesn't exactly sound like fun."

Having bemoaned my shift in responsibilities from extractor extraordinaire and Glitter runner to general with a desk and Q-forms several times to Matty, I sighed. "I miss having fun. Hell, I miss *being* fun."

Matty's grin increased. "I don't believe you ever were."

"The hell you say." I gave him a playful push, and he laughed. "I was once fun and very…shiny."

A thick eyebrow went up on that handsome face. "I believe the current expression now is *cool*. And *shiny* was only from that Old Days show you are so enthralled with and made me watch."

"You liked it. And I believe the show and the word are going to make a comeback." I laughed. "So, I was too once shiny *and* cool!"

He stepped back and made a sweeping motion toward his vehicle. "You need to prove it. Come on a quick mission with me this morning." His eyes twinkled and he waggled his eyebrows. "There's some art that needs to be liberated." His voice went up at the end of his comment, cajoling me.

Truth be told, I love art heists. There's usually some great story behind the rationale someone is paying to have the piece lifted, and the places that we have to break into are not only appropriately challenging, but also typically quite swanky.

I only paused for a second. "Fantastic!" I stripped off my officer vest and dropped it on the table near the comfy chair in the living room, leaving me in black leggings and a black fitted tunic. "I'm in. Let's go. But I have to be back in time to make those meetings." I pulled the door shut, and we started to head to Matty's forest-green sporty vehicle.

"Don't worry, General. I'll have you back in time to be

boring again." He slung an arm over my shoulders, and my insides rolled as his touch sent a quiver through me.

"Fuck you, Major." We both laughed as we slid into the vehicle. He turned away from the base after departing from my little white house. "Where are we flying out of?" I asked.

"Headed to the cave. Thought you and I could take your *Coupe*." He looked over at me and then reached out to stroke my cheek with the back of his hand. There was unmistakable desire in his deep, dark eyes.

The start to our dating life has been stymied throughout the weekend. Our Friday night first date was cut short by Cal Greene when he presented me with Sunniva, one of the freed souls, who brought with her the stunning information that my past enslaver, Rob Abernathy, was now the kingpin of the human trafficking trade on New Earth. That situation required my attention so entirely that I had sent Matty home after he fell asleep in my office chair, head on my desk, around three bells. I, on the other hand, continued with my calls to Kenichi Tsukasa, my friend and a yakuza boss in Edo, and with Phil Reston, now the attorney general of the Federal Alliance of Nations and newly married to the recently inaugurated FA president.

By the time we saw each other again on Saturday evening, Mama, my brothers Peter and Paul, and my sister Mimi were over at my place for dinner with their partners and all the kids. Matty squares beautifully with my family, but all those bodies in the house left no time for the two of us to have any privacy, and I wasn't about to have my first kiss with Matty in front of my adopted siblings, much less the passel of nieces and nephews.

Sunday was no better for the two of us as I had promised the kids a day trip into District One to see a show and have lunch. Matty was a great sport and joined us. We happily got to hold hands throughout the performance, but again, no first kiss amidst the boys climbing on me, asking for any number of treats. In a sweet moment, Grey even slipped her hand into Matty's as we walked to lunch, which made me smile, both at her comfort with him and at how much he took such an immense move in stride.

That night, I had a W-Mech board meeting with Tom Pikari and the rest of his board. W-Mech is the business using Will McCloud's stability mechanism that Tom had developed and I had financed. Though Will had been killed by Rob Abernathy four years earlier, breaking my heart and almost my mind and devastating the unit we all were a part of, his brilliance lived on, being put to use via Tom's professional acumen. Delightfully, the business was booming.

Matty was the first person since Will I had taken to the cave and the old airfield where my late father, Teddy, and I had spent so many hours. Now he, Peter, Paul, and I were all working on restoring the collection of Papa's vessels that had been languishing on the makeshift flightline. I smiled, "The *Coupe*, huh?"

The *Deuce Coupe* was what I had named my favorite small, sleek, and very fast vessel that I had poured my heart, soul, and skills into both before and after Papa left it to me. "Sounds cozy." I decided to try what I hoped was a sexy smile, though it could have come across as slightly creepy since, Sweet New Earth, I was searching deep into my body-memory for how to act alluring. It had been literally years since anyone had looked at me with the ardor I wanted to see from Matty.

The hungry look he returned reassured me that my ability to be attractive was still intact. A thrill that went beyond the excitement of our upcoming marauding mission shivered through me.

Matty briefed me on our mission as we drove. A very

wealthy couple was divorcing; the husband had possession of a landscape painting by a twentieth-century artist named Thiebaud that had been in her family for generations, and she wanted it back. She wanted it back to the tune of a half-million markers. So, we just needed to get in, get it, and get out. Without getting caught or killed, but that was always the trick, wasn't it?

"Oil, right? On canvas or paper?" I asked.

He grinned and nodded. "You do know your stuff, Gen. Canvas—so, you are going to roll it…?"

"Paint-side out, of course," I said, returning the grin with aplomb. Canvas and other fabric bases are what traditionally have been used for oils, especially old ones like the one we were going after, and the surface will invariably crack a bit when rolled. By carefully rolling them paint-side-out, the cracks will "heal" once the piece is re-stretched and reframed.

I turned and began to rifle through the materials in the tiny back seat of the sporty vehicle, murmuring my checklist of the inventory. "Acid-free paper, die-cut padding, gloves, transport tube, inner tube, tape… Looks like you have everything."

"Not my first art heist." He turned the vehicle onto the dirt road that would take us to the cave where I kept the *Coupe*.

We arrived and together wheeled it out from its place in the cave. I started to gather the materials from the back of Matty's vehicle to pack in my black crossbody bag and his backpack. I leaned down far into the back seat to grab the tape that had rolled to the floor, and when I retrieved it and stood, Matty was standing and staring, an unmistakably wanton smile curving his face.

"I think there's something else on the back seat floor. You should look again." He tipped his head and peered.

I laughed. "Lecherous approval noted. But, sorry, I got everything."

Matty covered the space between us in just a few steps. Before I could say anything, he was in front of me, holding my face softly on either side with his warm, gentle hands. "We are long overdue for a kiss, Kat Wallace." His voice was husky and came out in a low growl.

My breath caught as I looked up at him, taking in his eyes with their impossibly long lashes, the lines of his cheeks and nose, and the scrubby beard he wore. My gaze finally landed on his deliciously full lips. *What have I done so right that I managed to be here in this man's arms?* He wouldn't come for the kiss unless I consented. "So long overdue...," I said, closing my eyes and leaning my mouth toward his.

"Kat, are you just going to peer out that window, or are you going to get us out of here?" Matty's voice startles me back to the present, where I am peeking down at the grounds through a tiny space in the closed drapes. A flush has blossomed on my face at the memory of our first kiss, and the warmth on my skin is magnified as I watch this man who holds my heart and my desires fire out the mostly shut door once again.

"Oh, you're doing fine. Don't be so impatient, summer child." I make my banter light to cover the passion growing in me. Refocusing, I open the curtain for a bit more light and pull my newest purple rope out of my bag to tie a slippery hitch around the leg of one of the sturdy display tables that are bolted to the floor.

Matty gives a snort. "Summer child now, am I? I'm down to my last magazine."

"Well, then we should go... Oh, look at that medallion!" The display cases hold old coins and medals and other emblems. After tying off the rope and standing, my eyes pause on a walnut-sized silver—or maybe pewter—medallion emblazoned with a Jolly Roger. I'm not big on much jewelry, but this piece makes me happy. But, sadly, I have no time to find and jimmy the lock, as the resident security force is practically at the door.

"Okay, Matty. Get ready. I'm going to break the window, and then we can slide out and hightail it home."

"Hightail it? That's my North Country girl," Matty says between shots.

His North Country reference contains a tease, but he is one of the few people, along with my therapist, Ruth, whom I share my North Country memories with: the awful ones, the tender ones, and the funny ones. Besides, I find I like being referred to as his girl. My face glows with pleasure as I give a quick kick to the window, shattering it. I jerk down the drape and lay it over the sill to protect us from the ragged edge, then throw the end of my rope down. "It only goes partway," I say, sliding over the edge. "We'll have to jump at the end."

Matty murmurs an acknowledgment, then slams the door and braces it with a chair. I am over the side and out of view by the time the second sound of glass shattering reaches my ears. I pause in my rappelling, concerned for a moment, but it is alleviated as he swings over the windowsill and starts his descent.

After I jump to the ground, I wait for him to join me, pulling my pistol to be ready for any further pursuers. He lands heavily next to me and, with a firm tug, releases the rope, wrapping it in several loops and slinging it on his shoulder. "Let's go, General," he says.

We run toward the cover of the Caribbean forest that will shield us until we reach the beach and the *Coupe*. On our way across the vast garden lawn, we dodge behind a large boulder and pause for a moment, to get our bearings and catch our breath. As our backs press up against the cool stone on the hot June morning, the sounds of renewed pursuit reach us. We confer on directions and then spend a brief moment just gazing at each other and grinning foolishly.

We start our hard run toward the jungle edge. I want to laugh but need every bit of oxygen to make the sprint. I am exhilarated. I haven't had this kind of fun since my missions with Papa. We make the tree line and continue on, leaping over fallen logs, stones, and boggy areas. A tremendous sound of machinery erupts behind us, and Matty says, "What in the fuck?"

Over my shoulder, a small, enclosed tank is advancing along the rough path between the trees. While the tank itself is not large, it has a pretty big gun attached to it that is currently being leveled in our direction. "Split!" I yell and Matty veers to the left while I veer right, both of us running at top speed to stay ahead of the tank.

From a distance, Matty calls out, "Abatis!" *Perfect idea.* I pause, pull out my explosives, and begin applying them to several trees. I glance up, peering across the distance, and see that Matty is doing the same. He glances up almost at the same time and grins, then blows me a kiss. I make to catch it and realize that we are being ridiculous, but my heart is overflowing with delight. I calculate the direction my trees will fall, and I know he is assessing this too. Seconds later, we each run a distance away and hit our detonators, collapsing the trees into a tangled mass the tank will not be able to negotiate. My run begins again as I veer back toward our original path. Within minutes, Matty comes from the opposite direction, a look of sheer joy on his face.

We say nothing, conserving our breath until we are back in the *Coupe* and skating across the lagoon toward open water, about to be airborne. Then we begin to laugh.

"As I was running, I thought of my name for you," Matty

says as our laughter subsides, and he keys in our destination into the navigational computer.

I pull the yoke back, and we rise into the air, "Oh, really? Don't keep me in suspense."

My eyes are on the sky and my instruments, though I can't help but steal a glance his way. As his eyes run over me, I feel as if he is caressing me with his hands, and the flush from earlier returns. He says, "You are the brightwork of my life."

I consider this. Matty had introduced me to this term earlier this spring when we had gone out on his sailboat that had a deck and cabin made of wood that shone and sparkled and needed ongoing cleaning and polishing to maintain its shine. That wood, he had told me, is called brightwork. I raise an eyebrow and posit the qualifier he had put with the word. "I'm an awful lot of work?"

He roars with his big laugh. "That you are, Kat Wallace. You are so much work, but you are the most brilliant and beautiful person I think I have ever seen. You, motorcycle warrior, are truly the woman of my dreams."

Love and Delight, both dressed like a couple of ancient Greek gods in flowing white robes, are dancing and leaping in my head, giving high-fives and giggling. They bump into my eyes, and a few tears leak from them. "How'd you ever get so lucky?" I quip, but as he leans from his navigator's chair toward me, my heart expands in my chest and my tone becomes serious. "And how the hell did I?" I breathe.

Then, flying through the sky, we share a second, tender kiss. Though this time I keep one eye open on the horizon as we head to drop off our prize and collect our markers.

TWO

Workweek

Monday, June 6, 2366. Bosch Hall. Thirteen bells and twelve minutes.

Miles looks up from his desk at me as I walk into his office breathless and slightly less disheveled than when I arrived, thanks to Betsy's ministrations. He makes a big show of turning completely in his chair to look at the old-style floor clock that stands at constant attention against the wall behind his desk. Then he turns back and looks again at me, both the question and the critique reflected in his eyes.

"I know. I'm late. I'm sorry. Had an unanticipated…meeting…early this morning that ran a bit over." My cheeks are flushed both from rushing back to the base after securing the *Coupe* and from the delightful way Matty wished me a good day when he dropped me at the door to Bosch Hall before making his way to the Force hangar.

A lone eyebrow shoots up on Miles' face as he gestures to the small balcony that overlooks the entrance to the hall and the green. "Betsy and I saw the last part of your 'meeting' with Major Warner, if that's what you kids are calling it now. I also saw in my daily reports that Major Warner had picked up a premium item extraction mission and that it was already marked as completed this morning. Coincidence?"

My thumbnail goes between my upper teeth, which I know is my tell, but this fact seems to matter little as my master commander seems to have all the facts about Matty and my little outing already. "Umm…maybe?"

Miles grins and shakes his head. "You actually do have to stop taking those kinds of risks, Kat. You have larger responsibilities as you prep for taking on the MC position."

"I just wanted to have a little fun." I shrug and flop into my seat at the left corner of his desk.

"You and the major certainly seemed to be enjoying yourselves in front of the hall." He looks down, face expressionless, and scrawls his signature across a sheet of paper, which he then sets in a basket marked *completed* on the far corner of the magnificent mahogany desk.

I clear my throat, but before I can answer, he continues. "According to Betsy, who heard from your assistant, Olivia, the two of you have finally come to grips with the fact you have been a couple for the past several months. I feel good that the top position in Bosch is going to someone with such astute insight." The tease in this statement is clear.

Now I raise both my eyebrows and placidly say, "I think our allies will rest easy, and our enemies will take heed knowing that Bosch will soon be led by someone with the energy and vigor of youth." It is work to keep the smile off my face, but I do it.

Miles locks eyes with me, and there is a crackle and crunching sound. The ball of paper hits me squarely in the face, and I laugh. "Resorting to violence, huh?"

"I believe you fired the first salvo. I am deeply wounded." A grin has spread across my friend's face. "But seriously, Kat. I need you to lead, not be on the front lines. It's one of the trade-offs of taking on the path of command."

"I know. But it was an art heist. I couldn't resist." I grin back.

Miles nods and gives a sigh. "I did enjoy those back in the day. But let's move to current business. Before you give me a report on the Abernathy/kingpin issue, I'd like to discuss some of the transition details, starting with dates."

"Oh really? How's the place in District Four coming?" Miles had said he intended to retire after he and his husband had finished the renovations on their beachfront house just outside of Saltend. I selfishly keep hoping they will have termites or something to slow the process.

Miles knows this and shakes his head slowly. "I'm sorry to inform you that everything has gone smoothly. This past weekend, we painted and I installed the shutters."

My stomach drops and my mock horror is only partially mock. "Not the shutters!? That means you are…" I wait for him to finish the sentence, and he obliges.

"Done. The house is complete. I will inform the council that my final day will be at the end of next month. We will have the transition ceremony with this current class's graduation."

His face has a relaxed smile on it. *Of course he's relaxed—he's about to retire.* "That's less than eight weeks from now." I hear the terror in my tone.

"Again. It's that astute ability to evaluate a complex situation that lets me know I've made the right decision." Now there is a full-on tease in his voice.

I let out a deep breath. "Fuck you."

"Excuse me, General?" He looks sharply at me.

I grin. "Sorry. I mean, fuck you, sir."

"That's better." Miles leans back and smiles.

I relax in my seat and consider a topic I have been meaning to broach. "So, Miles, the council has to vote to approve me, correct?"

He nods. "Yes, that is what the charter calls for. It's usually just an automatic vote. Though perhaps we could get Bosch Intelligence to get a move on their Howard Archer investigation before I announce."

I snort. "That little weasel needs to be caged. I'll talk to Cal today and see if they have the kill-off-Kat leak ready." I pull out my device and make a note. "But I have a request that isn't part of the charter."

"Let's hear it." Miles intertwines his fingers and rests his elbows on the arms of his big wooden chair.

"I tease about youth, but I am markedly younger than the rest of the generals at the table. And I am the most recently elected." Miles nods and his brows come together in the way they do when he is carefully listening. "I want the members of the General's Table to vote on my appointment as well. Before it goes to council."

Miles looks away from me, his eyes slowly traveling up and down and side to side as he considers my request. His lips purse and relax, and finally, he looks back at me. "That is one of the best suggestions I've heard. You need this table to support you, and I believe they will. Asking for a vote shows them that you respect and value their views." He nods and makes his own note on his device. "I'll call a Table meeting without you, make my recommendation for MC, and let them know you have requested a vote of confidence." He smiles. "That's the kind of thinking that tells me you will do well at this job, Kat."

"Thanks, Miles. I will need each of their support and

talents to be successful." I give a deep exhale as I had been worrying about this issue.

Miles scrolls over his device and opens a document that I can't see from where I sit. He looks at it and then at me. "Now, your commission will leave a space at the table. So, we need to discuss your replacement. It is customary for the outgoing MC to appoint a general to replace the one taking over the master commander position. But I want to designate someone you want to work with, so let's talk Special Project general."

I know immediately that I want Gia, who has been my friend ever since my second enlistment and who stepped aside and supported my rise to general when she easily could have been elected, but I'm uncertain how to present her name without it seeming like I want my friend at the table. Which I do. But it is more than friendship that makes her the right person for the table. Gia is one of the hardest workers I know, and she is brilliant at reading people and situations. And she's a far better team player than I ever have been or will be.

Miles continues, "I believe, given your rank jump, we should pull the candidates from the commander pool. There are several well-qualified individuals, and keeping it to the commanders for appointment is just good politics and better optics."

My brows furrow as I tap my lips with my first and second fingers, considering how to word what I want to say. "I get that. Politics, no matter how much I dislike some of its false faces, is part of my job and yours. And while we want stability at the General's Table, now is not the time to fall back to only the old guard. The Burn the Ship anti-trafficking project of mine is moving away from being a special project and becoming a BPF focus. I want to see BtS continue, but a new general will have their own priorities for the job. I'd like to have someone at the table who brings the energy of new ideas and fresh perspectives."

Miles nods. "Understood. That's why I am asking for your input." He taps a few times on his device, looks at it, considers his work, then taps again a few more times. He looks at the screen and then at me. "I have a short list of three, and I have prioritized them." He takes his handheld device and passes it to me.

I smile. Number one on his list is Commander Gialani Ka'ne, soon to be General Ka'ne.

∽

Monday, June 6, 2366. Bosch Intelligence Building. Fourteen and a half bells.

"You seem eager for me to get you killed, Kat. What's your hurry?" Cal Green, my friend and best contact in Bosch Intelligence, pours a cup of coffee and hands it to me as I sit on his desk, a small, neat stack of papers to my left and a framed picture of Cal, his wife Eva, and their two curly, red-haired, round-faced children on my right.

The cup is sturdy and glazed in sage green with a golden drizzle over the top half, and the fragrance of the coffee is seductive. I slurp it cautiously to avoid burning my tongue. "Well, can you keep a secret?" I maintain my poker face as I ask this.

Cal turns his freckled face to me and scratches his own mop of red hair while he shakes his head. "Nope. It's not in my nature. That's why I went into intelligence."

I laugh. Man, the intelligence gags never get old for me. "Miles is retiring, and he'd like to not have to listen to Howie rant about his replacement."

Both of Cal's pale eyebrows come up, and I see his smile as he tips his head and points to me, eyes widening in inquiry. I nod in confirmation.

"Knew this day would come. Teddy always said you were the future of Bosch." He regards me, and his smile broadens. "So, the brash, boisterous, full-steam-ahead Corporal Kat Wallace, the woman whom I spent a good portion of my teen years crushing on, whom I served more bourbon to than anyone except Teddy, has grown to finally become Bosch's leader."

"You poured a good drink in those days, Cal." I shake my head, remembering. "Earth, I was so sure of everything then. No shades of gray. Everything was either black or white. Wrong or right. My way or no way. I hope I have grown."

"You have, but don't set aside the spirit of that bold, young woman. It's that fervor that makes you right for the job." He walks over to me. "Let's see how it feels." He salutes me, clapping his right fist to his chest and then dropping it. "Master Commander Wallace."

I slip off the table to stand and return the salute, breathing out a horse-lips sigh. "Sweet New Earth, that sounds crazy."

"Nope," my friend says. "It sounds just like what Bosch needs." He picks up his coffee cup and lifts it to me. "To Bosch and its brilliant and remarkable future under your guide." We toast, and I am warmed by his confidence.

"Okay, then. Let's plan your death and get Howard Archer's ass in prison or on a sandbar."

The evidence is strong that seven months earlier, Howard and Eliot Conrad, the commander who ran against me, passed information that led to attacks on all my units and the slaughter of one of them. Those bastards are guilty of murder and treason as far as I am concerned, and I would have simply disappeared them if I hadn't been committed to upholding Bosch justice.

Both Conrad and Archer want to see me dead, and Cal's team is banking on that motivation for the final piece of evidence. They plan to leak false information to Howard on my alleged location during a mission. Howard will likely send Conrad in to kill me, and then *snap*—the trap will spring shut, and the traitors will be ours. "Can I get a few moments alone with them after you pick them up, Cal?" My request is nonchalant, though my hand can't help but finger the eight-inch, bone-handled knife strapped to my right thigh.

He hoots as he pulls up his calendar and starts to arrange his team's final planning meeting. "Hell no. I want to see them survive to be publicly humiliated and convicted of treason. You'd return them in several small boxes." He nods toward my blade.

I grin. "Can't blame a girl for trying." I move to leave. "Okay, I have a comm to Phil Reston scheduled. Need to see if he will be able to unseat Abernathy from the VP position."

"Things may get dicey with that. I need to check on the 3-P agents in the field." Cal jots another note down.

The prepare-position-protect program Cal and I piloted last fall with the input of generals Baradash and Patel is one of my favorites. As part of the *prepare* segment, I was able to train agents in some of the techniques Teddy taught me way back. Now *positioned*, it remains to be seen if they will need to implement the *protect* portion of their training.

I open the door. "Bye, kid."

Cal raises his hand to bid me farewell, intent on his own projects. "See you, almost MC."

I shake my head at the title and head back to my office.

Monday, June 6, 2366. Bosch Hall, my office. Sixteen bells.

"I'm telling you, Kat, there's no evidence." Phil's voice comes through the comm speaker.

I frown. "But my source is certain. There has to be something that links Abernathy to the traffickers."

"I am not doubting your source, Kat. What I mean is, there is *nothing*. Here, we have a man who has clearly stated his support for legalizing trafficking throughout the FA, but when I go looking for any hard evidence of connection or even association, there's nothing. Not even a recording of him making such statements. The only time there's such a dearth of documentation is when someone has spent the markers and the time to be certain that the trail will run cold. In my opinion, it's damning, but I need more than my opinion. I think we have to find his people and get them to flip."

I consider options. "I'll call a couple folk from my Glitter days. I imagine I can find somewhere to start from one of them." I pause, chewing my lower lip. "Our source's ex-lover is the past Scanian cartel leader. He could provide definitive proof."

"Hartvig? Well, sure, if Abernathy hasn't buried him yet."

Memories of the graves I dug in Bellcoast for Abernathy bubble to the surface, and I run my finger over the scar on my neck. "He likes to inflict anguish over the long term. My read is, he'd leave him alive to suffer the enslavement of his family."

At this, Phil's voice rises. "Kat—that reminds me of something I have been waiting to tell you. We tracked the identity of the North Central Continent cartel leader. You will love this."

My pen is at the ready to take the name down. "Okay then, let's hear it?"

Phil lets the moment extend for effect. "And the winner is…Amelie Coates of Fairneau."

The name hangs in the air, and I can't speak for a moment. Madame Coates has worked closely with the Bosch Pirate Force since well before I was a new recruit. I almost got court-martialed after reacting to her practice of keeping enslaved people to work her elaborate estate. "Are you kidding me, Phil?" I whisper.

Phil's chuckle comes through the speaker. "I would not do that to you. But I remembered your story about recruitment when our intelligence picked up her identity, so I wanted to be the one to tell you."

"Does Bosch get to pick her up?" My voice reflects my growing glee as I picture the event.

"You mean, have Bosch do some unofficial FA dirty work, get paid, make my life easier, and make *you* happy? Sure, I suppose." I can hear the pleasure emanating from him.

I laugh, delighted at this turn of events. "Thanks, Phil! Send me the details, and I'll get a unit on it. Maybe I'll even go along for old times' sake."

"I'd like to see that."

"I'll get some photos for you. And I'll give you the *friend* price." Phil's big laugh rumbles as I finish. "And I'll scrabble up some contacts that can provide evidence on Abernathy."

We click off our comms, and I sit back, feeling deeply satisfied. Things are coming together. The target my Ambition and Revenge have painted on Rob Abernathy's back is starting to grow brighter and clearer. *You are going down, you asshole.*

Tuesday, June 7, 2366. Ruth's office. Seventeen bells.

"So, you and your friend Matty have finally started to see each other romantically." RTT's voice holds the same amused it-was-so-obvious tone both Matty and I have heard over and over since Friday. It's only Tuesday afternoon, and I can count over a dozen people who have responded this way.

"I'm not sure whether to be entertained by that response or annoyed by it." I look up from my seat in the big gray chair, an easy smile on my face. "But since I've heard it so much, I shall opt to be entertained. And pleased."

Ruth smiles. "Even the most self-aware person can have blind spots. Especially when it comes to places they feel vulnerable. Does this new aspect to your relationship with Matty create feelings of vulnerability for you?"

My grin wavers as I shrug. "Not when we talk and laugh and do regular things, but…" I trail off, hesitant to give voice to something that has been moving from a niggling concern to a full-fledged anxiety.

Ruth simply sits with a pleasant look on her face ready to listen.

I sigh and figure I should just say what I'm thinking. I pause my thoughts for a moment to physically envision the personified emotions I am feeling, something I started doing for Matty early in our friendship.

Shame has on the clothes of a North Country preacher, all in black with that special blue collar common to the fundamental folk. Its hair is stringy and gray, greased and combed back. It has sharp features that look as if it has smelled something spoiled and long, tapered fingers with knife-like nails perfect for pointing out flaws. Insecurity wears no clothes and morphs back and forth from being very round and hunched, with its head tucked into its shoulders, to slowly narrowing and fading to the color of the background, becoming practically invisible. It constantly shakes its head side to side. Both emotions try to grasp at me and explain how unwise it will be to say what I am about to. "She'll laugh at you." "She'll tell you that you deserve to feel like that." "You can't be helped—why bother?" In my head, I growl and stomp my foot at them both, then turn my attention to RTT.

"I'm afraid to have sex with Matty." I am surprised at how clearly I have stated my concern, and I raise my eyebrows at my clarity.

Ruth nods. She doesn't laugh or say anything shaming, causing the me in my head to stick my tongue out at Shame. She does say, "I think it shows significant growth for you to admit fear, Kat. Have you considered why you feel that way?"

I certainly have thought about why. Once Matty and I actually started holding each other, touching and caressing, and now kissing, I have been trying to understand my reluctance and worry. My fear. Now I nod, attempting to put what I have considered into words. "Well, one—I'm definitely the reacher. Have you seen him around base? He is so fit and so gorgeous and has dated plenty of almost equally beautiful women. I mean, I like my body, but in comparison, none of them have had babies, and none, as far as I can calculate, are a few years older than him, like I am."

"You are feeling insecure about your body, and you are making comparisons." RTT states this with no judgment in her tone. It's as if she is summarizing my statement. Then she makes a quick entry in the notebook she holds. *Great, I've created a future talking point.* "What else?"

How does she know there is more?

Because you've been coming to her for years. She knows there always is more—she just has to poke a bit. "Umm…" I squirm in my seat and bring my knees up to rest my chin on them, effectively creating a wall I can peek at her over. "Well, while there have been quite a few, well, more than that, but…ummm…" I glance over at the fireplace that sports its summer wear of fresh flowers and three unlit candles of varying sizes in the firebox. I rub my brow. "Well, I've been subject to, let's just say, many sexual encounters…over the years in the North Country and while enslaved. The truth is, I've only had two…" I hold up two fingers to demonstrate the significance of the small number. "…consensual lovers: Zach and Takai.

"Zach was sweet and gentle in comparison to the others and actually seemed to care how I felt. But then he got shot. Takai was a bit hesitant at first, uncertain of what he could do. I think my past frightened him a bit. We had some very nice times early, if memory serves. But sex became pretty perfunctory, especially after the boys, and then moved from occasional to sporadic to rare. At least for me. Takai apparently was so bored, he had to wander the globe looking for interesting places to put his dick." I cringe a bit at the venom in my comment, but, clearly, I have not moved beyond the hurt yet. "I can never again be in a relationship where that sort of thing is considered acceptable."

Shame pauses as if listening to someone else and then, seeing an opportunity to pile on, whispers to me, and I hear myself say, "I only thought about having sex with Will, and then he was killed." I let my head fall back against the chair, remembering. I sigh. "I wouldn't say I have a great track record." I glance up. Ruth's face still looks equable, so I continue. "Matty has been with lots of really lovely and very sexy women." I look at her again as she placidly waits for me to bring this to a close. I wrinkle my nose, scrunch my face, and say, "I am terrified I'll be a disappointment to him."

She shuffles through her notes for a moment, reading, then I see her left eye slightly close. Ruth has very few tells, but I have come to know this tiny expression shift. It happens when she composes her thoughts before speaking, a behavior I admire and have tried to incorporate myself—with varying levels of success. She says, "You have said you are comfortable talking with Matt about anything. Do you think talking about sex will be different?"

My thumbnail slips into its thoughtful space between my front teeth as I take this idea into consideration. "Well…no. Probably not. But I'd like to be as spontaneous and exciting as his past lovers—no, actually, I'd like to be more so." I give a rueful laugh. "But between my job, which requires so much focus; my three kids, who are still figuring out this new post-divorce life; my yakuza nanny, whom I love but is present in the house quite a bit; and the rest of my life: Mama, brothers, sisters, in-laws, nieces, nephews—hell, even my ex—spontaneity is kind of non-existent."

"It sounds like you have built the experience, and what you think it *should be*, up in your mind."

"Uhhh, yeah. Again, have you seen this man?"

Ruth's therapist persona breaks as she grins. "Actually, I have. Who hasn't? So, I honestly understand what you are saying and can empathize with you to some extent. But, Kat, take a closer look at yourself. You are a vibrant, beautiful, desirable woman in her prime. You are every bit Matt Warner's equal. Maybe you are less experienced sexually, but think of what fun it could be to learn from him?"

I can't help but giggle, and color rushes to my face as I consider that scenario. To my delight, Ruth joins in with a small laugh of her own. "Don't let shame and insecurity get the upper hand, Kat. Those emotions don't tell the truth. And they'll keep you from having the fun and the relationship that you deserve."

In my head, I see the two emotions wrinkle their brows in

dismay at both this statement and RTT's unwillingness to fully personify them. They take a reluctant step back, and then another, growing smaller and less clear. I nod, think about taking Major Warner to my bed, and grin. "You're right, as usual, Ruth. I do deserve happiness. And fun." I feel a lightness inside of me, but in a dark corner in the balcony of my mind, Remorse sits forward, bringing Shame and Insecurity near. He looks at me dubiously, whispering, "Fine, have your fun, but you know, if you do, something bad will happen to him." The lightness now feels tethered, and I wrinkle my brow.

Ruth's voice interrupts my thoughts. "Now let's talk about your sense of false responsibility when it comes to another adult's safety." I glance appreciatively at her and turn a cool shoulder to Remorse, who looks unconcerned but lets the darkness fall back around him.

THREE

Decisions and Intentions

Friday, June 10, 2366. The ocean. Twenty-one bells.

Finally, quiet. Matt realized it was actually far from quiet as he listened to the halyard clink slightly against the mast; the gentle creak of *The Rune*; the easy summer waves that broke rhythmically against her sides, sending up a mist of sea spray; and the stray cries of a pair of gulls as he sailed into the twilight away from Saltend Harbor. *But at least they're sounds I understand*, he thought soberly.

The week had started so well: he and Kat adventuring together, partaking in a little piracy, escaping by a narrow margin, getting well paid. And kissing. He decided that was the best part, finally being able to taste those lips that had played in his mind for months. Then he reconsidered. No, the best part was holding her, feeling her strong body pressed into his. No, it was talking with her; hell, just being with her was best.

But the rest of the week had swung from abject boredom to exhausting pandemonium. It wasn't work that was the problem. It wasn't Kat either, as their twice-a-week empanada lunches had shifted ever so slightly into romantic trysts, complete with some passionate kissing behind Dario's Empanadas Everywhere food truck.

No, it was the chaos of each evening at Kat's house. He had been there many times before, but usually just for an evening once a week or so, and the kids always seemed so civilized. But this week, he saw that they were fully kids. They argued ceaselessly with each other, sometimes loudly, but often just picking at one another with sharp tongues and words. And Kat just let it happen, only stepping in when one child or another did something egregious.

There was a reason he never wanted kids. He remembered how angry and mean he used to be as a kid, picking fights with his brothers and with his classmates until the fights escalated into blows. He had no desire to see that played out again.

And the time and energy they required. He and Kat had few free moments together already between the demands of her work and his. And the children seemed unwilling to allow them any opportunity for togetherness in the evenings, with one or the other popping up out of bed just as the two of them settled on the sofa to talk, kiss, and caress. This rather surprised Matt as the kids had been the ones to jumpstart the romance between Kat and him, just a week earlier. Now they seemed inclined to block any progression of it. But he had tried to be patient, knowing they were unused to sharing their mama with anyone else.

For his part, Matt was more than ready to explore the mysteries of Kat Wallace's body. A body that was sinewy and muscular in parts and soft and yielding in others. He knew there were more delights to be discovered, but Kat was hesitant to move their passionate moments to the bedroom. Matt couldn't blame her. *Damn you, Takai*, he thought.

Kat's ex-husband's philandering had taken a toll on Kat's

ability to trust a man's word, and she had made it clear even before they had started down the path of romance that she would never sleep with a man again if she wasn't positive he would be exclusive and faithful. Of course, if Takai hadn't been such an unmitigated shit, the marriage might never have ended, and Matt wouldn't be able to kiss his favorite general at all. But he still felt a tiny bubble of anger, easily controlled but present, when he thought of the pain the man had caused his brightwork girl.

Tonight's theatrics, though, had been the last straw. He finished work early in the day after his Butler unit had completed another successful night raid and burn of a waystation north of Toronto. While the BtS missions were necessarily violent, which Matt and his unit found emotionally exhausting, six more souls were free of enslavement, and yet another message had been sent to the traffickers to reconsider their profession.

Matt shook his head, considering how gratified he had felt earlier in the day. He had gone shopping and then headed to Kat's to make a dinner of spicy shrimp tacos with his special mango salsa. He had scored the mangoes on a recent Glitter mission and was excited to share them. Riki, the enormous Edoan nanny who Kat's yakuza friend had assigned to protect the children, had been very intrigued with the meal, so Matt packed him three to take home. Kat had arrived as he put the food on the table and was delighted with the surprise and the special treat of the tropical fruit, but Kik and Mac had sullenly poked at the food, complaining, "It looks weird" and, "It tastes weirder."

At one point, Kik pushed his plate away from him and said, "Papa makes really good shrimp." His face held an insolent expression that clearly was meant as a challenge, and Matt was surprised at the irritation such a small person could evoke in him. He tried to respond the way he had heard Kat react, saying, "I worked hard on that for you and your family. I think you could be nice about it."

To which Kik responded, "I don't have to be. You aren't my papa."

And Mac murmured, "Nope. He isn't."

Kat intervened then, asking them to leave the table, which they did amid loud protests and slamming of plates and doors. She had said to him with a shrug, "Sorry. I guess they are just getting used to you being here." *Here* clearly meant more than the dining room table.

When Grey, who Matt had felt was fully his ally, looked over and coolly asked, "Why are you here so much? Don't you have your own place? And actually, the boys aren't wrong. You aren't our papa," Matt had stood up, leaned over, and given Kat a quick kiss, saying, "I'm obviously not welcome here tonight, so I'm leaving." Then he paused and said, "Kat, I don't think I'm cut out for this." Matt cringed, remembering his words and seeing how they hit his Kat as if he had slapped her, which would never happen. But she had simply given a pressed-lipped smile and looked at him, nodding. "I get it. You didn't bank on a package deal." At that point, he had simply turned and walked out the door, getting into his vehicle and driving nonstop to Saltend and the peace and freedom of the sea.

Now, as he lay on the deck watching the stars appear in an almost moonless sky, perspective began to swirl in his mind, and he didn't feel peaceful; he felt like a coward. Two seven-year-olds and an eleven-year-old had said some mean things to him, and he had thrown his adult version of a tantrum and stormed out. Not exactly a grown-up response. A whisper in his mind then queried, *But am I a grown-up?* He began to ponder the question. His first answer was, *Of course, I am. I'm thirty-four years old. I am a pilot in the BPF. I head the Pilot's Coalition. People listen to me. I'm known for being skilled, thoughtful, and calm. Those are all adult skills and qualities.* He smiled to himself, pleased he had answered the question correctly, and for a few moments, he was able to enjoy being stretched out on the six-meter wooden boat his grandfather had given him. Then the whisper returned, and he could hear its skepticism. *What about outside of work, Matt? How's that personal life?*

At first, he was offended by the insinuation. He had friends. He got on exceptionally well with his family. He began to reflect on his myriad romantic relationships. There had been many, particularly in the years after Rita. He was careful to keep things light and fun. He had always felt he was more than fair, making his parameters clear to everyone he dated from the start: no commitment, no messy entanglements. *Why was that?* he pondered for a moment. Well, because he didn't like messy, and he didn't intend to get married or have kids.

He paused for a moment and, for the first time in his life, considered what a child of his might look like. The faces of his nieces and nephews swam in his head. It would be nice if the child had Kat's smile. Stunned by the path his mind had taken, he shook his head as if to reset it. If he had learned nothing else this past week, it was that kids epitomized messy entanglements and aggravation. Then he thought about how Mac's face glowed when they were playing guitars together and how Kik always had a joke for him. And Grey was so much a copy of her mother, with her quick mind and tenacity.

His thoughts shifted to Kat, as they had begun to do constantly over these past months. He pictured her flash-and-glow smile, her eyes when they connected with his, relaying her thoughts. Her thinking was so akin to his. On missions, they had found that they moved in concert as if in a neatly choreographed dance. He had never met anyone who worked as hard or took her work as seriously as Kat. But even so, she was still the person he had the most fun with. He had laughed more in the past year than he had since childhood. And he had revealed more about himself, even the deep, secret parts that he usually hid away, sure that they'd be too ugly for others to accept. With Kat, he felt free to just be himself.

While he had teasingly nicknamed her "Brightwork," he knew that he had never been in a relationship that was so easy and comfortable. In every romance before, when the fun part shifted to the daily grind or the woman he was with started to want him to step up and be more a part of her life, he had bolted, moving on to someone new and exciting and starting the cycle again. *Very grown-up of you, Warner.* Was that his intention with Kat? He held his breath, waiting for the answer as the warm, salty breeze ruffled the sails. He sat up, looking at the barely perceptible horizon. The sea, a deep blue-black, came up to meet the dark canvas of the moonless sky, strewn with its innumerable stars. He automatically checked his lines and sails as he kept his trajectory for the open ocean. He knew the answer.

No. I want to know her more deeply. I want to keep laughing and keep feeling fully me. I want to share every new experience, mission, triumph, even failure with her. Sweet New Earth, I want a life with her. He reached his hand into the water and felt the rush of the sea as *The Rune* skimmed its surface. *She has kids.* He nodded to himself. *I like those kids. Except for tonight, we get along well.*

His annoyance and irritation sat back, and love smiled knowingly. Matt grinned at what Kat would say when he told her that his mind was taking on her tendency to personify feelings. *I got mad because I wanted to please the kids as much as I wanted to please Kat and it didn't work. Damn. I care about them and what they think and do.* He played with the tiller, making tiny adjustments to either side, and then he started to tack as he made to come about. His mind asked quietly, *Where are you going?* That was a question he had often asked himself. But now he knew. He had a few things to do first, but then he was going home. To the woman he loved and to her family, which might become his.

∼

Saturday, June 11, 2366. Bosch, my house. Twenty and a half bells.

We come back to the living room from tucking the kids in, and Matty takes his spot on the couch as I pour two glasses of summer wine. I walk over and hand him his, my eyes broaching the subject of the night. He shrugs, which makes me smile. As I settle next to him, our empty hands intertwine as we both take a deep draught. I set my glass on the table behind the sofa, right next to the three tiny, framed pictures of the kids when Grey was four and the boys were just a year old. Matty releases my hand as he twists to set his glass down, and then he pauses, looking at the pictures.

After a twenty-four-plus bell absence, the front door opened before dinner tonight and Matty had stepped into the kitchen, kicked off his shoes, and received hugs of greeting and murmured apologies from each child in turn. Then he gave me a small kiss, holding my eyes with that smile of his, and asked, "What can I do to help?" So, we fell into our budding dinner routine.

Now, I ask, "So what made you decide to come back?"

"I missed you, Kat," he says simply.

I give a small chuckle. "You didn't leave because of me." I say the next part gently. "Matty, the kids are still here. They are still and always will be part of me and my life."

He picks up the picture of Kik and studies it. Then does the same with Mac's and Grey's. More than a minute passes as he does this. "I missed them and their ridiculous loud, chaotic shit."

I stay silent.

"If I hadn't come back, I would miss hearing about what happened at school today. Grey has that girl she's been fighting with, and there's that boy that Kik wrote the story about. Also, Mac wants to learn sweep-picking. I couldn't miss those things."

I grin. "Well, shit. They got you, didn't they?"

He gives a small laugh but looks a bit perplexed. "I guess…"

"No." I say with a chuckle, "They did." I shake my head and run my fingers over the front of the pictures. "I mean, I get how they got me. They came out of me and looked all squished and helpless and beautiful, and then nursed and got me high on mama hormones, and I've been chasing that high ever since. So, I fell for them and still hold onto that love, even when Grey yells she hates me, and the boys try to pummel each other into oblivion." Matty tips his head back and gives a silent laugh, but I continue. "But somehow, they have reeled you in, even though it's been one helluva week. I mean, they've been fully on edge, trying to figure out what this…" I gesture back and forth between Matty and me. "…means for them, and I know you weren't having fun during all the tumult; no one was. I even felt like hightailing it myself a couple of times." I smile, knowing how much he likes that particular expression.

I pick up my glass and take a sip of the dry, white wine. "So, what changed then? Because these are the same kids as last night, though they had their sweet faces on tonight. There will still be chaos and mouthiness and aggravation as they find their ways, Matty. But for me, I have put all my markers into the game with them, and those markers stay in the pot. I am all in, and I am all in for the rest of my life."

Matty takes the glass from my hand, sets it aside, and with a gentle touch, turns me to face him. His expression is intent, though his eyes are soft. "Okay then. I decided three things over the past twenty-four bells: one, I love you." He pauses for a moment, and I am surprised by how much it means to me that he has said that simple phrase. He takes a deep breath and says, "And I haven't said that to someone other than my parents for over six years. But you—I love you more than I ever thought I could love another person." He tenderly strokes and studies my face with two fingers tracing one side of my forehead, my cheeks, my nose, and my lips, extending their soft touch to my left ear and tracing my scar across my neck and to my collarbone, causing a small, electric thrill to radiate through me.

"Two, I want to see how those three people who emerged from you grow and change—I mean, they are so much like you, but so much their own people. I am fascinated. You…" Here he presses his lips together a bit before continuing. "…and, I guess I have to give Takai some credit as well…" I snort derisively as he continues. "…have raised them with love and support and acceptance, not the pain and neglect you dealt with so early. So given how amazing you are, what remarkable things will they be capable of?"

I laugh a quiet laugh. "If you mean they are the undamaged versions, I am delighted to have you see them that way. Because that has been my aim from the start."

He nods and smiles. "And you have succeeded and are succeeding—so, so well." There is admiration in his voice, and it makes me feel a bit teary.

"And three?" I ask with a swallow, wondering what is next.

"Hang on." Matty stands up and walks over to where he dropped his shoulder bag and brings it back to the sofa, settling it on the floor near his feet. I look at him and wrinkle my brow as I peer at the bag. He takes my hands in his. "Three: It's not just *you* that is all in. *We* are all in." Now he gestures between the two of us with one hand, keeping a gentle touch on me with the other. "We pool our resources in the pot, Brightwork, and we will be drowning in riches. I am all in. As long as I can be all in with you." His voice is lush with emotion.

His words seem to tug my breath from me and fill my heart simultaneously. I pull a hand free and reach up to touch his cheek, where I catch a single tear that slips down and bring it to my face, mixing it with my own. I feel my heart expand as he looks tenderly at me.

He reaches down and pulls a black, flat, rectangular box from his bag. "So, Kat Wallace. You and I, we are not the marrying kind. And you have made it clear that you will never again wear a ring that says you belong to some man."

Curiosity and Tension vie for top position in my mind as he continues to speak with so much fervor.

"But I think…" He laughs a small laugh that I realize is self-deprecating. "…I have finally grown up. I am done running from happiness and sabotaging my own life. I want us to be at each other's sides and be a part of the incredible things we each can do and, even more, the astounding things we can do together. I will never attempt to possess you or limit you or lock you away from the world. And I may be an ass, but I will always be the ass in your corner." Now I can't help but laugh as he echoes that early exchange, and he laughs a bit as well, but then says as he looks into my eyes, "I want us to wake up every morning and go to bed each night having decided that together is where we belong. You are my best friend, my

Brightwork, my heart's desire, and…" He looks pointedly at me. "…you will be the only lover I will ever have for the rest of my life. And that's a guarantee."

I am overwhelmed with emotion and want to answer as beautifully as he has, but there is a tight lump in my throat, and as I try to talk, I can only muster a breathy "Oh, Matty." He pauses and squints slightly as if trying to assess my meaning. I close my eyes, take two breaths, and am finally able to swallow. "I could never say what I feel as beautifully as you do, but I'll try." I open my eyes. "You are my best friend as well—the best friend I have ever had, and I know some remarkable friends. Also, I have to pinch myself on the regular to be sure I am not just dreaming when I feel your arms around me. Between you and Ruth, I am working on my 'I am not worthy' feelings."

His hand strokes my cheek, and there is love in his face, so I go on. "You are constant and honest. I know I can depend on you, and I don't depend on many people. I love having someone in my life who knows me so well and is so much like me that even the lousy parts of me come as no surprise or disappointment." I pause and look shyly at Matty, having confessed earlier in the week my worries about being a lesser lover than what he is used to. "I do want to be your lover, always. And it will happen…" I sigh a little and shrug. "…soon? some time? eventually?" Matty chuckles and draws me close to his chest. His heart beats strongly, and he kisses the top of my hair. I murmur as I rest my head, "And truly, the idea that I could wake up in your arms each morning and fall into bed with you each night is the most amazing gift I could ever imagine."

He pulls me back with a start. "Gift! I almost forgot; this is for you. No ring for you—but this—consider it a pledge of my love." He hands me the flat box. I take it into my hands and regard it. It isn't black as I originally thought, but a deep, deep blue, made of some kind of leather. I press the small, silver clasp to open it and can't help but gasp. Nestled on a bed of cream-colored velvet is the strand of black pearls I last saw Matty's mother, Mae, wearing back in February. Now, however, there is a familiar medallion attached to it. It is a walnut-sized pewter circle emblazoned with a skull and crossbones—the Jolly Roger. It is the piece I admired during the art heist. My fingers trace the image in small, soft strokes. The smooth coolness of the metal is offset by the dents and dings from the artist's small hammer. "How…?"

"You said you liked it, so I smashed the glass with the butt of my Scorpion and liberated it for you." Matty's voice holds pride as he relays this.

A smile stretches across my face. "Well done, Major." I look at him. "But these pearls. They belong to your mother."

He shrugs and looks a bit chagrined. "Well, honestly, the last time I was home, back in May, she came up to my room and handed them back to me. She said, 'I suspect you may want to give these to someone else someday. Hopefully, soon.' Which, at the time, made no sense. Now—apparently, she knew about us before we did, like everyone else on this island."

I chuckle and look again at the pearls, then at Matty. I do like Mae Warner. Now, though, I can't help but tease her youngest son, "Well, that sounds a lot like your mother broke up with you."

Matty's laugh rings out for a second before he moderates the volume with a cautious look toward the door that leads upstairs and to the kids' rooms. He leans toward me and says conspiratorially, "My brothers would say it's high time."

I join in his laughter, and then he reaches and takes the necklace from its box. He gently loops the pearls around my neck and fastens the latch. I touch the medallion and feel the weight of it and of the pearls. Standing, I move to take in my reflection in the front window, the pearls against my blue, Saturday work shirt. Matty's reflection is behind me, his face aglow as he smiles at me from the sofa. I run my fingers along the pearls, feeling their slightly ridged texture and admiring the tiny irregularities of each and how their luster catches the light.

"You still need to tell me the story of how you came by these, but first..." Taking a deep breath, I summon all my courage and turn to face my best friend.

What I say next comes out in a voice, husky with emotion. "Matthieu Warner, I love you. As that famous bard had Beatrice say to Benedick, 'I love you with so much of my heart that none is left to protest.' I love you for all the things you are and all the things you do." His smile broadens as I speak. Now that I have said this, most of my worries, fears, and trepidation roll away, and I know what I want. I lick my lips and bite my lower one. "I think I would very much like to take you upstairs and show you exactly how I feel about you."

I look with mounting desire at this man I love and trust. I reach out to him, my breath coming a bit faster as he stands, his eyes reflecting the passion growing in mine. "You can spin me the pearls' origin story before we fall aslee—" But my last word is cut off by Matty's mouth, ardently finding mine, and I feel myself lifted into his arms.

FOUR

Tracking the Kingpin

Monday, June 13, 2366. Bosch Hall. A bit after ten bells.

"You have an office?" Paddy looks around my general's space in Bosch Hall and gives a low whistle. "Pretty fancy for an old Glitter runner." He grins at me. Paddy has aged a bit, though he still reminds me of a fighter gone to seed. Ruddy faced and broad shouldered, he is able to carry his prosperity belly easily enough. I suspect his hair is beating a rapid escape, but he has camouflaged its absence by shaving his head.

My face is neutral. "I'm not that old, Paddy." His grin drops. "How about you cut the crap and tell me why it's been so hard for me to get in touch with you? Almost as if you were avoiding me." Paddy squirms slightly in his seat and glances over to the door. But he can't escape from me. I've sat him in a straight-backed chair that is just a touch too small for him to be comfortable in.

I have my big, leather chair on wheels that I purposefully lean back in and spread out my arms and legs, wheeling slightly side to side, keeping my eyes on him at all times. The message is clear. I own this space, and Paddy Owens is here at my request and won't be leaving until I allow it.

He shifts his heavy body in the tight chair, trying, without much success, to reposition his legs. He leans a bit forward. "No, Kat. I'm here now. Why would I be avoiding you?"

I lean to the side of my oh-so-comfortable chair, resting my left elbow on the wide arm, and tap my lips with my forefinger. "Well, that is the question, isn't it, old friend? And until we get a clear answer, let's have you call me General Wallace, shall we?" It isn't a question.

Paddy has been around enough that he doesn't spook easily, so now he laughs. "Kat, you're getting a bit big for your boots, aren't you? You've always been brash and cheeky, but you've never turned on your friends."

Perfect lead-in. I now lean forward, both elbows on my desk, and I fix him with my stare. "Well, Paddy. I *am* General Wallace, and the word is *you* are working for Abernathy. So, let's discuss who the turncoat actually is."

Paddy's face drops and his eyes widen for a moment before he plasters on his poker face.

I don't wait for a response but continue, "And if you haven't realized it yet, this is not a social visit. It's a questioning session. And if I don't like the answers I get here, you and I will step away from this civilized workspace, and I'll grab some tools for an interview—the way Teddy taught me."

"Now, Kat—I mean, General Wallace, no need to go to those extremes. We go way back. I… I…have been working for the vice president, but under duress, to be sure." Paddy's round face has gone quite pink as he protests.

"How long?"

"Uhh…" Paddy lets his breath out as he looks anywhere in the room but at me. But I've played poker with Paddy, and he's not that good. I simply have to wait for him to show his hand. He knows that the techniques Teddy taught me to encourage people to readily discuss subjects they would prefer to remain private are no bluff, and he definitely does not want to be on the receiving end of them.

Slowly, he says, "A few...years..." He glances to see my reaction, but I am careful to keep my expression unchanged. No tells in this game. The slow reveal now becomes cards slapped down on the table in panic. "It started when I was running reconnaissance for you. For that woman thrall you were planning to grab. He got wise and I had to give him information or I'd have been dead. I mean, it worked out, right? You got her out. But then Abernathy had his claws in me and...and...I did what I did because I had to. You see that, right, Kat...General? You see it, don't you?"

My mind is spinning. Paddy gave Abernathy the information on the mission that led to Will McCloud's death. While my face is still impassive, I see myself using all the tools in my interview kit to cause Paddy the same pain and anguish he'd caused me. I wait, though. There are more cards in his hand, I am sure of it. I simply raise my eyebrows.

Paddy is nervous and drops a pair stashed deep in his coat pocket. "I was glad you didn't get killed in that Parida mission. I mean, surprised, but glad."

What the fuck? You did set me up. I wondered. I blink and attempt to look disinterested. What else does this scared, scheming weasel have to show?

"And then he made me into some sort of chauffeur, ferrying that DeLeon fellow who seems to be his second to be introduced to Archer." Paddy snaps his mouth shut, realizing too late he has most definitely overplayed his hand.

That's a full house.

I stand up and walk around my desk, watching Paddy's face as he clearly is cursing himself inwardly for his loquacity.

His eyes dart several times from the floor to my face as I stand in front of him and then boost myself to sit casually on my desktop, tilt my head, and inquire, "So, Paddy, explain to me why I haven't killed you yet?" I know Paddy hears the threat inherent in the question. And I actually am very curious as to why I have not.

It is to his credit that he doesn't shrink back at that point. Instead, I watch as a remarkable transformation takes place. This nervous fish starts to shapeshift into a shark—a shark with rows of sharp teeth. He leans forward, "Because, I have information on Vice President Rob Abernathy that he doesn't know I have." The shark raises the bet.

The start of a grin crosses my face before I can shut it off.

The shark continues, "I would be delighted to share that information with you, Kat. As a friend." He attempts to create a look of innocent generosity on his face. *Nice work getting back in the game, Paddy.*

"And, Friend-Paddy, what will this information cost me? And why will I not just water cure it from you?" I smile in an equally innocent fashion. I intend to win this pot.

Now Paddy relaxes back in his chair. This is his kind of gamesmanship. "Well, Kat, I know you don't like to hurt your friends. And this is detailed information. You wouldn't want it garbled with me talking through a mouthful of water." I snort and he gives a laugh as well. "And it won't cost you a thing. I owe you."

Now I know the price will be steep. My eyebrows go up, demonstrating my growing skepticism.

"Okay. I'll give you the information. Free of charge. Of course, if you think it's worthwhile, I wouldn't say no to some means of defending myself from Abernathy and his minions."

"Of which you are one," I say pointedly.

He waves the comment away with his hand as if that fact is inconsequential.

The value of whatever intelligence he provides next is unlikely to be of greater value than his connecting Abernathy, DeLeon, and Archer. But I'm in the game, and nothing ventured… "Let's hear the information."

"I need a pad of paper and something to write with." When I start to frown, he says with enthusiasm, "You want me to get it just right."

"Fine." I stand up and go back to the working side of my desk, extracting both a pencil and a pen, as well as a notepad with the emblem of Bosch and the words *From the desk of General Katrina Wallace* at the top in a flourish, from the drawer. "Here." I hand him the lot. "I wasn't sure you knew how to write."

Paddy chuckles at the dig and begins to wrinkle his brow as if he is either concentrating or constipated. After what drags out to be close to two minutes, he selects the pen and begins to write on the notepad. He reads it back to himself and then crosses out a line and rewrites. Then he hands it to me. On one line are the letters "NC" and then a string of thirteen numbers. Below it, first crossed out and then rewritten, is an "S" and a second string of thirteen numbers.

I look at him and he grins. "Seriously?" I say. "I'm going to need more than this if you'd like to leave my island with all your fingernails."

He laughs. "How about if I tell you the NC stands for New Caribbean and the S for Sarapion?"

I look at the numbers with this insight. Both of these nations are renowned for housing banks that provide strict identity protection for investors. These banks also have a tendency to casually disregard the source of the markers being invested, and they pay great dividends. I start to grin. If it's what I think it is, then this is a royal flush. "These wouldn't be bank account numbers, would they? Belonging to the human trafficking portion of Abernathy Enterprises?"

Paddy's foxy smile returns. "Well, that business goes under the name of JourneysAbroad. There's a logo and everything."

My smile shifts to a sneer of contempt. "That's disgusting." But I file the name away to give to Cal.

"Maybe so, but quite lucrative. As you will see when you investigate those accounts. Now about my means of defense." Paddy's confidence is back in full.

I cross my arms. "You want me to give you weapons from my armory? Why? You'll just sell them."

He laughs. "That is likely. But I will keep one or two for myself, and isn't a nice profit the best protection?"

I regard this man who I have done so much business with over the years. "Okay, Paddy. If these numbers check out, I'll see what I can do to get you a crate or two of last year's guns." I will keep most of the firing pins, though I keep this information to myself.

He pops up from his chair, which almost comes off the floor with him, and leans over my desk, extending his hand. "It's a pleasure doing business with you, General Wallace."

I shake my head as I reach out to take his hand. While I'd like to beat the hell out of him for his betrayals, I've won this hand neatly, having gotten more intelligence than I expected. But Paddy is still a shark. I'll speak to Demery and warn him to keep blood from the water.

∼

Monday, June 13, 2366. Bosch Hall. Sixteen bells.

"Good morning." I smile as I hear the comm pick up. "How are you this morning, my friend?"

"Just finished my morning stretches before getting down to some early business. But it's not morning where you are, Kat-san. To what do I owe the pleasure of this comm?" Kenichi Tsukasa, my favorite yakuza boss, sounds strong and healthy. I definitely do not ask him about what business he has this morning as it is best I don't know.

"I have a request for you. Or actually, for your accountants."

"You are like my own child, Kat-san. If I can assist in any way, I shall. Please, enlighten me."

"Well, there are some markers in two accounts, one in the New Caribbean and one in Sarapion, and I'd like to quietly transfer the balance out of both accounts into…different accounts," I say with the barest hint of a smile.

"Ah. You wish for me to have my accountants do your banking?" Tsukasa asks.

I laugh a bit. "Well, the accounts aren't exactly mine."

A chuckle comes through the comm. "But you'd like to have the markers from them?"

"No, thank you. But I do have some ideas about where they could go." I grin to myself. This will be fun.

Wednesday, June 15, 2366. Fairneau. Nine and a quarter bells.

"Coming into Fairneau, Gen," Matty says.

I am sitting in the jump seat of the Butler Unit vessel watching my friends at work as we head to take Amelie

Coates, hyper-privileged landowner turned human-trafficking cartel boss, into custody—a task I am more than eager to be a part of.

Blond-haired, handsome Aaron, the navigator, is studiously checking and rechecking landing coordinates while Rash uses his quick eyes and hands and even quicker brain to assess the various switches and levels that a good flight engineer uses to check their vessel's air and water worthiness. Tania, with her orange, asymmetric hair, and Bailey, with their dozens of tiny, dark braids now sporting several sparkling beads at the ends, compliments of their latest partner, are more relaxed since there is little chance we will need heavy weapons, but they still periodically check their rail guns and assess for risk.

I say off-handedly, "I am so excited to see that woman's face when we tell her she's going to jail. I feel kinda bad—I am getting a better present than you did, Matty. And it isn't even my birthday."

We celebrated Matty's thirty-fifth birthday the previous night, and along with a very nice, very spendy bottle of rum and a cheesecake I actually made from scratch, I threw a party, and we hosted his parents and his siblings, nieces, and nephews, along with all of my family. Mae had come to me in the kitchen while I was plating the birthday cake and slipped her hand into mine and gave it a squeeze, whispering, "I don't know when I've ever seen Matty this happy."

I grinned and whispered back, "I'm glad. I'm the happiest I've been since the boys were born. And he is somewhat less work than twins."

Mae had laughed her charming laugh and, leaning in, added, "Your necklace is very lovely. I hope you enjoy it as much as I know Matty enjoyed giving it to you."

I flushed, mostly with pleasure, tinged with a bit of self-consciousness, thinking about what else was given and received that night along with the necklace. My fingers reached up and touched it where it lay on my simple black sheath dress. "I love it. I may have to rethink my mostly black wardrobe and find some things to show it off in a manner befitting its beauty." Though at this, I flushed again as I recalled Matty, sitting up on one elbow the night I received the gift after we had made love a second time, tracing the pearls and the medallion and beyond with one dark, copper-colored finger while he looked at me with so much love and devotion. He had said, "Nothing you wear these with will ever compare to how lovely that necklace looks against your beautiful, bare, pale breasts." And he had punctuated the words with kisses that made my heart and body flutter.

Now Major Matthieu Warner expertly lands and parks the vessel in the Fairneau airfield. He pivots his pilot's seat to the center, a move that all units know indicates some important instruction is about to be conveyed, so all attention is directed toward him. Then, looking directly at me and raising his eyebrows, he says for all of Butler Unit to hear, "Oh, I don't know. I'm pretty sure the present you gave me this morning is worth several cartel-boss collars." And he follows this with perhaps the dirtiest smile I have ever seen from him. The vessel carrying our friends erupts in hoots and laughter, and I move from a moment of shocked embarrassment to join them in delighted exuberance. I suppose I am learning some things.

Wednesday, June 15, 2366. Fairneau. Ten bells.

"I don't know what you're talking about," Amelie Coates blusters. She has definitely aged, though not dramatically. Her hair is still yellow, though it has the slight brassiness that dye gives. She still seems to float about the room, though now the float is more like a slow bob. One aspect of her that is unchanged is the fact that she is still accompanied by her doting lady's maid, a young thrall she keeps enslaved. It is not Beth, who Madame Coates had renamed Rosalind, the enslaved young woman who attended her on the day of my first Glitter mission some seventeen years earlier. That mission was a shitshow of an experience that left me, Teddy, and Bosch changed—mostly for the better.

"Do you remember me, Madame Coates?" I use her last name and title as it is considered rude among the wealthy of Fairneau, and I have no interest in being polite to her.

She scoffs like a woman who couldn't be troubled to remember anyone not in her social circle. "Oh, you Bosch, there's always some new upstart trying to make trouble. It wasn't like that before...." She now looks at my face for the first time, leaning in and retrieving a pair of spectacles from around her neck to better study my face. I attempt to reflect the young woman I once was to help jog her memory.

She gives a gasp. "It's you!" She draws back. "You are the source of all the issues I have had with Bosch these past years. After that rude visit, your master commander came to me. I thought he was going to apologize, but instead, he insisted on buying the freedom of all the thralls I kept at that time. And he insisted that I provide payment to my other workers. Which I was forced to do until he retired and then was killed." She pauses and looks me up and down. "Wasn't that at your hands?" She steps back and holds up her hands as if the very sight of me offends her, which it probably does. "You disgust me."

I nod pleasantly and turn to the rest of the unit, who stand relaxed, but ready, in the exquisitely appointed parlor that looks over the meticulously cared-for gardens, and tell them,

"She remembers me." I see more than one smile suppressed. I tuck away the delightful information that Papa had quietly paid for Beth and Karl and whoever else had been given Shakespearean monikers to be free. He had never told me he had done that, and it makes my heart expand with love for him even more.

I turn back to this cartel boss in a sea-blue dress. "I am proud to secure the disgust of someone who traffics and exploits men, women, and children through this section of New Earth. We are here on a mission from your homeland, Eternia—a place where trafficking, thankfully, is illegal. You are under arrest and will be transported back to Eternia to stand trial for your crimes." A photo is taken by Bailey with a brisk click, and I grin inwardly at the envelope I shall present to Phil.

∽

Wednesday, June 15, 2366. Fairneau. Ten and three-quarters bells.

I escort Madame Coates by the elbow from her mansion, her hair clip now loosened, and her thinning hair unkempt from her raging about the parlor, to the Butler vessel. The enslaved people who work in and around her property line, up on either side of the road to the flightline, watch with interest, worry, and, I imagine, hope. Bailey, Rash, and Tania move from person to person, speaking quietly to each in order to inform them of their freedom and to discover what transport arrangements need to be made.

As I walk, I observe the faces, most of them a deep brown and most looking quickly to the ground when I make eye contact. They are clothed in either the brown homespun of the outdoor enslaved worker or the modest, but customary, regional style of the indoor thrall.

About halfway to the flightline, I notice, standing back a fair distance from the small crowd, near a livestock fence, a very pale, very blond man. His clothes are noticeably clean and, while they are somewhat worn and not traditional to Fairneau, are obviously expensively made. Fairly tall, his familiar face is long and broad, and his eyes are sharp, observant, and a surprising deep-brown color that looks striking against the pallor of the rest of him. Most notably, he has only one hand. His right arm ends at his wrist, and the stump looks well-healed and properly cared for. Apparently, Madame Coates is also harboring someone who is persona non grata in the trafficking circles. Interesting. I am delighted. Two bosses for the price of one.

I pause and stop Madame Coate's walk of shame momentarily, asking Aaron to finish escorting her. Then I turn back and walk over to the pale man, who, unlike the enslaved, looks me in the eye with no semblance of subservience. "Eric Hartvig?" I ask without a smile.

He acknowledges the name with a small nod. "I am not a citizen of Eternia. The FA cannot arrest me." He speaks in formal FA, but there is a clear Scanian accent, much like Sunniva. His tone is haughty, but there is a haunted look in his eyes.

I nod my agreement. "We are not part of the FA, nor has the FA hired us to bring you in. But I would like to speak with you personally. May I invite you to Bosch as a guest?" These words stick in my throat a bit because I despise all that he has done to afford the expensive clothes, the polished words, and the air of privilege.

He looks around at the thralls and the unit ministering to them. "I don't know…"

My patience frays. "Look, Hartvig. You can come as a guest or come as a captive. It makes little difference to me, but it may make a difference in whether we extend to you our help finding your family."

At the mention of his family, I see the facade of his previous self cave in, and he looks at me with eyes that implore as he grasps my arm with his remaining hand. "You would help me?"

"No." The hope in his face crumbles as I say this. "But I would help your children and your wife. They did not ask for an immoral, grasping, bastard of a father and spouse."

The ousted cartel boss of the Scanian cartel looks suddenly old and beaten, but I don't care. I need something from this man, and I have spoken the truth about his family. They didn't choose him, but they have suffered from his actions. He nods. "I will come. As a guest. And I will provide whatever is necessary for help to bring my family home."

FIVE

Plans into Action

Thursday, June 16, 2366. Bosch Hall, my office. Seventeen and a quarter bells.

I collapse into Matty's chest when he comes to my office at the end of the day. "I don't wanna go home. Don't make me," I moan.

He pats my head and gives me a quick hug, then, taking me by the shoulders, moves me back. I stare down at the floor, dejected. He lifts my chin, so I am looking at him. "It's your house. You made the invitation. I think you have to show up."

I squint and grit my teeth, groaning. "This is your fault." I watch Matty's eyes widen and his eyebrows raise in that sexy way they do when he is bemused. A small smile is on his face.

"Oh, really?"

I nod. "Yes. You should have stopped me when I made the comm inviting them."

"Sounds like buyer's remorse," he laughs.

I give him a soft punch on the shoulder. "I never consult with Remorse when I buy things. But I definitely do when it comes to inviting my ex and his new little family over for dinner." I have agreed to Takai taking the children to Edo for a month. And at some point, and I can only assume there was alcohol involved, I decided that it would be in the kids' best interest for them to see all the adults actually behaving as adults. So, I came up with the plan to have us all have dinner the night before they would leave for the four weeks. I'm an idiot, clearly.

Matty throws his big arm over my shoulder, then reaches over and picks up my fish leather bag. He hands it to me and says in a cajoling voice, "You said you wanted the kids to see you being civilized."

"Can I change my mind?" We close my office door. I glance over to Olivia, who is wrapping up her work for the day. "Bye, Liv. See you tomorrow unless I get arrested for murder—again."

Liv glances up and smiles. "Have fun with Takai. At least you get to play with a baby."

"How will I be able to tell the difference between the two?" I say with disgust.

Matty raises his hand in farewell to Liv as he shepherds me to the door and says, "She wants to decline being civilized."

"I feel that way every time I go home for the holidays." Liv laughs. "See you tomorrow, General."

Thursday, June 16, 2366. Bosch, my house. Twenty and a half bells.

"I think I have a couple extra old baby blankets upstairs. Let me check," I call as I prepare to take the steps two at a time. When I get upstairs, I pause and rest my head on the wall in the hallway, resisting the temptation to pound my head against it. Little Sumiko, only a month old, is sweet, as all newborns are, and Hayami, while still petite and delicate with long black hair now done up in a messy bun, is clearly in the overwhelmed place of having a new baby as she figures out nursing and surviving on two hours of sleep at a time.

The children are quite taken with their new little sister, with Mac playing a song for her and Kik reading to her from one of his books. Grey is being solicitous of Hayami, making sure she has water and a snack as her Mama M instructed her to do for postpartum mamas. And even though she is undoubtedly exhausted, Hayami is as kind to them as she always has been.

It's just…Takai. He is still Takai—a pedantic windbag who disapproves of all things Bosch.

I sigh, go into the boys' room, and then pull open the deep drawer behind their bunks and select three baby blankets, putting them to my nose to both assure myself they are clean and free from dust and to catch a scent of my past.

RTT has said that betrayal on the level I experienced in my marriage can cause a person to shun another relationship and view intimacy as something to be avoided. After much discussion, she thought I was ready for this, since Matty and I are together, and I don't shut myself off from him. But RTT focuses on my emotional health and doesn't consider the part where I still want to smash Takai's face in.

Having Takai in my house just irritates the hell out of me. He is still tall, dark-eyed and dark haired, with just a hint of gray at the temples. It has always astonished me that Edoans don't seem to age. He is also still quite cultured and dashing with clear views on what is right and what is wrong. No big surprise where I fall in that dichotomy. All the little digs about pirates being rambunctious and the morality of Glitter and whether food should have sauce. I feel like I have been deflecting and redirecting barbs all night long. It's a good thing I have become versed in politics; otherwise, I don't think I'd be setting the example for my kids that I am going for.

I look at the two suitcases and two backpacks sitting neatly by the door. I can't believe the kids will be gone in Edo for four entire weeks. We've never been apart that long. A few days, sure, maybe even a week. But even when I was in my darkest place, having time with them was like feeling my soul washed by a warm spring rain, refreshing and revitalizing. But all three are excited to go and be back in Edo; Kik, in particular, has been practicing his Edonese. They want to see their obaachan and the friends they have there. And, of course, have ample time with their papa. Though he was a lousy husband, he has always been a loving father, so I guess his demise at my hands will have to remain a fantasy.

I head for the stairs and consider. Like me, Takai seems actually happy in his new life, even content. I do worry, however, that his wandering will re-emerge, and the pattern will play out again. But Ruth and I have agreed that is not my concern other than to protect my children.

"Here we go, Sumiko! Nice, soft, clean blankets, compliments of your big brothers and sister," I say in that sing-song tone almost all adults use with infants as I come back into the room. I look and Hayami is nowhere to be seen. Takai sits in one of the gray chairs, reading a story out loud, with both boys on his lap and Grey leaning on the chair back, listening. Matty is in his usual place on the sofa, and he is holding little Sumiko on his knees, leaning in and making silly faces at her.

He looks up. "Hayami was going to the head with the baby, but I offered to hold her." He flips a cloth onto his shoulder, then raises the little wrinkled child there and begins to gently rub her back. I feel a stab of desire. I bring the blankets over and give him a quick kiss and then sit down next to him, whispering, "After the kids leave tomorrow, I'll explain to you exactly how attractive you are to me right now." He grins and chuckles a low chuckle, and Takai looks over at us and raises a single eyebrow. Four weeks without children. Huh. I guess I'll find some way to fill my empty hours. I put a bit of Bosch sauce on the smile I send to Takai and snuggle closer to the man I love.

Friday, June 17, 2366. Bosch Hall. Twelve and three-quarters bells.

"Hey, Miles, what's up?" I am combing through a handful of papers as I walk into his office. I plan to use them to create a brief to send to Phil Reston, showing Abernathy's connections to trafficking, and I want to put the strongest evidence first. "I only have a few minutes. It's the kids' last day of school, and they leave this afternoon for Edo."

I had just returned to my office from a scheduled meeting with Etienne Winter, the quartermaster, when Olivia, my assistant, handed me the papers I had requested and informed me, "MC wants you in his office now."

I sighed and said, "Seriously, it's not on my calendar." I love visiting with Miles, but I needed to get this brief done and sent before I left early today.

Miles doesn't respond as I make my way for my chair in the left corner in front of his desk. As I approach it, I see feet in very nice, very familiar shoes where my feet usually go. Perplexed, I drop my hands holding the papers and see Gia sitting in my usual chair. She smiles, but there is tension behind her expression. I glance over to Miles, whose face is easy and relaxed. I realize that, oh shit, he hasn't asked her about the generalcy yet. This must be it, and he's called me down to be a part of it.

"Hey, G—err, rather, Commander Ka'ne." I give Miles an impatient half-scowl.

His face remains pleasant. "Have a seat, General," he says, motioning to the chair that sits on the right side.

I try to quietly stack my papers as I sit down, but several slip from my hands and float to the floor, one going under Miles' desk. The rest crunch loudly as I belatedly tighten my grip. "Shit. Sorry…." I drop to my knees to pick them up, setting the original pile in the chair. I swipe at the strays and toss them on the pile and then flatten myself and shimmy partway under the desk to grab the final one that has come to rest near Miles' feet. As I back out and start to rise, I misjudge the distance and smack the back of my head on the desk overhang and exclaim overly loudly, "Ouch. Fuck." I back fully up and, kneeling by the chair, slap the last paper on the seat and rub my head.

I look over and see that Gia no longer looks tense; instead, her hand is across her mouth, and she is shaking with suppressed laughter. I can't help but grin sheepishly. I glance at Miles and see he has a pleasant, patient smile on his face. Realizing I am holding things up, I rise, turn, and sit as fast as possible, right on top of all the papers I had placed there. They crunch in dismay. I decide to pretend I don't notice and sit back, but the papers slide toward the edge of the chair and cause me to slip forward, requiring me to stomp my feet in front of me to avoid ending up back on the floor. Miles shakes his head and opens his lips to show me he is literally biting his tongue.

When he finally speaks, he says, "Nice to see you've perfected your general's entrance, Kat. Or was that a comedy routine? A good thing, either way. You may need a job soon."

Now I chuckle and stand, quickly gathering the papers from under my butt. I stack them to the side and sit back. "Ha. Ha. Sir."

Now the master commander of Bosch gives a laugh and begins to inform Commander Gialani Ka'ne of his retirement and the succession plan. I watch her eyes and smile get big at hearing that I will be assuming the MC position and then watch her jaw drop and her military comportment waver as he asks her if she will accept the general's position.

"Are you kidding, Miles?" she says with just the slightest elevation in her voice. She looks over at me. I grin and shake my head. She gathers herself and stands, then salutes. "It would be my honor to serve Bosch at the General's Table." Her salute smartly comes down and she remains at attention, but I see her blink her eyes just a bit more quickly to stave off tears.

Miles looks at me. "Now, see? That's how it's done."

I roll my eyes, stand, and salute him, threatening ever so slightly to embellish it with a middle finger before dropping my hand. "How's that?"

He tips his head. "Hers was better. Maybe she should be MC instead?"

A sharp intake of air comes from Gia, and a panicked look rolls over her face. "Don't worry, G," I say. "He's probably only half-kidding." I walk over to the elegant cabinet that holds the crystal glasses and liquor bottles and open it, selecting Miles' favorite glass, then mine, then the next nicest one. I transfer a very small pour into mine and a regular, small pour into the other two, carrying them over and passing them around. "I have three minutes to drink on this, and then I have to get back to work." I raise my glass. "To General Ka'ne. Now the world feels in balance."

Friday, June 17, 2366. Bosch Hall and environs.

The clocks ring fourteen bells, and I am headed out the door to home when Cal shows up. I don't break my stride as I head for the steps. "Walk and talk, kid. I have to get my kids and Riki on a vessel to Edo for a month." I contemplate Takai's reaction when Riki shows up, packed and ready. Among the many and legion things he doesn't approve of—me, Bosch, weapons, fun, sauces—Riki makes that list. Takai believes there is no use having him in Edo, saying, "Be reasonable, Kat. It's Kiharu. There's never any threat there."

I didn't want to argue—well, not much—nor tell him about the time his mother tried to have me killed, so I just waved my hands noncommittally, but I'll be damned if I'm going to chance another kidnapping—or worse. Where the kids go, Riki goes.

"A month? I can't even imagine," Cal begins as he hustles to keep up with my fast stride.

I throw a hand up. "Don't start down that road, or I'll be sobbing."

Cal nods. "Okay, I get it. Here's good news. We've scheduled your murder."

"You do know how to cheer a girl up! When?"

"This coming Wednesday. In Mynia."

I chuckle. "I've got a bit of history there."

"That's why we picked it. Actually, Metztli still remembers you, reasonably fondly. She told the female agent we sent in that you 'had the makings of a leader—given time.' Pretty prescient." Cal grins.

I chuckle a bit, though with a pang of sadness as I remember the crazy mission when Metztli, the matriarch of Mynia, tried to trade with me to take Will McCloud and Tom Pikari as thralls. It took a couple of years for that relationship to be renewed, given the fact I had my vessel blow a hole in her roof, but she started it.

When we reach the base gate, he stops. "I still have work to do. Not like you upper echelon folk taking holidays."

"I'll trade you my quartermaster meetings for, oh, just about anything," I say with a laugh.

"No thank you. Take care, Kat. I'll be in touch after we arrest Conrad."

I wave and head to send my children thousands of kilometers away for a month.

SIX

Diamonds, Kisses, and Tea—Just Your Usual Week

Wednesday, June 22, 2366. Bosch Hall, my office. Fifteen bells.

"Kat! It worked! We got him!" Cal comes into my front office, eyes alight and the bounce in his step practically a hop, where I am quietly talking with Olivia about my calendar, waving a small device.

"Who? Conrad? What about Archer?" My eyes go wide, and a grin spreads across my face.

With a shake of his head, Cal says, "Archer has 'conveniently' taken an off-island vacation, according to his secretary. It doesn't seem to be a well-planned one, though, as his place looks like he ran in, threw stuff in a bag, and caught the first transport he could out. Which is probably exactly how it went down. We're guessing Conrad notified him somehow when he was nabbed." Cal leans on the wall, breathing heavily. "But don't worry, we are tracking what vessel he was on, and we've got people waiting at his house. We've also taken his wife and kids into 'protective custody' and removed all comms from them. Here's a surprise—the kids don't seem too broken up that dear old dad is going down."

I snort a laugh. "I imagine he wasn't exactly a stellar parent." I point at what Cal brought with him and knit my brows. "What's on the device?"

Cal looks at his hand as if he forgot he was holding something. "Oh, right. We make sure to have video evidence these days of any arrest missions whether on or off island." He holds it up to me.

"Seriously? Let's see it!" I motion Cal into my office and pull a chair around for us to both watch. He takes his seat and sets the device on the holder that sits on my desk. I slide into my chair, and as he hits play, he says, "Just video, no audio."

At first, we just see the water as the vessel silently lands.

"What kind of vessel did you send in?" I ask.

"Just some old clunker dolled up to look like that *Deuce Coupe* of yours," he says without looking at me.

I scowl at him. "The *Coupe* is not a dolled-up clunker. It is small and magnificent and can outfly most of the BPF vessels." I almost punctuate my statement with a "so there" but restrain myself.

I see him grin without looking at me. "You certainly got the small-vessel-elitism from Teddy. Should we have borrowed the real thing?"

I shake my head as the vessel rolls up past the beach until the ground is firm below it and stops with its nose between a couple of trees, the camera pointed at the path to a small clearing. "Hell, no. I don't let just anybody fly my baby."

Cal gives a chuckle. "Okay, now watch." He points to the screen.

A woman, all dressed in black with a helmet and face mask and a dagger on her right thigh, appears in the camera's view and starts to walk away from the vessel. She walks with a swagger I have been told is a bit of a trademark of mine, and I grin, but within seconds, she falls to the sandy earth. I startle and grab at Cal's arm.

"Sweet New Earth, Cal!"

"Just wait. We have her outfitted with a couple layers of some of the newest ammo-proof clothes." He seems calm, but she is unmoving on the ground.

A man approaches and looks around. His face is visible—Commander Eliot Conrad. He walks over to the woman, who he believes is me, and shoves "the body" with his foot. Then he cocks his weapon and points it at her—*my*—head. My eyes go big, and I hold my breath.

Quick as fire, my impersonator rolls and kicks his legs from underneath him, his gun arm flying upward, and while the report of his pistol can't be heard, I see the spent casing fly. A couple more kicks and punches, and she has him fully on the ground. I can see her talking and yelling and wish I could hear what shit talk she is saying. She kicks the loose weapon aside and rolls him to his belly. She takes out arm restraints and pulls his arms behind him, keeping a foot in the middle of his back. Once restrained, she disarms him of several other weapons, and then she reaches up and pulls off her helmet, and dozens of thick, black braids fall out and her face is exposed.

"It's Diamond Miata!" I am delighted. Diamond is one of the most beautiful women I have ever seen, and her skills are astounding. She can shoot a marble to pieces at five hundred meters—every time. I've never seen anything like it. She is also a fierce hand-to-hand fighter. Her name derives from her choice in jewelry. She has several diamond studs all along her ears, three that run down the back of her neck, one in her nose, one in each eyebrow, and one in each hand in the skin between her thumbs and forefingers. Not exactly regulation, but given her skills, the Force has decided to let that slide. There are rumors that the diamonds extend to other parts of her body. Matty, unfortunately for him, fumbled his date with her close to two years ago so is unable to confirm or deny the rumors. I'm okay with that.

Cal nods. "Yeah, she really wanted to be part of the 3-P Program, but was too…" He frowns as he searches for the word he wants. "…sparkly. We needed people who could blend in, and even without the diamonds, she does not blend in. So, we offered her this mission."

"I'm feeling pretty good that you had her as my double." I smile. "I'll take that as a compliment."

We watch as she hustles Conrad toward the vessel until they both disappear from view. Cal turns the device off and stands. Then he smiles. "You know what? She said the same thing about you."

I laugh and finger the top of my ear. "Well, isn't that nice? Maybe I should get some diamonds…"

Cal laughs as well. "I'll keep you posted on Archer's movements. I'm going to be interrogating Conrad myself."

I nod. "Well done implementing your plan, Colonel. Sure I can't help with the interrogation?" I figure I may as well try.

"That little toy you keep strapped to your leg, Kat Wallace, is infamous." He gestures to my thigh, where my bone-handled blade rests. "The punishment to kill a Bosch citizen is still banishment, whether they are treasonous or not. And I want to keep you around, so no." He shakes his head but does not look particularly regretful. "I'll keep you and the MC informed on any information I glean."

I laugh. "All right then. I'll wait to hear from you."

∼

Friday, June 24, 2366. The walk home. Twenty-two bells.

The moon shines down practically full and illuminates the road and its grassy shoulders as Matty and I walk back from Barton's. It has been a hot, sticky day, and the cool of the night is welcome. A few drinks have made us a bit giddy as we laugh and joke. We are swinging our linked hands, and I start to skip, but then he stops and pulls me back to him. He looks at my face with that amazing smile of his and leans down, and we kiss. It's a great kiss that becomes several great kisses. It continues on despite several vehicles that drive past and slow to see their lights catch a couple in a passionate embrace on the shoulder.

We finally pull apart and continue walking. "You have survived week one without the kids," Matty's warm, deep voice rumbles.

I look up at him and grin. "Well, I have missed them, but the daily early morning calls from them helps, and…" I reach a finger up to softly touch his face. "…you have done an excellent job keeping my mind off of their absence."

The past week has been one of the most passionate of my life. We have been together every night, sometimes at his apartment and sometimes at the house. We have now made love in the kitchen, the washroom, and the front room of my house as well as many times in the bedroom. We have laughed, played, and not put clothes on for the day until absolutely necessary and then removed them as soon as we have gotten home. I have to say, watching a man of Matty's physique cook dinner in nothing but an apron is a sight to behold.

He grins back. "Oh, it's most definitely my pleasure." After a few more steps, he says, "You know…" He gives a small shrug. "…I miss them too. But you know what I don't miss?"

I do know. "Not having to put pants on before we fall asleep?"

He laughs. "That's the one. I mean, I still am not used to waking up and finding a selection of children sprawled over the woman I love. Though I will grant you, they look pretty adorable, all cuddled up with you."

"I had not slept naked for almost a decade. It's very luxurious. And those three are pretty sweet when they are cozy and asleep. I mean, after all, they're quiet." I give a laugh that ends in a wistful sigh.

Matty releases my hand and slides his arm around my shoulder, pulling me near him. "How about we head out on an adventure this weekend? Do something the kids don't want to do but still explore somewhere we can go with them when they are home later this summer?"

"That's a great idea, but where…?" I work to think through the layer of wine fuzz in my brain. "How about the artist community museum in District Five? That would be boring to them, but I've always wanted to go. And I heard they have opened a tree climbing park, with obstacles and ropes near there, so we can scope that out!" My wistfulness has subsided as I think of finding places to take them.

"Sounds perfect." Matty gives my shoulders a squeeze. "Now let's get home and leave our clothes at the door." He takes off running down the street toward my—our—little white house with its beautiful blue door.

Friday, June 24, 2366. Kiharu. 7:30 p.m., Edo time.

Yumiko Shima carefully poured the tea she had painstakingly prepared in her kitchen. There were the three small cups of hojicha for her grandchildren, a cup of sobacha for herself in her preferred delicate ceramic cup, and a large cup of strong black tea for the brutish foot soldier.

She paused and glanced into the small round mirror framed with cloisonne cranes. She smoothed her black hair and tucked a small strand back into the tidy bun she wore. Her sixty-seven year old face pleased her. Her skin was still fairly smooth and pale without age spots or significant wrinkles. She gazed into her own dark eyes and then looked at the door of the kitchen.

She slipped the small, flowered pillbox from her apron pocket. She opened it. Inside were some of the pills that had been prescribed for her late husband and Takai's father, Shigeo, to alleviate his pain and help him rest before his death. She had been very careful to cut them into quarters as his doctor had recommended, and he had cautioned her to only give them every few hours, so she had many left over. She frowned as she looked at them, considering the man's size. She selected three, dropped them into the cup of black tea, and stirred until they dissolved.

She dropped the pillbox back into her apron pocket. Then she added a small bit of honey to mask the bitter taste and set all five cups on a tray. Taking off her apron and hanging it on its hook, she carefully lifted the tray to carry to the living room where the oversized shin'nyū-sha[1], who the pirate had sent, sat with her precious grandchildren.

Tano Macrae and Kita Keaton both stood up when she came in, and Tano took the tray from Yumiko and set it on the low table in the living room while Kita walked her to her comfortable chair. They were good boys. She doubted it had been the pirate who had actually taught them proper manners; more likely, it was something they learned from her son and his lovely new wife.

Aika Grey, though, worried her. The girl had lovely manners, to be sure, but Yumiko could see her marauder-mother in her behavior, and it unsettled her. The children should be in Edo. It was the country of their birth. But Takai had told her that he had agreed to them living mostly in Bosch. She'd see about that.

"Are you children excited about our outing tomorrow?" She smiled and nodded to Tano as he handed her the teacup with cherry blossoms she favored, then she watched carefully to be sure he and Kita distributed the rest properly. The big man took the cup that had been prepared for him and took a large, polite slurp, nodding appreciatively to his hostess.

Grey enthusiastically replied, "Oh, yes, Obaachan! I do love being surprised. I can't wait to see where we will go. It sounds like a great adventure for the day!"

"Yes, anticipating the surprise is sometimes the best part. However, you will enjoy yourselves when we arrive as well." Yumiko had told her son she wished to take the children on an extended trip, but he had said, "Not this visit, Mother. I'd like them to stay close. Let's keep it to day trips only." Yumiko appeared to acquiesce to her son, but after all, how often does the vice president of the Federal Alliance invite one to his home? It was only for a week.

In diplomacy, it was occasionally better to beg forgiveness than to ask permission. Her son had no interest in interacting with the vice president. She had tried to tell Takai about her interaction with this powerful man on Friendship Day in Truvale earlier in the month, but he became angrier than she had ever seen him. Clearly, the pirate's fabrications still held some sway over him.

So, she had bought and packed extra clothing for the children into a new bag, and that case and her carryall were tucked in their spot in her closet ready for the trip. She and the children would be picked up very early in the morning by a special auto sent by the vice president and taken to his personal airship. The big intruder would still be snoring due to the effect of the medicine as they departed. By the time he awoke, they would be halfway to Haida and the elegant estate of Vice President Abernathy. She smiled to herself. She was a good grandmother. She was looking out for her sweet grandchildren, her mago, because oftentimes, who you knew was more important than what you knew.

Saturday, June 25, 2366. Kiharu. 10:45 a.m., Edo time.

Takai was in his study reading when he heard a loud knocking at the front door of his home in Kiharu. He stood and opened the study door; along with the loud pounding, he heard the voice of Riki, the yakuza foot soldier his ex-wife had employed to watch their children in Bosch and had imposed upon him for this holiday.

"Shima! Shima! Open up! Where are the children?"

Takai arrived at the door almost at the same time Hayami did, her eyes wide and little Sumiko held closely in her arms.

"What is he saying about the children? I thought he went with them and Okaasan?" Her voice carried an edge of concern.

Takai smiled his easy smile. Women worried so much about children. "I am sure it is all fine," he said and opened the door.

Riki spilled into the front room. He did not even pause to take his shoes off but walked in and looked around, almost frantically. "Are they here?" he asked in a demanding voice as he scratched his chest and then his nose. Riki was usually well put together, but now Takai observed his hair was uncombed, and he still wore pajama bottoms and a knit shirt. He kept shaking his head as he looked around the room.

"No, Riki, they are with my mother. Weren't you there last night? You had insisted you accompany them." There was impatience in his tone. Takai did not like this man, this criminal, spending so much time with his children. He appreciated that Riki had kept them safe in Bosch, which was by far a more dangerous place than Edo, but here he was unneeded. Takai took both Kat's insistence and the man's presence as an insult.

Riki squinted at Takai and then, as if remembering himself, slipped off his shoes and nodded respectfully to Hayami. "I was at Yumiko's home last night. We planned to leave this morning. My alarm was set. But I did not hear it. I woke only a few minutes ago, and they were gone."

Takai nodded. It was becoming clear to him what had happened. "Did you have too many whiskeys last night? It looks like you did."

"No. I do not drink when I am caring for the children. I had only tea last night. But I was very tired when I went to bed."

Takai shrugged and with a knowing smile said, "Well, my mother is simply taking them to see the flowers in the mountains up north. They will be home by dinner. Perhaps you should go to your place and sleep off your 'tea.'"

Riki opened his mouth and started to respond, but then stopped and looked at Takai. Takai knew the animosity he felt ran both ways. This man was one of the yakuza boss's men, and the yakuza boss was loyal to Kat as was this Riki. But this was Takai's home and he made the rules here.

Riki picked up his shoes and walked to the door. "Please comm me as soon as they arrive home." He turned to Takai's new wife and nodded. "Excuse my intrusion, Hayami-san." He slipped his footwear on and went out the door. Takai watched as he pulled out his comm and dialed, putting it to his ear and beginning to talk intently. Undoubtedly calling his puppet master on the city-ship. Criminals always assumed the worst.

～

Saturday, June 25, 2366. Kiharu. 6:00 p.m., Edo time.

Takai ran his hands through his dark hair that was starting to pick up a few strands of gray and paced the front room, looking at his comm for perhaps the twelfth time in the past half-hour. Though his mother had given no specific times, he had assumed they would be home for supper. Or that they would comm if they decided to eat at a shokudo. But there was no comm and no message.

He was not exactly worried; it was likely the visit from that foot soldier had created this unease. He punched in his mother's number and listened to it buzz several times and then drop off, not even going to the voice message box. Then he once again punched in the numbers for Grey's comm, the one he had disapproved of. Kat had given it to their daughter for this trip without discussing it with him. It, too, buzzed unanswered until it went to her message. "I'm doing something more fun than talking on a comm. Leave a message, and I'll tell you about it later." He had left three messages. This time, he simply turned it off, his handsome face tight and concerned.

"Hayami, I am going over to Mother's in case they go there first." He slipped on his walking shoes and headed over the few streets toward his family home. They had simply gotten caught up, enjoying the late afternoon sunshine and the flowers. That was what he hoped. That was what he had told Hayami. But as he walked, he recalled how his mother had tried to convince him to let her take the children on an extended trip…somewhere…. He didn't recall where she had mentioned that she was going or if she had even specified a place. He had told her no, but he knew it would be just like his mother to go ahead and do as she saw fit. When he walked up the path to the elegant home's door, he saw Riki sitting on a chair in the front garden, stone-faced and arms crossed.

"Where has she taken them, Shima?" He unfolded his arms and held out a small metal pillbox with a carving of a lotus on it that Takai recognized. "This was in the kitchen in an apron pocket. It has sleeping medicine in it. Your mother drugged me to keep me from traveling with them."

Takai analyzed the possibility quickly, basing his conclusion on his lifetime of experience with his mother, and decided that the scenario Riki presented was very likely. He looked at this man who obviously cared for his children. "That's ridiculous. Why would you think an old woman would do something like that? It really just shows that the criminal mind assumes the worst." He walked around Riki and, slipping off his shoes in the genkan, walked into the house he had grown up in.

As he walked in, Riki stepped in as well and said in a voice that was not loud but held power, "Shima, your veracity is poor, and it tries my patience. I will get answers. If not from you, from elsewhere."

Takai paused and gave a short nod. Then, he walked first to look into the guest rooms that the children would occupy. The boys' room was clearly identifiable. There were clothes strewn about, and one futon was clearly not slept in while the other looked as if two small typhoons had blown through it. The second guest room was a bit tidier with clothes simply piled near the futon.

He pulled the door shut and moved into what had been his parents' bedroom, now only his mother's tidy space. He opened the sliding doors of the closets and looked down at the floor of the one closest to the window.

He heard Riki's voice. "It's not there. That's where my mother keeps her suitcase as well." He allowed a moment to pass before continuing, "I have contacted Tsukasa-san and now have people investigating all forms of transit both within and away from the island today. But it would help if you know where they have gone. Where are they, Shima?" His voice was insistent.

Takai wrinkled his brow and felt his breath come more quickly even as his thoughts came slowly. Her suitcase was indeed gone. As were his children. Where could his mother have taken them? Why would she have done this? He looked helplessly at the large man with the serious face. "I... I don't know."

Saturday, June 25, 2366. Bosch, my house. Five and a half bells.

I stretch and shake my head as the buzzing of the comm stirs me. I open one eye partway, glance at the time, and realize I must have overslept a bit because I am usually up to comm with the children around this time. I close my eyes against the morning light streaming in the window, push the on button, and sleepily say, "Good morning, darlings! I'm afraid Mama had a bit of a lie-in. How are you?"

"Kat? It's Takai. We have a bit of a problem here. I don't know where the children are."

Both of my eyes open immediately, and I sit straight up in bed, the sheet dropping off my naked shoulders and exposing my body to the cool morning air from the window. Matty's head raises from the pillow as I say stridently, "What the fuck do you mean, you don't know where my babies are?"

Part II

SEVEN

The Monster

Monday, June 27, 2366. Bosch, my house. Four and three-quarters bells.

The horizon is a deep pink that fades into a sky streaked with gold, and a few clouds are turning purple with tiny pink edges. The trees are dark silhouettes against the magnificence of the morning show, audience members to a play that has repeated daily since the beginning of time. I have my own place in the audience, watching from the front porch as I lean on the white door jamb, staring.

I smell the coffee and sense the warmth of Matty as he places my mug in my hand. "Did you sleep at all?" His warm voice rumbles as his arm goes around me.

I don't answer but continue to watch the colors shift and change. "All three of the kids love sunrises. I mean, they should." My voice gets husky. "They are always up so damned early, and I can't count the number of times I've barked at them for waking me up." I take a sip of the steaming coffee, and it struggles to get past the lump in my throat. "I wonder if they are up early, watching it now?" Emotions begin to build. "Matty, what if I never get…?"

He takes my cup and sets it with his on the stoop as he wraps me up in both his arms and pulls me against his shirtless chest. "Kat. We will find them. We will bring them home. And we'll never let them out of our sight again." There is emotion in his voice as well, and the two of us stand, holding each other. I allow myself a few minutes of tears and take the comfort offered by this man who has been at my side almost continuously since Takai called to tell me our babies and his mother were missing. Then I feel his body give a small shake. I know his tears have started, and I reach up to kiss them away.

I look up at him and nod. "We will. We will find them soon." There's a noise in the house, and I turn my head to see Mama, up from where she was sleeping in Grey's room, looking as bereft and bedraggled as I imagine I look. Matty opens one arm. She comes close, and we stand with our arms around each other as the sky shifts to an ordinary blue on a day that is anything but ordinary.

Monday, June 27, 2366. Bosch, my house. Nine bells.

I come awake with a sudden gasp and am disoriented. My body stays still as my eyes shift in the room, and I relax, realizing I am on the sofa in my living room, asleep on Matty's chest with his arms about me. Then I remember and the heaviness settles in. Matty wakes with the same suddenness as I sit up. We look at each other, and I lean in to kiss him, hoping for this magic to fix the horror. And for the tiniest moment, it does. We move apart, and I smell eggs and toast.

I stand and pull my nightshirt down over my naked bottom. "Mama? Are you cooking?"

In the kitchen, Carisa and Aaron are at the counters preparing breakfast. Carisa presses her finger to her lips. "She fell asleep about half a bell ago. It was hard to convince her to move from where you were."

"What time is it? How long did we sleep?" I am still groggy. Matty comes in, lays a hand on my cheek, and grunts a greeting to our friends as he makes his way to the toilet. *That sounds like a good idea.*

Aaron shakes his head. "It's about nine bells. You two only slept for about three hours, I figure." He points to the food Carisa is plating. "We are on breakfast today."

"I don't think I can eat." My voice sounds dull and blank.

Carisa comes and takes my hand. "No, first we will go upstairs, and you will shower."

"And pee," I say flatly.

Her smile is gentle. "Yes. You should do that as well. Then shower, then eat. Matthieu, you as well." Matty has come back in and nods obediently. He takes my hand from Carisa, and we head upstairs.

Monday, June 27, 2366. Bosch, my house. Ten bells.

Matty and I sit at the table pushing the eggs around on our plates more than actually eating any.

"What did Riki say?" he asks.

I sigh. "He and Kenichi are trying to track how they left Kiharu. They don't even know if it was by vessel, ship, or vehicle. They could be twenty kilometers away or two thousand. He did say he had found the comm I gave to Grey in Yumiko's kitchen stuffed back in a drawer. All my missed comms and messages were on it. So, they don't have any way to contact us." I hear a disgusted sigh from across the table, and I am right there with it. "Takai is contacting all of Yumiko's local and diplomatic contacts. But so far, nothing."

In a sudden appearance, Anger and Hatred join forces and bubble up in me at Yumiko, and I slap the table. "Damn her to oblivion! How dare she?! How dare she take my children!? I can't just sit here, doing nothing. But…" I pick up my plate and fling it across the room at the wall, and it shatters, shards of plate and bits of egg and toast flying everywhere. Then I grab Matty's plate and lob it, hitting the same spot, a mass of plate, eggs, toast, butter, and jam spattering the wall and scattering across the floor. I reach for another missile, find my coffee mug, and pull my arm back to launch. Then I feel Matty's gentle grasp on my arm and the hand that grasps my cup.

In my ear, I hear his voice, deep and calm. "No, you love that mug. Grey made it for you."

I drop my arm and look at the mug. It is a bit lopsided and glazed in purple and blue. On one side is a heart she had traced with her little girl finger. I collapse in Matty's arms and sob, pulling the mug to my chest like it's my child.

Carisa and Aaron appear through the kitchen door. "What happened?! Are you both okay?" They stop short as they take in the scene: food spread over the far wall and me, a mess, wrapped in Matty's arms.

Aaron looks at Carisa. "I'll get a broom." I feel Carisa gently rub my back.

"Oh my…" Mama's voice. I turn my head from where it is burrowed in Matty's chest and guiltily realize I pulled her from her sleep with my tantrum. Her eyes move slowly around the room, and there are dark circles under them. Her face is a bit pale, with wrinkles on it that I haven't seen before. There's no reassuring Mama smile. *Everyone is broken by this, not just me.*

I take a breath and shrug off Matty's embrace. "Mama, I'm so sorry I woke you." I walk over to her and smooth a strand of silver hair from her face. I fashion a smile. "I kinda lost it." My Grey cup is still held to my breast, and I hold it out to her. She gently takes it and looks at it with tears in her eyes.

"Kinda?" I hear Matty give a small chuckle.

Suddenly Anger whispers to me, and I turn on Matty, stamping my foot and raising my voice, practically spitting at him, "Well, why not? Aren't you angry? How can you be so calm?"

I see him take a step back, but his eyes stay on me. I don't see any hurt or anger in them, just the warmth that has always been there, and now I can clearly see his love. He furrows his brows as he gazes at me standing, ready to fight. Aaron stops in mid-sweep, and a glance passes between Matty and him.

This beautiful man sighs as he steps toward me slowly like I'm some wild animal he doesn't want to spook. "I told you. I don't let myself get angry since, I don't know, I was maybe twelve. I had a real bad time with my temper as a kid, and it got me almost expelled, and it cost me a few friends. So now I have to keep it under control." His voice is even, but there is a sense of plea in it.

His stories surface in my mind, and I remember his description of a schoolyard fight with his ex-best friend. I soften. "I'm not mad at you, Matty. It's just… This waiting. Not knowing… My babies… I need to protect them.… I can't lose them like…" I feel my knees go loose, and I sink to the floor. I put my head in my hands and start to sob anew. Matty's big body folds down to the floor next to me, and he gathers me up and pulls me into his lap, where I continue to cry as he holds me close, kissing my hair.

A knock on the door startles everyone.

~

Monday, June 27, 2366. Bosch, my house. Ten and a half bells.

The boy who rode up on the bicycle and knocked looks around the room with big eyes after Carisa invites him in. I recognize him. He works weekends down at one of the shops and always helps the older folk with loading their groceries. One time, he even went home with one of the really old ladies, put all her foodstuffs away as directed, and then washed the dishes in her sink. She was so thankful, she tipped him fifty markers, and I remember her saying to Mama that he was going to grow up to be a good man. But for the life of me, as I sit cradled on the floor in Matty's lap, I can't recall his name.

Mama, a bit of pink now in her cheeks and her soft, everyday smile on her lips, has shifted into Mama mode, and she is clucking over him. He makes eye contact with her and also with Aaron and Carisa, studiously avoiding looking at half-naked Matty and the odd general of the BPF currently sitting on the floor in a man's lap with egg on her wall.

In his hand is a large plain envelope.

"I was asked to deliver this to this address and to be sure it went to General Wallace." He glances around the room, and I know he is hoping he is wrong about who he thinks that is.

I sigh and uncurl myself from Matty. Standing, I swipe at my eyes and my nose and straighten my shirt, glad I opted to put pants on after my shower. I shake my head and say, "I'm General Wallace." I make no excuses for anything.

He hands me the envelope, and I nod. Aaron pulls some

markers from his wallet and tips the boy who moves quickly back to the door and, without looking back, jumps on his bike and rides away.

With Matty at my shoulder, I open the envelope and pull out a letter-sized photograph. There is a pause as we both stare.

I drop to my knees, the photograph fluttering away, and I vomit, placing more egg and toast on the floor beneath me as I hear a roar of fury from the man I love as he flips the table onto its side, scattering the rest of the morning's repast.

Aaron yells, "Matt! Not the—!" The front window shatters as a chair flies through it to land in the front yard, causing a breeze that allows the photograph to dance back into my vision.

There sitting on an elegant sofa in a room with blue walls is Rob Abernathy. My ex-mother-in-law sits primly next to him, clear pride written on her face. My daughter stands between his legs, smiling, her head tipped onto his cheek, and dark-haired Kik and sandy-haired Mac are happily settled, one on each of the monster's knees, laughing.

EIGHT

Planning the Shit out of a Mission

Monday, June 27, 2366. Bosch, my house. Eleven bells.

I slowly rise to my feet and wipe my mouth with the back of my hand. My stomach is completely empty now, and it makes my thoughts sharp and clear. I lean down and reach for the photo where it has settled face-up on the floor. I look at the room, ignoring the faces. *Study the light, Kat. What plants are outside the window? What kind of decor?* Any clues that can tell me where this picture was taken... I feel Matty at my side, gazing and analyzing as well. I murmur, "There must be more than this picture."

"I'll look," Carisa's soft voice says, and the envelope rattles. She gives a small gasp.

"Let me." Aaron's voice now.

There is an intake of breath and Carisa says in a steady voice, "No. I can do it. I need to do it." I glance up and over to where Carisa stands, an envelope in one hand and a small, cream-colored piece of paper in the other. Aaron's arm is protectively around her, but he is gazing at her with admiration and now, I see, with love. But I can't react to that. I have to get the evidence. I have to get my children. I have to plan. Carisa begins to read, and it is as if her voice changes and the room falls away:

Dearest Mary,

Perhaps I should address you formally. What do those pirates call you? General Wallace?

How delightful it is to host your darling, half-breed children. Be assured, I am giving them everything they ever wanted or desired. Just as I did for you before you showed me how ungrateful you were. Hopefully, they won't disappoint me in the same way.

Their grandmother does not seem to appreciate how fortunate they are to have one of our race offset her and her son's inherently lesser genetic makeup. She seems quite critical of you, in fact, using the term "pirate" in a remarkably disparaging way. But I, on the other hand, know you quite intimately and would never denigrate you. In fact, while the ambassador feels you are an unfit parent, I anticipate that even a pirate feels something for their offspring. In fact, I imagine you are feeling quite dismayed by their absence. So, I offer you a trade. Bring me something I would value as you value them.

But you get plenty of negotiation in that profitable Glitter trade, don't you? So, let's make this fun for both of us, shall we? I understand from your children that you quite like seek-and-find games. So, I will give you three clues, one a day, and you can try to find me. And try to find the children.

But remember, all games come with a time constraint. And in this one, children can become so tiresome. One week from today, the boys will be sold off. Perhaps as a pair, though it really would have been more profitable if you could have made them matching. Either way, they will fetch a fine, premium price. You should be proud.

And then there is your lovely Grey. I can see the same spice growing in her that you carry. I'm saving her. For myself, for later.

In case you choose not to make the trade or fail in the attempt as is your wont.

I'll send clue #1 tomorrow.

With fond regards,
Rob

P.S. Grey tells me that you have taken up with one of the dark pirates. Really, Mary, I would have thought you could do better. Nevertheless, bring him along.

I'll send him the way of that last young man you brought into my home.

Carisa stops and looks up from the paper, her eyes wide. "Oh, Kat." Her voice, while stunned, holds its normal music now. She stands in my front room, Aaron at her side, and I am disoriented. How was it that I could hear that monster's voice pour from her petite frame?

Matty touches my arm, and we connect and study each other's faces. The fury that overtook him earlier is being tied, restrained, and confined as my tactical partner emerges, both of us detaching from our emotions to create strategies that will achieve the mission goal: retrieve the children. I glance away for a moment to keep my other goal private: kill Rob Abernathy.

We bring the table upright and lay the photo on it. Matty says, "We need maps and your friend over at BI to get us up-to-date information so we can go in."

I am about to chime in with my own thoughts when the word "we" recalls the final line of the letter, stirring my memory and bringing with it the echo of a shot and so, so much blood. "No. You aren't coming. This is between me and him. No one else."

Aaron remarks, "C'mon, Kat, you can't do this alone," causing me to whirl toward him fiercely, ready to fight.

One of Matty's hands goes up, staying any further comments, and the other settles gently on my shoulder. His face appears in my line of vision, and it calms me slightly. "Okay, Kat. Let's assume you go in alone. But that doesn't mean you plan it alone. Let's use the tools and the people we have and plan the shit out of this."

I reach up and touch his face, feeling the beard that is two days thicker than usual. Tears threaten as I look at him, envisioning him blood-covered, gray, and still. I whisper, "I can't bear the thought that he might kill you. I'd rather die myself."

He gently kisses my forehead. "I understand. Let's make the plan. We can adjust as needed." His voice is strong and reasonable. He is whole and well and here with me. I return to allowing my brain to work the problem without the visions of blood and pain. I nod and we go to work.

Monday, June 27, 2366. Bosch, my house. Twenty and a half bells.

Matt walked down the stairs after holding Kat until she finally fell asleep. It took almost an hour and two shots of her favorite bourbon. He had sung and then hummed and then just held her silently as she lay on his chest with him rubbing her back, fingers entwined in her curls to massage her head. When her breathing had been slow and steady for several minutes, he had gently slid from beneath her, settling her head on her favorite pillow. The evening was still very warm, but he slipped a light blanket over her and made sure the windows were open to catch any breeze. Then he made his way through the darkening room and went to talk with the friends gathered downstairs.

He paused to use the toilet and then, after washing, splashed water on his face. He contemplated his reflection in the washroom mirror, rubbing at his beard that desperately needed trimming and then staring hard at himself in preparation for what had to be done.

He appeared in the front room. The unit was there in its entirety: Aaron, Bailey, Rash, and Tania. Gia Ka'ne was there as well, as was the old member of the unit, Demery Ludlow. They were all sitting with seats pulled close together, and Matt could hear the murmurs as they spoke in low, serious tones. Aaron finished whatever he had been saying and looked up. "Warner. Come sit." He cocked his thumb toward the couch.

Matt walked over and slid onto the sofa in his favored place as Rash moved to the center. A dozen eyes scrutinized him. "So, where's Miriam?" he asked automatically as he began to shift his weight to get the cushion just right. Kat's mama had arrived at the house a few hours after they had gotten the call from Takai and had barely left since. He knew it was a comfort to both Miriam and Kat to be together at this time. He got that. He'd found himself calling his own mother for reassurance and support.

"Carisa walked her home and is going to stay with her for the night," Aaron said.

Matt nodded as he rubbed his tired face. "That's good."

"So, Warner. We need to talk." It was as if the whole room held its breath as Aaron spoke.

Matt figured he knew what was coming. He'd anticipated it, and in fact, desperately wanted it, but he couldn't request it. It had to come from them. "Sure, Aaron. What about?"

Aaron's voice was low but strong. "About this ridiculous plan of Kat's to run this mission solo. Matt, you can't seriously be considering letting her run this rescue alone."

Matt looked around at the group for several seconds then gave a rueful grin. "Well, first of all, none of us, me included, can let or not let Kat do anything. The woman does as she pleases, and I, for one, love that about her and, mostly, wouldn't change it for the world." He saw nods of agreement, but the faces stayed serious and the eyes glued to him.

"Second, we all know that Kat is probably the most skilled, most talented extractor in the Force, and it's not unreasonable, after what happened to McCloud, that she would want to avoid that sort of risk again." Everyone except Tania furrowed their brows as Matt said the name of their fallen unit member and friend. Still, Tania had heard enough Will McCloud stories to know to reach over to Bailey's hand and give it a squeeze.

Matt regarded his friends, "For Abernathy, everyone is expendable with a single shot at his whim, whether it advances his cause or not. But he will hold his trigger for Kat to keep her alive, for reasons I care not to contemplate. No, she will not put any of us in the line of fire again."

The tension from his listeners mounted, but he pressed on. "And three, it's Kat's children who are endangered." Now he saw faces start to drop in incredulity, so he shook his head. "But—hell, no. I don't care how good she is; I don't care if it is likely I will take a bullet; I am not going to stand by and simply send her in on her own with a kiss and good wish." At this, the entire room exhaled.

"Well, good," Gia said. "Because neither are we."

Matt gave a low chuckle and thought about how fortunate he and Kat were to call these people their friends. "I figured as much. But it will take far too much energy away from the project to argue up front with Kat about it. As we get more information, let's quietly make a complementary plan with hers, and I'll work on getting her to accept it, if not outright, at least as backup."

There were murmurs of agreement, and then Matt and the team settled in to outline the start of their own coordinated rescue plan.

∼

Monday, June 27, 2366. Haida, Karuk Estate, 9:00 p.m., Haida time.

"Good night, Obaachan." Grey reached up to kiss her grandmother on her wrinkled cheek. "I'm going to stay with the boys for a while and tell them stories. They are feeling homesick—for Papa." Grey smiled her most charming smile, the one that made almost all adults, except her mama, acquiesce to any request. She could feel her brothers' scowls behind her but ignored them.

Her grandmother smiled and nodded. "I understand. I gave the vice president a note to send to your papa, assuring him we are safe and well and on a delightful little holiday for the week. I'm sure your papa will write back soon, and I shall share it with you all. Don't stay up too late, dear ones. The vice president has promised you can ride some of the ponies in his stable tomorrow." Grey, with Kik and Mac peering behind her, watched as their obaachan slowly walked, in the old namba style, back to her room, dignity pouring from every step.

Grey turned to her brothers and sighed as she closed the door. "She is so proud to have brought us here." She saw Kik and Mac nod in agreement.

Mac spoke up, "Why'd you tell her we were homesick?

We're not." Then he frowned a little. "Well, not a lot. I do miss talking to Mama at night, but that's not the same."

"Yeah, I miss our comms too, but I'm not sick," Kik added.

Grey shrugged. "I know. I just wanted time for the three of us to talk." The three children moved to the corner farthest from the door and sat down crossed-legged on the thick, soft rug and leaned in. Then they all looked around as if they expected to see someone watching them. Grey knew who she wished was there—Riki. "Obaachan said Riki would come a little later. Do you guys think it's weird he hasn't shown up yet?"

Kik answered this. "Yeah, it's strange he isn't here, but maybe it's like Obaachan said—he needed to see his Edoan family."

"Maybe." Grey looked thoughtful and then added, "I thought it was fun here at first, with all the toys and treats, but Vice President Abernathy—I mean 'Mr. A.'..." She repeated the name he had requested the children call him. "...gives me the creeps, especially how he talks about Mama. He is always asking about things she does and who she knows. I wish we hadn't talked so much about Bosch and Mama and Matt that first night."

Mac jumped in. "He keeps talking about how he gave her a necklace a long time ago and she always wears it. And she hardly ever wears necklaces, only on special occasions."

Grey saw Kik nod vigorously in agreement as she thought about this. "It's also the way he always smiles with his mouth but not his eyes. He hardly ever looks people in the eye, and the couple times he did with me, I felt scared." She felt her brothers reach over to touch her arms reassuringly.

Suddenly, something occurred to Grey, and she took a quick breath in. She let it out with a "Nooooo."

"What?" Kik asked.

"What is it?" Mac said almost simultaneously.

Grey ran her finger from her ear to her collarbone over and over, staring at her brothers. "You don't think...?"

Kik wrinkled his brow and looked so much like Papa when Papa was offended by something. "No. He's weird, but nobody would do something like that."

Mac shrugged and looked thoughtful. "Somebody had to have done it. But Mama always just says she got it long before we were alive."

The three children stared at one another, considering this.

Mac spoke first. "We should just tell Mr. A. we need to comm our mama."

"Yeah, he hasn't said 'no' to anything we've asked for," Kik agreed.

Grey took charge; after all, she was the oldest. "We have to be careful. Obaachan said she forgot to bring my comm, and Mr. A. says comms don't work out here, but that doesn't make sense. What if there was an emergency? Still, I don't think we should ask. But if any of us find a comm and can use it safely, we should call Mama."

"Or Papa," Kik said automatically.

Grey nodded. "Well, yeah. But let's comm Mama first. She and Matt will come and get us."

"But Mr. A. said he sent her that picture from our first day here, so she must know we are here," Kik protested. "And Obaachan said she sent Papa a note."

"But she gave it to Mr. A. What if he didn't send it?" Grey wrinkled her brow in concern.

Mac's face was very solemn. "Do you really think Mr. A. gave that scar to Mama?"

Now it was Grey's turn to shrug. "I don't know. But I don't think we should ask him. And if we can get a message to Mama—or Papa—yes, Kik, then we should. And we shouldn't tell Obaachan what we are thinking. She might tell him. Grown-ups might not understand."

"Riki would," Kik said wistfully.

"Yeah. But he isn't here. So, we have to be in this together, like in that story Mama read us—all for one and one for all. We meet after lights-out every night and talk. Okay?"

Grey spit in her hand and held it out. After only a moment, her brothers did the same, and they all shook on it in turn.

NINE

Clue #1

Tuesday, June 28, 2366. Haida, Karuk Estate. 5:50 a.m., Haida time.

Grey was watching the sunrise over the hills in the screened porch, or veranda as Mr. A. called it, as she lingered over the toast with extra fresh butter and jam. Her brothers had finished earlier and run off to explore the gardens with hedges that formed a maze on the east side of the house. The first night they were there, they had sat on the west side in big comfy chairs, watching the sunset over the ocean and toasting marshmallows in the big, stone fire pit. That night, Mr. A. had warned them not to play on the west side because there was a part where the bluff dropped off sharply to the sea, and the fence had broken during a storm, and it was dangerous. He admitted that it was very pretty, but they could only go on that side with a grown-up.

Susan came over to her. "Are you done, Miss Grey?"

Grey smiled at the tanned, ample woman who had long hair she wore in a braid and a blue pinafore with an apron tied over it. "Almost. But I can wash up when I'm done. Mama always says not to make more work for people."

A soft smile came over Susan's face. "Your mama sounds very kind." She reached across the table to get the plate that had held the pile of toast that the children devoured. As she did, the sleeve of her white top pulled back, exposing her forearm and her tattoo.

Grey looked at it curiously. She saw lots of tattoos on Bosch, but she had only seen this one twice. "My mama and my Aunt Carisa have that same tattoo." She pointed at the raised, rough circle with a T-shape in it.

Susan stopped and looked at Grey. She frowned and was silent for a bit. Then she pulled her sleeve over the brand and said, "Well, isn't that something? You go play now. I'm going to get your grandmother's breakfast together."

Grey smiled and carried her plate to the kitchen, where she did as her brothers had done earlier: washed it carefully and set it on the counter to be put away.

Tuesday, June 28, 2366. Haida, Karuk Estate. 6:15 a.m., Haida time.

Grey was just about to go outside to find her brothers when Mr. A. appeared.

"You know how you told me about that marvelous treasure hunt you had?" The tall, blond man put his hand on Grey's shoulder and looked down at her.

Grey wanted to shrug the hand away, but she didn't. "Yeah. That was fun."

"Well, come into my study for a moment. I want to make one for your mama, and I want your help. It's hard to find

Karuk Estate, and I wanted to invite your mama here but make it a fun seek-and-find game. She likes games, doesn't she?" The words that came from his mouth were light and friendly, and Grey wanted to leap with joy at the thought of Mama coming there, but something whispered to her to be careful.

"Sure, she does. Doesn't everybody? I'd like to help." Grey smiled that adult-pleasing smile and thought, *And I'll try to tell her just where we are.*

∽

Tuesday, June 28, 2366. Haida, Karuk Estate. 7:00 a.m., Haida time.

Grey ran as fast as she could to the gardens, weaving in and out of the hedges, calling in low tones, "Kik, Mac, where are you?"

After several minutes, she knew they were hiding, and while she wanted to get mad, she decided that she wouldn't because what she had to tell them was too important. She could have searched and found them, but instead, she said a little louder than before, "Mac, Kik—I have a secret and won't tell you." Then she sat down under the black-eyed Susan flowers and wondered if she should pick some to take to Susan-in-the-Kitchen. Within a minute, her brothers appeared.

"What secret?" Mac asked as he and Kik slid next to her, their pants' knees filthy with dirt and plant stains.

"There's actually three things." Grey looked all around her and then leaned close to her brothers. "One, Mama doesn't know where we are. Mr. A. wants Mama to come here, but for some reason wants to make it hard for her. He is sending clues to her about how to get here." She saw the boys look at each other and frown, so she pushed quickly on. "Two, he wants *us* to help him write clues, so I tried to put something in that would help her. So, if he asks either of you, you have to do the same." Both boys nodded vigorously.

Mac paused. "But we really don't know where we are either."

"That's stupid," Kik retorted and kicked at his brother. "We are here. We know that."

"Well, yeah. Obaachan said we were going to Haida, and that's a city. But we haven't seen a city or even a town," Mac said matter-of-factly and kicked back a bit.

Kik frowned. "I guess. But Mr. A. said that from the bluff, you can see the Great Ocean and Ohlone Bay at the same time."

Grey said, "That's a good clue. And we know Haida and the Great Ocean are all the way on the other side of Central Continent from Bosch." All three children paused, thinking of just how far away they were from their home.

Grey broke the silence. "I heard Mr. A. call this the Karuk Estate, but I couldn't get that into a clue." Grey was frustrated that Mr. A. was so specific about what hints were to be in the rhyme. It did not make sense to her to send her Mama anywhere but here. But she had done her best.

Kik turned to his sister. "You said three things. Is that the third one?"

Grey nodded and leaned in closer. "When Mr. A. opened his desk to get paper, I saw two things: a gun and a comm."

Her brothers' eyes went wide.

∽

Tuesday, June 28, 2366. Bosch, my house. Ten bells.

My dining room has become mission central. The window is gone, but Matty has cleaned up the broken glass and wood and tacked some screening over it. He started to apologize, but I stopped him.

"No need, love. Just channel that shit into getting the kids home." I was even able to give him a grin. "That was actually pretty impressive. Remind me to stay behind you if you ever get angry again." He had snorted a half-laugh as he continued his temporary repair job. Me, I'm carefully putting every moment of anger and rage into a special box inside my chest. I intend to open it and let my furor fly when I am within killing distance of Rob Abernathy. I will use any weapon available, even my hands.

I walk into the dining room and see Cal and Aaron poring over maps marked with all the known properties of the FA vice president. There are at least two dozen, mostly on the Central Continent but with a few in the Old Europe cities and one even on the southern tip of Africa.

Gia and Bailey have taken the original note to the science labs on the base in hopes that some analysis of it might provide a clue as to where it was written. All we could assess from the photo was that it was taken in the morning. Plant life outside the windows was obscured because of the elegant, sheer drapes that covered them. Close examination could only pick up varied hues of green, with patches of red and some purple. So, at least we knew it was in an area with lush plant growth—though, given his wealth, the locale could even be a desert that he was irrigating for his own indulgence.

The bicycle boy, whom I have been told is named Martin, but goes by Marty, had little information about the envelope. He works at L&G, a mid-sized grocery several blocks outside of my usual shopping territory. Apparently, the Central Mail Service keeps a shelf for packages and mail drop-offs at L&G. The envelope, not addressed, but with a note directing it to me, had been dropped there after the usual CMS morning pick-up, though neither Rusty nor anyone else at the shop could recall seeing it appear or had any clue who might have dropped it there. Lucia, one of the owners, did some sleuthing and had Marty ride it over.

Neighbors and some folks from the kids' schools have come by with food and support. I am touched by their concern but disconcerted, even angered, by their appearance, so similar is it to the flow of comfort and generosity that happens when a loved one dies. And my children are very much alive.

Miles actually came by the house and assured me that I had the full weight of the Force at my disposal. It was a deeply generous offer from a man I am proud to have called a friend and an ally for over fifteen years. But I don't need the Force. I am doing this on my own. I will get my babies back, and the only blood spilled will be Rob Abernathy's. And maybe a trickle of Yumiko's.

Tuesday, June 28, 2366. Bosch, my house. Noon.

Clue number one arrived at noon tucked into a bouquet of two dozen roses delivered by Roxanne, a lovely older woman who owns the Chime and Leaf florist shop. She said the order had been made by comm, but the note for it appeared on her front counter after she had been working on arrangements in her backroom.

"I didn't hear a soul. And I have a bell on the door." Her round face was a bit perplexed as she answered Rash's questions about the note's origin. Then she turned to me. "I'm so sorry to hear that the children and their other grandmother have gone missing." She patted my arm. "But don't you worry. Old ladies like us always take care of the little ones in our care. They are likely just out on a lark."

I press my lips together and nod slightly. Old ladies like *her* perhaps, but not like Yumiko Shima. No, she delivers children to hell. I hold up the envelope in my hand. "Thank you, Roxanne. I'm going to read this now. Just let us know if there are any more similar comms."

She nods and then, with a pat on my cheek that almost brings me to either sobs or screams, turns back to her delivery vehicle and drives away. I rip into the envelope, Matty at my side and a mixture of friends and family close by as I begin to read aloud:

Dearest Mary,

Well, I had simply intended to write a short clue, but Grey assures me that you enjoy them in poetic form.

She said that your dusky…

I stop and scan the next lines silently.

…friend did this for you and for her and her brothers in little rhymes. While I cannot approve of such a match, as they are much better off with one of their own kind as are we, at least you have chosen one with some intelligence. It is very unusual as I am sure you know as that island of yours is full of them.

My eyes narrow as I remember my dad in the North Country saying something similar about *kinds*. I am at once furious and embarrassed. Matty has read the lines silently as well and gives a summary to the room. "Unsurprisingly, the man is a skin-bigot. He underestimates us. Let's be sure to use that to our advantage." I hear murmurs of agreement from our people. I continue reading out loud, squeezing Matty's hand in mine.

Anyway, with your sweet daughter's help, I have constructed this clue that will lead you to a second, final clue for the day. Please know, she and the boys are so excited to be the ultimate treasures you are seeking in our little game—ah, the naivete of a child.

While leeward is where we be
 Sobayton Bay is a bit seedy for me.
 But it is a place for a pirate's spree.
 To Fairneau Island with all haste, you should speed
 And to my instructions pay careful heed.

Head down to the warehouse of the number three dock
 And be sure you are there before two o'clock
 We have a mutual friend who we know is quite garrulous
 And if you aren't right on time, that may become perilous.

With fond anticipation,
 Rob

There is just a brief beat as I take this in. "Fuck. It's gotta be Paddy."

"It's almost half a bell past noon now. We are cutting it close," Matty says. I glance up and the room is in motion, but in an organized way. Aaron is on a comm, calling for a vessel, and Rash is at his side, saying something about one with the new engines.

Carisa comes and takes the flowers. "I'm going back to the university to research Abernathy's movement pattern. It might narrow the options. I'll take these over to the hospital on my way. They can brighten someone's day there."

As I go to put my shoes on, I feel strangely glad that I finally can do something other than wait. Cal approaches. "Let me go with you. I was in deep cover there, following Paddy at the first of the year. I think I know exactly where this note is sending you."

Matty doesn't even pause as he hustles out the door, staying at my side. "Get in the vehicle, then." Cal starts to trot to catch up and squashes himself into the tiny back seat of my small, black vehicle. I accelerate to about as fast as the little machine can go, once we are out of the neighborhoods, and head directly to the base airfield.

Tuesday, June 28, 2366. Fairneau, Sobayton Bay. Thirteen bells and a half.

"We need to go faster," I implore our driver. "It's an emergency."

The driver whom we hired to meet us at the Fairneau airfield is implacable. "Do you see all these autos? All these people? I can only go as fast as they move." The vehicle comes to almost a full stop, slowly creeping along with the many others on the road. Horns honk, and through the open windows, expletives abound. Sobayton Bay is rough, impoverished and looks like something out of the twenty-second century.

I expel a deep breath and drop my head back against the rear seat where Matty, Cal, and I are crammed together, hot and sweating. I grab Matty's arm and look at his timepiece. Half-past one bell.

A motorbike zooms past us and then another. We all look at each other, and Cal throws open the door and calls to the driver as Matty and I tumble out after him. "Thanks. Good luck getting out of this mess."

I step in front of a kid on a motorbike. "Can I buy it?" I shout and wave some markers. The kid frowns and shakes his head, maneuvering around me and taking off.

"How rude," Matty says, having had the person he just tried to buy a bike from display his middle finger before kicking off and throwing dust up in our faces.

"We might as well just run," Cal says with a shrug. And so, we take off down the crowded sidewalks toward the smell of fish to find dock number three.

∼

Tuesday, June 28, 2366. Fairneau, Sobayton Bay.

"C'mon, it's almost two bells!" Cal shouts and continues our sprint. Just like the rest of the city, the docks of Sobayton Bay are teeming with people and vehicles on a Tuesday afternoon. There are twelve separate docks, and number three is almost all the way to the end.

"We should have fucking water-landed. We could have gotten closer," I pant to Matty as I once again dodge sideways to avoid being bowled over by a large cart of goods pushed by some burly guy in a sweat-stained work shirt. I am only partially successful this time, crashing my shoulder against the far corner of the poorly stacked trolley with a grunt. I stagger slightly sideways as the cart tips a bit, a package from it falling to the ground. Quick as fire, some half-grown kid nabs it and runs in the opposite direction, with the pushman yelling half-heartedly after him and then grousing loudly at us as the cause as we move quickly away from him.

Matty reaches out to steady me. "You okay?"

"Fine," I say with disgust, though my shoulder really did take a blow. "Did you see that?"

He gives as much of a laugh as he can while running. "Yeah—shit literally falls off the back of a truck in Sobayton. And no to the waterworks. We would have never found a place to dock our vessel. Look at all the ships and boats tied up all along these docks."

I nod, glancing at the cargo ships and fishing boats that populate the water surrounding the docks. "And it would have been stripped for parts by the time we got back," I say as I run.

After another few minutes of weaving and dodging, we arrive at dock three. There are three warehouses. We stop, catch our breath, and stare first at the one large brick building and then at the two wooden ones, both with peeling paint, one dirty white and one a sad, graying blue.

"Which one?" Cal asks. "Was there a clue in the rhyme?"

I pull the letter out and scan it again, the men reading over my shoulder. Cal makes a face of contempt. "Fucking skin-bigot."

"If only that was his worst quality." I am surprised I can quip at this point, but it helps. I concentrate as I look at the buildings. "What time is it?"

Matty checks his timepiece. "A few minutes past two."

"Fuck," all three of us breathe together.

Then it clicks. "The blue one!" I yell and start to run toward it.

"You mean the one with smoke coming from the door?" Matty asks.

"Shit. Yes." I run up the steps and try the door, thankful it is cool, but it is also locked. I don't even think about my pick-kit as I start to kick at the entrance.

"If I may?" Matty asks.

"Do it!" I shout.

He kicks the door down, and we run onto a broad, open floor. There's no product of any kind here, only empty crates and some gunny sacks, but the smell of smoke is strong. I am positive we need to find its source. Cal is shouting our location through his comm to the fire brigade.

"This way." Smoke is roiling from under an office door on the far side. Matty starts to chamber a kick, but I turn the nob, and the door swings open. The smoke is thick, and we start to cough. As fresh air comes in, flames rise from several small cans sitting atop an old desk.

I run back out and grab some sacks, and we smother the small fires somewhat; the smoke begins to clear.

I am blinking my eyes, which have teared up from the noxious fumes.

Matty is wiping his eyes as well and turns his head. "Oh, fuck. Kat, look."

He is pointing to the far wall, which had been obscured by the smoke. I smear at my eyes and squint. There, in front of the wall, hanging upside down is Paddy Owen's body, suspended by the ankles with a rope from the warehouse beams. There is drying blood on his slack face that seems to have run from his open mouth over his cheeks. It somewhat obscures his eyes, which are open and staring. His arms hang down toward the floor, and one hand is discolored.

Helluva way to go, buddy. You've spun your last tale.

Suddenly, the bells of the fire brigade grow very loud and then come abruptly to a halt as we hear the shouting of firefighters. We turn and, through the open door, see them run into the warehouse, hoses at the ready, setting up to douse the room we are in with seawater.

I spin back to squint at Paddy's corpse and see something smeared on the wall near him. "Stop them!" I yell and Matty and Cal immediately run toward the crew and start waving their arms.

I am methodically checking the room for any tripwires or traps as I make my way toward Paddy. Matty and Cal return, accompanied by a tall woman in fire gear who holds a large bucket and douses the cans thoroughly. Steamy smoke billows up, and she yells, "There's more fires. We need you out of here. Now!"

I shake my head vigorously and swerve away from her attempt to rescue me so I can get closer to the wall. "We need to cut him down."

As Matty drags the desk near the body, getting ready to climb up and sever the rope, I notice something on the floor just below Paddy's discolored open hand. The room is dim and smoky, so I squat down to retrieve it. A wave of revulsion comes over me as I reach for it and then quickly withdraw my hand. It's his tongue.

I stand up and can now make out the smear next to him. I point to the wall. "There's our clue."

Written in Paddy's familiar handwriting, in his own blood, are the words: *Central Continent*.

TEN

Clue #2

Wednesday, June 29, 2366. Bosch Hall, my office. Nine bells.

"It's just the first clue, Kat. And it is something," Gia says, trying to reason with me this morning.

I, however, am both disgusted and defeated. "Oh, sure. The field is now narrowed to nineteen known properties spread out over some eighteen million square kilometers, minus a million or so of utterly uninhabitable land. Of course, there could be more properties Abernathy has under assumed names. And we know he is keeping a close eye on Bosch. Why else would he have picked now to kill Paddy." I shake my head. I didn't trust Paddy and was pissed as hell at him, but I still enjoyed his shenanigans, and his death was grisly, to say the least.

Gia is, as usual, prepared with a response. "Well, that's about 490 million square kilometers we can disregard. I'll take it. Maybe the next clue will narrow it that much more."

A vision of one of my children, dead and hanging by their ankles, flashes into my mind. I quickly reassure myself, *He won't kill them. He needs them as bait.* This I am sure of, but

Doubt asks quietly, *All of them?* I squeeze my eyes shut against the tears that threaten and then growl to chase the vision away. "Yeah, the glass is fucking half full. But my children still spent last night and are apt to spend more nights under that man's roof and influence." I open my eyes and see Gia's face take my verbal blow and immediately feel bad for snapping.

We are in my office, but I am on the far side of the desk, sitting in the chair I had put out for Paddy, and looking at Gia, who is in my chair. She has been taking care of all the rote work business for me, including the Hartvig situation, since I learned the babies were missing, and I truly am beyond grateful. The entire world doesn't stop when there's a crisis, or we are in pain. Knowing I have friends like Gia to keep the ship steady is such a gift. In her face, I see the pain she carries for me. I give a half-smile and nod. "No, G, you are right. It is something. Thank you…for everything."

She smiles back. "They'll be home in no time. You know there's nothing the Bosch can't do when we work together. Now let's get some coffee and a pastry. You need food."

Wednesday, June 29, 2366. Bosch, my house. Noon and three-quarters bells.

I pace back and forth in the front room, going from one window to the next. I pause to step onto the stoop. My front door is wide open, and the breeze of this mild, late June day eddies about the room. Usually, it is very hot by now, so I try to be grateful for the cooling breezes, hearing Papa say, *"It keeps the bugs down."*

I scan the road in front of the white picket fence. Seeing no one, I sigh and step back, noticing a place on the door where the cobalt blue paint has suffered a blow. My fingers run over the dent, knowing it likely came from one of the kids as they bulldozed their way into the house. Any other day, I would rant at them for spoiling something I created and want to keep nice. But I can't today; they aren't here to listen or argue back.

On the side table, nearest the entry, where we keep pencils and paper, I pull out the tablet I placed there and write "door dent." I have started a list of things I will tell them about after they return home. It's what we planned to do during the month they were in Edo, though few things made the list early on since we commed each other every day that first week. Now, though, the list is getting long.

I never realized how much of my own life I share with those three. I wonder what is on their lists. When I had them here every day, it always seemed like I was the container—they were pouring themselves out to me—but now I see how balanced it was. *Is? Will be.* I breathe that last part out as a plea to the universe.

It's almost thirteen bells. I had a houseful of people until noon, waiting for the second clue. But when half-past came, and no clue appeared, I shooed them all out, telling them to go for a walk or get some lunch. I even convinced Matty to go upstairs and shower and shave. We both need a few minutes alone. My brain settles back to the question haunting the mind of everyone I know. *Where the hell is that clue?* I imagine Abernathy watching my impatience and taking what passes for joy in the man at making me wait. Hence, my attempts to act normally today…as if my heart isn't breaking more with each moment and my fury mounting. I sigh and head to the kitchen to make a plate for Matty and me from all the casseroles sitting in the icebox.

Wednesday, June 29, 2366. Bosch, my house.

I hear the bells chime seventeen times. Then, as the chimes fade, a delivery truck pulls up, bringing in a box. Cal and Rash are on either side of the driver before he arrives on my stoop. After they pause to let him make his delivery, they pull him aside to extract any information from him, but the story is like the past two. The box simply arrived at the service with instructions to deliver it here at this precise time. The driver does remember that a dark-haired man dropped it off, but that doesn't exactly narrow the field much.

Inside, I pull the expected cream-colored envelope from the box and dump the rest of the contents on the table. Matty and Aaron rummage through them. My eyes fall on the red-and-white striped shirt, an eye patch, what looks to be a peg leg, and a hook with an attachment that might go over an amputated hand. The idea of a false hand makes me think of Eric Hartvig, who is on ice in a nice-enough room in Bosch Hall. I wanted to put him in the cells, but Miles recommended a gentler touch until we gained all the intelligence he could provide. Gia and Cal have been conducting the talks.

Tania looks at the gear. "Does he want you to be a cartoon pirate?"

I look at her, my respect growing with every interaction. I give a half-grin, looking at the components. "Um, yeah. I think that's exactly what he wants." We roll our eyes in synchrony.

I tear the envelope open.

My dear Mary,

It is time for Clue # 2. I do hope you didn't become impatient waiting for this clue. It is really quite astonishing how quickly the week is going. I hope you fathomed how the first clue included a gift for you. Really, a man that is disloyal to his friends and employers

Blow the Man Down

really cannot be trusted, so I dealt with him for the both of us. I am sure you will demonstrate your appreciation when we next meet.

Today's clue also will help both of us resolve the thorny issue with our Mr. Hartvig, whom I believe is a guest of yours currently and, if you are quick, will give you some insight into finding me and your prizes. You and your band of pirates should find this one especially emblematic. And dearest, I had your son, Kita Keaton (Kik is such an undignified name for a young man), assist with this rhyme. I do think it is quite good, and your boy seemed quite pleased with himself.

Golden hour reigns—on the biggest ocean,
    Calmly rests the sturdy beam;
    Steady is the barque's proud motion,
    Peaceful is the sailor's dream.

Sailor, come, death is near,
    You are all oh, lone,
    Arise from your deceitful sleep;
    Sailor, ere the moon shall appear,
    Thou shalt slumber in the deep.

Lightly on the riven waves,
    Bounding swift, with murderous mein,
    Sailing to the sacred victims' graves,
    Lo, the pirate-ship is seen.

I've included some appropriate gear for you as your adopted people seem unwilling to dress the part. Good luck. Five days until market.

With excited anticipation for our reunion,
    Rob

I wrinkle my brows at Matty. "Isn't that...?"

"The old Tappan poem? Yeah. But he changed it a little, I think," Matty remarks with a thoughtful expression.

"So, what did he change?" I ask.

Bailey comes over, reaching out a hand for the note. "May I?"

I nod and relinquish it.

They read it first silently, then again, in a voice too low to be heard as I watch them mouth the words on the page. Then they turn, seeming to gaze out of the tacked-up screening. "The sacred burial section off Saltend just before sunset, at golden hour. That's most of what he altered, so that's got to be it."

"If you say so. It sounds reasonable." I turn to Matty. "Can you get us there?"

"Absolutely. But I want to take the unit."

"Fine... Let's go. We are cutting close as it is if we need to be there at sunset." I start to head for the door, but Tania stops me, handing me the box with the ridiculous items piled back in.

"You never know," she says with a shrug. I take it with a snort, and we all head for Matty's larger vehicle.

∽

Wednesday, June 29, 2366. Haida, Karuk Estate, 7:30 a.m., Haida time.

Kik skidded to a stop next to his brother and sister in "meeting place C" in the hedges. Grey had said they needed to "change up the ronder-voo point so the enemy can't track us." It was lots farther away from the house, and he could barely breathe, he had run so fast. Finally, he arrived, announcing to his siblings with some pride, "I did it. He wanted Mama to go to the Bosch burial place just after sunset, so I just wrote down an old pirate poem[1] and changed some lines."

His siblings nodded approvingly as he shared the details.

∽

Wednesday, June 29, 2366. On the *Rune*. Twenty and a half bells—sunset.

It's generally a two-and-a-half bell drive to Saltend, sometimes longer, depending on the road conditions and the time of year. This time, Matty shaves off a good ten minutes, so it is just before twenty bells when we all pile onto *The Rune of Bosch* and begin the half-bell trek to the sacred burial grounds where the Bosch find their final rest. I had visited it for the first time in March to commit the bodies of the Awilda unit to the sea after their murders at the hands of a group of now-thoroughly-deceased traffickers.

Matty knows this sloop, as he said, like an extension of his own body, a description which now intrigues me in a different way than previously. Oh, the complexity of humans: We carry pain and grief, worry and anxiety, and yet, still find room for love and desire. It is astounding.

I take the tiller while Matty tends to lines and sheets, but the rest of the unit passes the time cracking nervous jokes. Finally, tired of all the parrot jokes, I kick the box of pirate gear to them, and they take the items out and jokingly try each on, pivoting and modeling for each other to claps and laughter.

After about twenty minutes, Aaron calls, "Sail ho!" and points ahead. We all look. It is still small in the distance, and there is no sail, but we all most definitely see a boat at the burial grounds. We each use the bi-spy glasses in turn to peer at it, studying the old, rusty fishing boat sporting three of the newest Enna Zephyr motors on the back and carrying a crew dressed all in black and carrying significant weaponry.

We approach cautiously. Matty attempts to raise them on several channels, to no avail. I am beginning to wonder if their presence is just a coincidence when six crew members appear from below holding three long boards, which they lay across the back of the boat, placing weights on one end and leaving the other end to extend over the sea.

"I don't like this," I hear Bailey say.

"Agreed, it looks like...shit," I reply as three half-grown, blond, and very disheveled people are escorted topside, arms bound behind them.

"They're actually making them walk the plank." Aaron's voice carries disbelief. "They didn't even do that back in the day."

I shake my head. I learned early on after I arrived in Bosch that "back in the day," said in a certain tone, means the Golden Age of Pirates.

Tania and Bailey quickly evaluate the weapons differential. "We can't outgun them," Tania determines, with Bailey nodding their agreement. Matty heaves-to, and we all stand silently together, close enough now to watch what is about to happen.

The black-suited crew marches the three captives onto the boards. Then they add a twist, tying a rope to each person's leg. At the opposite end is a net that appears to have a heavy stone or stones in it.

"Fuck." I start to strip off my clothes and see Matty and Aaron and Tania doing the same. I know that Bailey is only a recreational swimmer, and Rash can barely tolerate seeing open water.

It all happens so fast. The blonds are compelled with guns

to their heads and shouts to move to the end of the boards, a crew member behind each carrying the netted weights. There is a moment when the crew pauses, and we hear one, perhaps the captain, yell in FA, "This is what pirates do now." All at once, what must be the three Hartvig kids are shoved off the end of the planks into the deep water of the ocean, their ankle weights pulling them down before they can even yell for help.

The four of us hit the water almost simultaneously and dive deep. I am getting close to one of them, but the water is getting dark as the sun sets, and I can't see well. I grab for the floating mass of blond hair and tighten my fist around it, but then feel myself being pulled down with the force of the stones. I release the hair and reposition, forcing my body further down and pulling my blade to slice at the rope. It comes away, and the rocks continue their descent, but the person I was after starts to float off, caught in a current.

Suddenly, they lurch back toward me, and through the dim ocean water, I see Tania, pulling the unconscious person upward with the pirate hook snagged onto the bindings of their wrists. *You never know, indeed.* We make the surface. The fishing boat is only a dot on the eastern horizon, but Matty and Aaron, each with a limp, blond Hartvig in tow, are boarding the *Rune*.

Tania and I drag our Hartvig along, alternately bobbing up to inhale air and then bobbing back down, pushing through the water until we arrive boat-side. Matty pulls us up, and we quickly evaluate our prizes. None are breathing, but all three have heartbeats. One after the other, they spasm and vomit their part of the sea onto the deck. Bailey asks, "Are we pursuing?" and points in the direction the fishing boat went.

Matty shakes his head. "No point—we'd never catch them, given the motors they have."

I nod agreement, so we turn the *Rune* for shore and radio

medics to meet us at the dock. We are halfway home when one of the two girls opens her eyes.

"You are safe. So are your siblings," I reassure her, glancing at her still-unconscious sister and brother. "We are taking you all to a hospital." I decide not to mention their father quite yet.

Her eyes are not well focused, but she grabs at me and croaks, "Our backs. I'm supposed to say 'our backs.'" Then she closes her eyes and sinks back into unconsciousness.

Matty, I, and the rest of the unit all practically shrug in unison, but we gently turn the three Scanian youngsters and cut their shirts with our knives. There, on each of their backs, are fresh, fairly amateurish tattoos. The boy has been inked with a rough compass rose with the "W" circled. The one who I think is the younger girl has a mountain range on her back, and the girl who woke briefly and spoke has one of fire consuming trees across her shoulders. That's our clue. And I have no idea what it means.

ELEVEN

Excuse Me, What?

Wednesday, June 30, 2366. Bosch Hall, my office. Nine and a half bells.

"It's on the west side of a mountain—and there's a fire?" I have said this with the exact same intonation three times over the past hour as Gia, Rash, and I sit in my office, coffees now cold on the desk, and stare at the easel holding a writing board. A large floor fan circulates the air that is already heating up for the day. I should close my windows and pull the curtains, but I crave the daylight even as sweat trickles down my bare arms. I'm glad the summer uniforms are sleeveless, with a sun-proof jacket for protection outside.

I moved mission central away from my home this morning at Mama's insistence. "You need a space to come home to, darling. Somewhere you can be just Kat, not the mission planner. Somewhere you feel safe to cry." It was a good idea. My walls were covered with maps with circles and arrows; lists of last known areas for Abernathy; drone photos of so many mansions I was beginning to assume all homes were intended to have wings, turrets, and formal gardens; regular photos of my children; and close-up ones of Paddy and the tattoos. I found myself slipping out of bed and staying up until just before dawn, trying to make sense of it. So, I nodded and then noticed that Mama did not look as broken as she did before the letters came.

"You look like you got some sleep, Mama," I had said. "And you seem... I don't know... Hopeful?"

She had smiled her warm smile, though it didn't glow as it did when she was really delighted. "I did, dear. And I am hopeful. The children were smiling in the picture, and he continues to mention them, which means they are alive. Now you and the BPF are planning to rescue them. And I believe in the power of those two entities because I have seen the strength both have." She put her hand on my cheek. "So, yes, I have hope because of the BPF, but especially because of you."

Mama also made me reschedule my hour with RTT, which I had canceled for the first time in years yesterday as I waited for the second clue to arrive. I reluctantly went to her office at seven bells this morning, a time I had never imagined that therapists worked. It turned out that it felt good to be in my familiar chair, speaking with someone who knew me well. I rub my knuckles on my left hand now and feel a small, shivering pain from the scrape they received from my swipe at the brick hearth as I raged and cried. So, Mama was right on two counts. I needed to talk with Ruth, and it was good to cry. And punch something. And, I think, I feel a glimmer of hope in me as well.

Gia leans back and stares at the board where we have transcribed the tattoos from the three young Hartvigs. "West is obvious. But the rest.... I don't know. The kids you brought in, they don't know anything about them?"

"Nope. They all have similar stories. Sold off separately in November. The boy was resold in early spring. Then about a week ago, they were all collected by the black-suited crew and put on the fishing boat. They had to work but were kept shackled and abused and threatened. A few days ago, each one was taken to a cabin in turn and tattooed and warned not to look. Then yesterday, the captain told them they were going to be tossed overboard, and if they weren't dead when they were fished out of the ocean, to tell whoever they saw to look at their backs."

The room has gone very quiet as I say this, and Gia stares and I watch her lip curve in disgust. "Sweet New Earth, Kat. What kind of monsters are these people?"

"Ugly ones...who do the bidding of even uglier monsters."

Rash takes a sip of the room-temperature coffee and grimaces. "Yeah. It's a helluva note that those kids are the lucky ones."

I nod in agreement. "Well, Hartvig is with his kids again. That's something. Can't say it will last long. He has to pay for his crimes."

Gia intones, "Which are many—even according to him."

I sigh. "Well, there should be another clue today. Maybe it will help make sense of..." A commotion starts up in the outer office, and we turn toward my closed door.

"But I need to see General Wallace!" We hear a young female voice, volume rising.

Liv answers in her level, no-nonsense voice, "You need an appointment, and besides, recruits need to speak to their sergeants or the officer in charge of recruitment. General Wallace is busy."

There is a long pause, and I can't help but grin, listening to Liv handle things so crisply. We all sit quietly, waiting to hear what is said next.

Boom! My office door crashes open and a young, round-faced, round-bodied recruit with limp, chin-length brown hair stands staring into the room with Liv rushing over and grabbing her arm. The recruit's eyes are wide, and she is breathing quickly as if she is shocked at what she has done.

"Recruit Porter, either you leave immediately or I will call security," Liv says with intensity.

I look at the young woman's face as she looks at Liv and then into the room at the three of us. There's a desperate quality to it, and yet there is also resolve. I stand. "No need to call security, Liv. I think I can manage one recruit."

Liv releases the young woman's arm and says, "Yes, ma'am." She looks at me, and I can tell she thinks this is a bad idea.

"Come have a seat, Recruit…Porter…is it?" I motion toward my desk and see Rash stand and point at the chair he had just occupied.

The recruit moves into the office and looks at Captain Holloway and Commander Ka'ne, who both are regarding her as she enters my general's workspace. She freezes. "Ummm…"

"Recruit?" Gia prompts in her usual business-like voice.

Recruit Porter looks back at the door that she forcibly opened, which I am now shutting. "Maybe I should come back another time." Her voice is small, and she looks at the floor.

"Nonsense. If you go to the trouble of busting down a general's door, you might as well come in and say your piece. Sit down." I point to the chair as I move around to sit behind my desk.

She sits and looks at her knees.

I remember the feeling of all the officers' eyes on me at my assessment hearing for possible court-martial, and so I try to ask as kindly as I can, though I am somewhat impatient, having more important things to deal with than this sad recruit's moment of strength that she clearly is now regretting. "What did you want to see me about?"

The recruit's eyes come up to meet mine for only a second, dart around the room, and then settle on the writing board. She stares at it and takes some deep breaths. "Ummm, everybody talks about everything here on base." She has the accent of someone who grew up speaking FA

I nod. "True. Go on."

Her voice is barely above a whisper. "I heard that your kids are…missing. All three of them."

I am not prepared for, nor interested in, the sympathy of some recruit, and I feel my shoulders tense. "Recruit Porter," I start to stand and say with a flat tone so as not to rage, "I appreciate your support, but yes, we are in the midst of attempting to find my children and bring them home. So, if you will excuse us, we need to get back to our work and you need to get back to yours."

Now she looks me directly in the eyes and says in a haunted tone, "He'll never let you have them back."

I freeze. While it is known my children are missing, the details have been kept private. "Who…" I find my voice is shaky and clear my throat to steady it. "Who won't let me have them back?"

I watch as this young recruit's body unfolds, and her chin comes up. "The vice president."

I sit back down in my seat, and, from the corner of my eye, I see Rash walk to stand in front of the closed door, crossing his arms. I put both hands on my desk. I'm not sure if it is to steady myself or keep me from pulling a weapon. I have not broken eye contact with this recruit. "And what, if anything, does a BPF recruit know about the vice president of the FA?"

A shadow passes over her face as she says, "A lot. More than I want to. He's my father."

TWELVE

Holy Shit

Thursday, June 30, 2366. Bosch Hall. Ten bells.

"Ho-ly shit," I hear Rash say. I completely agree.

Gia comes to stand next to me and puts her hand on my shoulder while she provides this young woman with a taste of her piercing stare. "Are you saying that Vice President Rob Abernathy…?"

"Is my father? Yes." Recruit Porter answers her in a voice that seems to be growing stronger. She looks back at me. "And I think he has your children. Because I heard him talking about three children before I left at the beginning of the month."

I shrug off Gia's hand and swiftly come around to the chair this plain young recruit sits in, spinning her story. I put both hands on the arms of her chair and lean threateningly in toward her. "Where? Where the fuck are they?" My voice is angry and demanding, and I see her draw back from me. I can feel my hand wanting to rise to strike her. I catch my breath as I hear Gia say softly, "Kat…"

I squat down, still holding the arms of the chair, and lean my head back, closing my eyes and giving a deep sigh. I open them and look at her, my face and my voice softer. "I'm sorry. Do you have any idea where they might be?"

Her eyes are wide like a frightened animal's. She shrugs and whispers, "Maybe."

I've frightened her, but her fearful face stirs a memory in me. "Wait here." I go to the door, and Rash steps aside, his comm in his hand. He says in a low voice, "I messaged Warner. He should be here in a few minutes." I reach up and squeeze his shoulder in appreciation, then go to Olivia's desk and request that she make a comm for me. I take a breath and return to my office.

I look at the recruit as Rash retakes his position at the door. I need to build a bridge. "Can I get you some water or tea?"

She looks at me with concern and shrugs a little. "Water might be good."

I go to the small cabinet that serves as my bar, grab a glass, and open the icebox. I take out the pitcher of cold water, pour some, and then bring it to her. She drinks a sip and then holds the glass in her hand. Her uniform has a name tag that reads "F. Porter." I nod at it. "F. Porter?"

"Flossie Porter. That's my Bosch name now. I couldn't very well enlist as Farris Abernathy, could I?" She shrugs.

I contemplate this as I sit back down at my desk. The names of the children of both the president and vice president of the FA are easy enough to find. Who is this recruit? I don't know if she is telling any kind of truth, though what would be the point of lying?

"Why would Rob Abernathy's daughter enlist in the BPF? It makes no sense. If you really are his daughter, then you must have had a pretty cushy life. Why come here? Did he send you to infiltrate? We need the truth." I keep my voice conversational, but I will get what I need from this girl.

She twists her face around, and it moves from what looks

like disgust to almost a smile. "He wouldn't trust me to do anything. He hates me. I mean, look at me. I'm not exactly the model beautiful daughter he would want." She swipes at her straight hair and shoves a loose lock behind her ear. "He said the Bosch were criminals and wanted to destroy him." She looks at me, and her eyes contain curiosity but not malice.

My eyebrows go up, but I stay silent.

"I've never belonged. Never fit into my family. I always used to make-believe I lived some other life—where people liked me and I could be happy and strong and brave, or at least not get hit and humiliated. Finally, one night, I overheard him talking about Bosch, and so when he was horrid to me, I decided to leave and be part of trying to destroy him."

I lean my left elbow on the desk, my thumbnail between my teeth as I listen and consider this girl. I say nothing, but I do understand the idea of not fitting in and wanting some other life. That was me as a kid back in the North Country. I got my wish here in Bosch, but the path here was ugly and painful.

"I've made a couple friends here, though." She sighs and her voice drops. "I'm not very good at being a pirate. My drill instructor always tells me I'm the worst." She pauses and her face folds in heavy lines. The kind I get when Shame and Insecurity are taunting me. "I can't shoot straight, and I always get knocked down in fights. And I am a slow runner."

Her story certainly plays at my heart, and I want to smile. But she could be lying and be placed here to slow me from getting to my children. "You understand if I am skeptical of your claim. My...experiences with whom you claim to be your father makes me highly suspicious of anyone who asserts to have been allied or related to him." I turn both arms over in an I-don't-know gesture.

She nods. "I get that." I see her look at my left arm and my thrall brand. Her eyes narrow and a crease appears between her brows. Then her eyes go to my neck and widen slightly. She leans forward and asks in a whisper, "Are you the thrall he calls 'Mary'?" She gapes at me. "I read the transcripts from the trial on the airship here. It is you, isn't it?"

I nod. "I'm no longer enslaved and haven't been for seventeen years, so thrall is not a descriptor I'll take. But yes, I'm the one who testified against him. Though in retrospect, I probably should have taken care of him the Bosch way. Sorry, Phil."

She tips her head. "If the Bosch way would have made him go away, I wish you had. Is the Phil you mentioned the same Phil who is the attorney general?" I nod and she smiles. "Oh, he really hates both of you. You're the 'evil woman' I've heard him talk about. And he says the AG is bent on ruining him."

I start to comment when there's a knock on the door, and Rash opens it. Matty stands there and looks in with concern and curiosity. Next to him is whom I had Olivia call.

Carisa looks into my office, and her eyes widen. "Miss Farris? What are you doing here, for goodness sake? Are you okay?"

Recruit Porter turns and stares at the lovely, petite blonde woman who steps in closer. Her face lights up in both recognition and what looks like shock intermixed with a touch of joy. "Ann? You're alive?" Carisa comes over to the recruit and reaches a hand out. Recruit Porter is crying now as she takes it; she looks at my friend and reaches out to touch her face. "He said he killed you. Because of me."

∽

June 30, 2366. Bosch Hall and the green. Noon.

I called Mama to come over to take charge of Flossie Porter. She doesn't want anyone to call her by her old name, though she doesn't seem to mind when Carisa does. The recruit says her favorite teacher in primary, a Miss Johanna, had accidentally called her Flossie one time and then kept calling her that as an inside joke between the two of them. Miss Johanna, in turn, had allowed her to call her Miss Jo. She drew the name Porter from someone who had worked for the Abernathy household not long ago who had been kind to her.

I've made two other calls—one to the OIC of recruitment requesting that Recruit Porter be given personal leave for a few days with no repercussions. The other was to Tommy Gallagher, who groused about being too old and not wanting to come out of retirement to drag "some infant out of their crib and make them a pirate." I told him he had the weekend to make a plan to whip Recruit Porter into shape and that I'd tell Teddy if he said no. He laughed and said, "Damn that man, still running my life from the great beyond. I'll be there Monday."

Before she went back home with Mama, I watched as Flossie and Carisa talked in my office, Carisa wiping Flossie's tears and reassuring her that none of what had happened was her fault. Flossie clearly adored Carisa.

She had been fifteen and sent off on a holiday when the rescue mission occurred. When she had returned to the New Detroit house, she went to her father's study to ask where Carisa, whom she knew only as Ann, was. Her father had clucked his tongue and asked if she had given one of her outgrown dresses to Ann. When Flossie said she had, he pointed out a small, brown blood stain on the floor. It was one of Will's we had missed, but he told her it was Carisa's and that he was forced to dispose of her because "thralls should not be that familiar with their owners" and perhaps Farris "should be more careful in the future." What a bastard.

I watched the two women recall their shared history, and something began to dawn on me. I am appalled at myself for not having considered it before, and I need to address it. So, I leave Gia in charge of waiting for the next clue and head outside.

Aaron, Carisa, and Matty all sit, chatting at one of the many umbrellaed tables. They are starting to open the bags that hold lunch, and I catch the scent of salmon empanadas. I slide next to Matty and give him a kiss, which I intended to be quick, but his hand comes to my cheek, and it extends. I hear Aaron chuckle, and we move apart, but only a little.

"So, what's the agenda for this lunch meeting, General? Plan an attack on Haida?" Aaron asks with a smile.

I am still unwilling to consider having any troops be a part of the offensive to extract the kids. I want to handle it solo. Get in, get out, get home. And now it seems possible. Flossie has told us where she believes the children are: an estate somewhere outside of the city of Haida, which, she pointed out while looking at the board in my office, is west of the Burnt Mountains—or what was known in the Old Days as the Sierra Nevada Range. So obvious once she said it.

I have Cal's people working to pinpoint the estate among the dozen or so luxury properties that are spread around the bay. That area hadn't even made the list of known Abernathy properties. We would have never gotten this close without Flossie. She said she only was there once when she was about five, so she just remembers a big house and garden and a high bluff with lots of seabirds.

I shake my head. "No. I…" I look at Carisa and tear up. My empanada-free hand slides onto Matty's knee and gives it a squeeze. He looks down at me, uncertain of what I am about to say. I give a half-smile. "So, for the past seventeen years, I have marched around, throwing my brand up, preaching about the horrors of human trafficking, and plotting my revenge against Rob Abernathy because of the abuse I suffered at his hands for a year and a half." I reach across the table now and grasp Carisa's hand. "But you, my friend, how did I not actually realize until today that you survived thirteen years with him? I could never have lasted through what you clearly did. You should have been the one seeking revenge these past years." I watch as Aaron's arm comes protectively around this tiny woman.

Carisa looks off in the distance for a few seconds, and I watch her face as her brows furrow and then relax. A small smile curves her lips, and she moistens them with her tongue and closes her eyes, giving a sigh. Then she looks at me. "Kat, I was good at blending in and being invisible on Bellcoast, and it helped for a year or so after you escaped. When Abernathy finally called for me, it was you who helped me survive. You had taught me to disconnect. And while that isn't healthy in this world…" She makes a circle with her finger. "…it was essential in Abernathy's.

"Once I was moved to New Detroit, things… Well, they weren't better, but his family was there, and he was in Truvale quite a bit, so the episodes were…less frequent. And I got to take care of the children. Farris—I mean, Flossie—was just seven when I arrived, and that was actually fun. One day, the year after I had been brought there, he came back to stay in New Detroit, and I heard him curse your thrall name. Oh, he was so angry. He took it out on everyone—the children, his wife, his assistant…and me.'

"Oh, Ris, I'm so sorry," I practically moan.

"No, don't be. I was glad he was angry, though not glad he

wasn't leaving the house. I didn't know exactly why he was so mad, but I knew you had done something to him, and that gave me hope. I believed that since you had done something once, you would do something more. And eventually, you did. You found me. You saved me, though I know the price was horribly high."

I take a sharp breath in, remembering. Now I feel Matty squeeze my thigh for strength. "We went in to get you out, Ris."

She nods. "And you did, Kat. You got me out, even if I was still a scared little rabbit."

"You're no rabbit," I say automatically, though, with Ruth, I am overcoming my distaste for the species.

"But I'm no avenger, either. I'm not a BPF pirate. I'm a researcher. And I know things about Rob Abernathy, and I'm learning more. I'll provide the information. You take our revenge." She squeezes my hand and smiles at me.

I squeeze back. "I will. For both of us."

She looks at Aaron, and their eyes speak to each other. Then he smiles and gives a small nod. She grins and looks back at me. "And I can't go off to battle anyway. Aaron and I are having a baby."

For the first time since Takai called about my children, utter joy floods me, and Matty and I leap up to give congratulatory hugs, kisses, and slaps on the back.

THIRTEEN

Clue #3
_____

June 30, 2366. Haida, Karuk Estate. 8:00 a.m., Haida time.

"So, did your brother and sister tell you what I am doing?" Mr. A. showed his very white teeth to Mac as they stood in the big, wood-paneled office.

Mac looked at the tall man and thought, *You cut my mama. I know you did.* "Yeah," Mac answered in what he hoped was his most cheerful voice. "We are playing seek-and-find for Mama to come visit us.

"That's correct. And it's your turn to help me with the clues. Does that sound fun?" Mr. A. spoke to them as if they were babies. "You can describe what it looks like here. Perhaps the flowers. But don't make it too easy for her. You know she likes a challenge."

Mac had never felt so much dislike for anyone before. Not even the kid in their class who made fun of Kik for having long hair and writing stories. He really felt the urge to hit Mr. A., but Grey had said they had to be careful. And if this man had cut Mama, who was the strongest, toughest person Mac knew, what might he do to a little kid who hit him? "Yeah.

Lotsa fun. Can I write it like a song? Matt and I like to write songs."

Mac watched Mr. A.'s false smile waver. "You and Matt. Hmm. Of course, like a song."

Mac sat down at the big desk and thought about all that he and his siblings had talked about and all the things they saw. *What might help Mama?* He wrote, crossed out, and then wrote again. He used the big dictionary to check on words, and he scribbled a few more out. He glanced up and saw Mr. A. sitting in a wing-backed chair in the corner nearest the door, looking at his timepiece in an impatient manner. Finally, Mac wrinkled his brow and put his thumbnail between his front teeth as he read over what he hoped was finished. "Okay, I'm done," he called.

Mr. A. hurried over and read it silently. "Hmph. Well, it's not as good as your brother's, but it will do."

Mac smiled inside because Kik had used an old pirate poem and just changed some words and Mr. A. hadn't realized it. Mr. A. didn't notice what Mac had done either. Maybe you didn't have to be very smart to be a vice president; maybe only a president did, and maybe not even then. Mama was smart, though. She would figure it all out. "Can I go play?" he asked, standing up and walking a few steps toward the door.

"Yes, of course," Mr. A. said without looking at him. Instead, the tall, impatient man looked at his timepiece and made a growling sound, then he took the paper Mac had given him and walked rapidly out of the room, breezing past Mac and leaving him alone. Mac stood very still, holding his breath. He heard the footsteps fade away down the hallway, and he remembered the third part of the secret.

Mama liked to say, "Quick as fire," so that was how Mac moved. He ran back to the big desk near the window and pulled open the top drawer. He grabbed the comm, stuffed it into his pocket, and started to close the drawer, then he paused for a fraction of a second, pulled it open again, and grabbed the pistol that was there. He knew enough to check that the safety was on, then he stuffed that, too, in his pocket—though it only fit in partway—slammed the drawer shut, and ran out the door Mr. A. had left ajar in his haste.

Thursday, June 30, 2366. Bosch, my house. Fourteen bells.

Clue three comes to my house in a box of chocolates, which, ordinarily, I'd be thrilled to have, but I want nothing to do with anything that comes from Abernathy. Mama is posted up at my place with Flossie, and she took the delivery. While mission central is now my office, Cal and Matty and I head over to evaluate this newest piece of information.

When we arrive, Flossie is looking longingly at the chocolates. I grin. "You can have them if you want them. I don't."

The recruit lights up. "I love chocolate!"

I open the box, and there is an envelope on top. I open it and lay it on the table for Cal and Matty and me to read, pushing the box of candy to Flossie.

Dearest Mary,

I don't know if you were able to solve my last clue or even if you were able to fully retrieve it. Hopefully, it will end poor Mr. Hartvig's search either way.

This clue was written, laboriously and at great length, by your duller son, Macrae. It does give you some images to search for, though market day is coming quickly, and I'm not certain you will be successful.

Kaleidoscopes of red and purple
> *Dance along the pathway's edge*
Above the bluff
> *The seagulls fly*
Rusty fence is broken off
> *Don't get close or you may fall*
Ukulele and guitars left behind
> *In Edo land*
Know that we cannot wait
> *For you to come and hold our hand.*

Please note, I am not without my own protective resources, so I hope you are prepared to lose some of your pirates as you come to attempt to retrieve your children. If you wish to simply surrender and present yourself at my doorstep, I am sure bloodshed can be kept to a minimum.

See you soon, one way or another.

Your owner,
Rob Abernathy

I read the poem over again and again. Definitely at the coast, but…

Flossie speaks up through a mouthful of chocolates, "He's not dull like my father says. He's really smart." She is peering at the letter on the table.

I look at her. "Yeah, he is. But why do you say that?"

She wipes a brown-stained finger on her uniform front and places it on the first line of the poem. Then the third. Then the fifth, the seventh, and the ninth. "See."

I don't see. And I'm about to say so, when Cal says, "Oh, shit. I see—Karuk. It's Karuk Estate."

She nods, reaching for another chocolate. "Yeah. I would

never have remembered the name, but when I saw the letters, it suddenly rang a bell."

I stare at her, unable to speak.

"Kat, show her the other clues," Cal urges.

I look at him and at Matty and Mama and shrug, taking the first two clues from my bag, along with the original Tappan poem, and lay them next to the third.

Flossie regards them for several minutes, then laughs. "I don't know what all the clues mean, but there are clues inside the clues. Damn, all your kids are smart." She points to the first clue, reading, *"While Leeward is where we be.* Leeward: the west. That is where they are. That's the first clue."

Now, she points to the first line of the second clue. *Golden hour reigns; on the biggest ocean,* and tells me, "They are next to the Great Sea. But this one is my favorite. It isn't in the original at all. *"You are all oh, lone…* Ohlone Bay. That's where Haida is. And then, of course, the really specific one your Macrae wrote for Karuk. This is fun!" She looks stricken with her last statement. "I'm sorry, I didn't mean…"

Cal has, along with Matty, Mama, and I, been staring at this plain, frumpy recruit who has all but told us she has no talents. Now, he interrupts her apology and turns to me. "Mine. She is mine after graduation. Is that clear?"

I give an actual laugh. "Hey, it's up to her. But it seems like a perfect fit."

Cal smiles at her. "Recruit Porter, correct?" Flossie nods and stands up a little straighter, though she has a smear of chocolate on her upper lip. "I'm Colonel Calvin Greene of Bosch Intelligence. Have you thought about going into codework?"

And for the first time, a real smile grows on Recruit Porter's face, and I see Farris Abernathy fade into history.

Thursday, June 30, 2366. Bosch, outside my house. Fifteen and a half bells.

I walk Cal out the door with the newest clue transcribed for him and tucked safely in his pocket. He seems happy, but there is something clearly weighing on him. "What's on your mind, Cal?" I say with as open a voice as I can currently muster.

He looks at me and narrows his eyes, and his smile is tight. "Apparently, my tradecraft isn't good enough to keep you from knowing when something's up."

I give a tired laugh. "I know you too well, kid."

"We, uh, picked up Archer yesterday."

I look at him, and my feelings are jumbled. The *me* before my children were stolen would have been whooping and leaping at this news. Now, all I can muster is a nod and a "Well done, Major—er, I mean, Colonel." It's a clear indication of how tired and distracted I am that I fuck up somebody's hard-won rank.

Cal just grins, and it's a real grin because, after all, his children are safe and well at his home. And for that, I am thankful. "Well, there's more," he says. "I've put Archer in a holding cell, way out in District Six, out of your easy reach. But we also picked him up with Alejandro DeLeon."

My head pivots swiftly to look straight at Cal. His grin increases. "Him, I put in a cell in Bosch Hall, and you are on the list to question him, starting tomorrow."

I consider this and let out a low whistle, and then say quietly, almost to myself, "Happy fucking birthday to me."

Part III

FOURTEEN

There's Something Happen' Here

Thursday, June 30, 2366. Haida, Karuk Estate. 9:30 a.m., Haida time.

Mac didn't stop running until he was deep in the gardens. He was breathing heavily, but he managed to give the quick, two-note whistle that he and Kik used to call each other. After a couple of minutes, he heard the unmistakable sounds of his brother and sister. At least he was pretty sure it was them. He scooted back into a hedge that had tiny, purple blossoms on it. There were bees all over it, and he didn't want to get stung, but if that was Mr. A. coming, things would be worse than a bee sting, Mac was sure.

From where he was hiding, he could see the pathway in the garden, and he saw two pairs of bare feet appear and then stop just in front of him.

"Where is he?" he heard Grey ask as she started moving in the systematic sweep Mama had taught them to find misplaced toys and lost shoes.

He started to crawl out from the hedge, and it made his

brother jump. "Mac! That's not funny," Kik said, scowling at him.

"I needed to be sure it was you two." He looked at them, and he could still feel his heart beating as if it were ten times its normal size. "Look." He pulled the comm and the pistol out of his pockets.

Kik and Grey stared, their mouths hanging open. Finally, Grey breathed out. "Oh, Mac, what have you done?"

∽

Thursday, June 30, 2366. Haida, Karuk Estate.10:00 a.m., Haida time.

"It needs its battery charged. It's useless like this," Grey said after pushing every button on the comm several times and still having a black screen reflect back to her. Disappointment flooded through her. She and her brothers sat in a tight group, peering at the device.

Kik said, "Maybe we should put it back. Along with the gun." He glared at his brother as he spoke that last word.

The gun now sat safely behind Grey, pointed away from all of them. Mac had reassured both her and Kik that he had been careful. But still, Grey had immediately demanded Mac hand it over. They never touched any of Mama's weapons, but they had watched her clean them and listened to her talk about handling them safely.

Grey had gone to the firing range on her eleventh birthday, this past May, and her Aunt Gia, who wasn't really an aunt but just a good friend, showed her how to shoot a lightweight pistol and a rifle. She hadn't hit much and found that it was really hard to make her shots go straight, and they were pretty loud as well. But it was fun, and she had asked her mama about more practice. Mama said there was plenty of time to learn.

"I think putting them back will be riskier than nabbing them," Grey decided. "Maybe he won't notice. Since the comm doesn't work, maybe he won't go to look for it. And there's no reason he'd look for the gun."

Mac reached for the dead comm. "Do you think Obaachan's cord would work for it?"

"No." Grey shook her head slowly. "I was looking at hers last night when we were saying good night. Remember how she came over and took it and said it didn't work?"

The boys nodded.

Grey continued, "Hers is a different kind—the kind you get in Edo, so I'm guessing the cord is different too."

Kik looked thoughtful. "You know, I bet there's a charging cord in the drawer. Grownups always keep them in spots near comms."

"That's a good idea," Mac praised. "One of us could sneak in and get it, and the other two could be on lookout. It'd be like an extraction mission."

The children often played missions where they rescued a toy and had to climb trees and wriggle under fences and take the stairs three at a time, sometimes firing on each other with small, soft missiles inside or water pistols with dye outside.

Grey considered the proposal. "We could do that, but first, we should hide the weapon."

Thursday, June 30, 2366. Haida, Karuk Estate. 9:30 p.m., Haida time

"Go," Grey said in a whisper to Mac as soon as she saw Kik's hand do a thumbs-up move through the second-floor stair railing. She looked left and right and gave him a little shove. Mac had on a black t-shirt and a pair of Grey's dark blue short pants. Kik had smeared mud on Mac's face and hands, and Grey had fashioned a bag for Mac to wear on his back like Mama did and put in the comm and a fork. "In case you need to jimmy a lock." Mac thought it sounded quite professional the way she said it.

They had put the gun in the wood box that was used for the firepit on the bluff side of the house and covered it with an old, greasy, red rag they found in the gardening shed. Since no one went on that side of the house, they figured it was the safest spot. Then they started their preparations for the mission.

Everything was ready before they were called to dinner, but they knew they had to wait until it was dark, and everyone was asleep. Mac thought it would be hard not to fall asleep, but his insides felt all funny. He could barely eat dinner and had used the bathroom about six times since they made the plan. He wasn't tired at all.

He scooted down the hallway, toward Mr. A.'s office, intent on getting the plug for the comm. He paused at the fancy double doors and listened for the two-note whistle that they had agreed would be used if there was trouble. He heard nothing. He peeked under the doors. The room was dark.

Slowly, slowly, Mac turned the ornate doorknob on the left side and gave the door a small push. He peeked inside. The drapes were drawn, and everything was very dark. He knew the desk was close to the window directly across from the doors. He dropped to his knees and crawled quickly over until he felt he was almost there. His eyes were getting used to the dark, but everything was still just large blobs of dark gray. He squinted and put his hand out as he inched forward.

It seemed to take forever, but finally, he came to a large, dark shadow, and his hand touched what was clearly the smooth front of the desk. He carefully felt his way around to the far side, feeling the intricately carved legs in the front and the back. Then he slowly stood and felt for the drawer, lifted it slightly, and opened it with just the slightest scraping sound. He reached in and began to feel around for the cord. There were papers and writing tools. In the far back was something hairy that made him jump slightly when his hand grazed it, but no cord. He stood and sighed. He would have to look in the other drawers.

He was feeling for the one on the left when suddenly, he was blinded by the bright electric lights of the room blazing on. He automatically put his hands up to shade his squinting eyes and looked in front of the desk. There was Mr. A., standing with a cord in his hand. And he wasn't smiling.

Thursday, June 30, 2366. Haida, Karuk Estate study. 9:46 p.m., Haida time.

The three children were seated in straight-backed chairs that had been brought in from the kitchen: Macrae on the right, Grey in the center, and Kik on the left. Mr. A. stood in front of his desk, holding the bag Mac had carried, facing them. A handsome young man, probably in his twenties, blond and similar in build to Mr. A., had come in shortly after the lights came on, hustling Grey and Kik roughly along, a strong grip on each of their upper arms. Now he stood behind them, still keeping one firm hand on Grey's shoulder and another on Kik's.

Mr. A. slowly opened the bag and pulled out the comm and the fork, considering each one before settling them carefully on the edge of the desk next to the cord he dropped there. He felt around in the bag and, finding nothing further, tossed it on the floor. "What were you planning to do with the comm, Macrae?"

Mac glanced over at his sister, and Mr. A.'s voice came up loud. "*Don't* look at her." It was a clear command, and Mac looked back at the man standing in front of him immediately. "The comm, Macrae?" His voice was regular at volume now.

Mac swallowed. "We were going to call our mama."

"Ahh." Mr. A. nodded and looked at Mac and then Kik and then Grey. "I see. And then, were you going to shoot her with the gun you also stole?"

This time, Grey answered and tried to rise but was forced to stay seated by the young man's hand. "No! Mac just thought it would be fun to play with."

Mr. A. tipped his head. "Really. And where is it now?" He was clearly addressing Grey.

There was the tiniest pause and then, "I got mad at him and told him guns were dangerous. So, I threw it over the bluff into the ocean." Grey was using her big-sister-know-it-all voice.

A single eyebrow came up on Mr. A.'s face, but he made no response. Instead, he turned to Kik. "You are awfully quiet."

Kik looked at the blond man who had blank eyes. "I have nothing to say to you."

At this, Mr. A.'s face curved into a smile, though it looked far from friendly. Now he addressed the young man. "Ashton, I've been heartless. These poor children just want to talk to their mommy." The children heard the young man snort while Mr. A. continued, "Well, I'll tell you what. Let's comm your mama."

Now the children all looked at one another, and no one yelled for them not to. It was Kik who spoke up. "Yes, please, Mr. A., may we?"

"Of course." The smile on his face now looked even more unpleasant. "But I would like to speak with her as well." He glanced at his timepiece. "Let's hope she wakes easily." He pulled out a small, very modern comm from his front jacket pocket and looked at Grey. "The number?"

Grey recited Mama's comm number and watched as Mr. A. punched it in. He was about to push "on" when he paused and smiled at them.

"You children do realize that you will never return to Edo or to Bosch. Your mother was a thrall, and that makes you thralls. Your very lives are maintained right now by my whim and even the whims of Ashton here." They heard another chuckle from the young man who was looking less handsome to them by the moment. "Keep quiet and do as you are told, and you may live to see another sunrise. Act out and you will see your siblings suffer at my hands."

He looked at the stricken faces of the three young pirates and smiled. "Now, let's chat with Mama, shall we?"

Friday, July 1, 2366. Bosch, my bedroom. One bell and three minutes.

My eyes pop open as I hear the comm buzz. I don't recognize the number, but I have been answering every comm since the children have been gone. I sit up and push the "on" button as

Matty rouses and looks questioningly at me. I shrug. "Hello?"

My throat tightens as a voice comes through the comm. "Mary, dear. How delightful to hear your voice. I cannot wait to see you soon."

I slap at Matty and click the speaker on my comm. I mouth "Abernathy" and flip the light on. "Mr. Vice President, where are the children?" I try to make my voice sound relaxed and conversational. I see Matty turn the recorder on his comm and set it near me.

The voice now comes across with a pouting tone. "Oh, Mary. Do call me Rob. I had hoped you'd want to chat a bit with me." There is a pause, and I can hear the slight hollowness that happens when the comm is switched to speaker. "But they are here. Say hello, children."

I hold my breath.

"Hi, Mama. I miss you." It's Mac.

"Oh, Mac, same. I love you," I say before I lean my head back against the wall and start to cry.

Now I hear Grey's voice. "Hi, Mama. Can you come get us?"

There is a short laugh in the background, and I feel my temper cut my tears off.

"Yes, Grey. I will. I love you," I say firmly.

Finally, Kik is on the comm and says, "We are okay. But we want to come home."

"Yes, Kik—you will. I love you."

I hear the children murmur in turn, "I love you, Mama."

Grey says, "Tell Matt we love him and miss him too." I hear the boys repeat the same sentiment in the background.

I glance at Matty and see him wipe his eyes and nose with the back of his hand. He leans in and says in a husky voice, "I love you guys, too. Sit tight. We'll be there soon."

The phone switches off speaker, and Rob Abernathy says with a lacing of venom, "Aren't you all the cozy little family? The children do so want to follow in your footsteps, Mary. So, I'll help. I'll be sure to get them their first tattoo at the marketplace—just like your first one. Maybe I'll even give Grey the same necklaces I gave you. One that sparkles…" His voice shifts to its most dangerous tone, the one that still sends a cold stab into me. "…and one that stays."

My anger boils over at this threat, pushing the old fear aside. "Listen, you bastard. I guarantee you will die at my hand, but if you even touch one of my children, I will make it take so long that you'll beg me to finish it, and then I'll make it hurt even longer. Is that clear?"

His response is a cold laugh. "I can't wait to see you and all your pirates soon, my dear. Everything is going to go my way. You kept me from what was due me before, but I will have it now. Remember, Mary. This is all because of you. Everything that will happen to your children, your lover, the pirates who you call family, even Bosch itself, is your fault." There is a tiny pause. "You should never have run from me, but now, perhaps you should run from Bosch *to* me."

The line goes dead, and I throw my comm across the room with a growl.

FIFTEEN

I'm Coming for You

Friday, July 1, 2366. Bosch, my house. One bell and six minutes.

I am up and pulling extraction clothes from their drawer and onto my body in seconds as I scrabble to find where my comm landed. As I rise from the floor with it, Matty stands in front of me.

"What are you doing, Kat?" he asks levelly, reaching out to me.

I shake his touch away. "I would think that would be obvious. I'm going to get my children. We know where they are now. I shouldn't have even waited this long. Every minute I delay, he might…" I can't bear to finish the thought.

"You just talked to them. They are okay. He said earlier that market was not until Monday. Let's…work…the plan." His voice is calm and reasonable.

I, however, am not. "No! We made a plan last night. I'm just turning up the clock on it."

"Kat, you know you can't go into a mission like this. Your judgment will be off. You have to—"

"If you fucking tell me to calm down, I'll cut your heart out." I feel for the dagger that I have yet to strap on.

Matty's fingers come to his forehead, and he turns from me for a moment. I take that time to pull my pistols for loading and strap their holsters on my back. My rifle is in the *Coupe*. I pull open the drawer that holds my blade.

He is back next to me. "Kat, what was Teddy's saying about mission prep?"

I glare at him, thigh holster in hand. "There's no time."

Now his voice comes up loud and commanding, "Dammit, Kat, make the time."

I square off and put my hands on my hips. "Don't you yell at me."

Now his eyes are flashing, and his voice is still loud. "I-1, Kat."

"No!" I yell now.

I-1!" he yells in my face.

I stomp my foot, then spin and head for the bedroom door. He is fast and cuts in front of me and stands, his big frame blocking my exit. "Fuck off, Matty. I'm going!" I yell.

"Fine! I will fucking pack your damn bag," he says with fire in his voice. "But first, you tell me: I-1."

I take a breath and work the angry kink in my neck. "I-1: initial information: plan one. Now let me pass."

"Nope. I want the rest: R-2, D-3, C-F. Go." His voice is lower now, but his body is still tense and ready to go toe-to-toe with me. "Let's hear them all. Every recruit knows them. And you got to learn them twice."

I roll my eyes. "As if I needed to learn them again." This was still a sore point for me.

"Great, then." He makes a little *c'mon* motion with the fingers of his right hand while looking expectantly at me.

I sigh. "R2: refined information: plan two. D3: detail work: plan three. CF: contingency plan: final prep. Go."

Matty nods. "And if you don't follow the steps?"

I move my jaw back and forth. "Bad plan: bad outcome."

"And what step is this plan on?" His volume is lower, and his shoulders drop their tension as he looks tenderly at me.

I blink and look out the window. I say with a moan, "Matty, I can't bear my babies being there."

Now Matty's voice has its usual soft, tender tone. "I know, my love. If they were anyone else's children, and you had to extract them, would you allow either of their parents to be mission planners?"

I shake my head. "No," I say, my voice almost a whisper.

"Kat…General, what stage is this plan?" he asks softly as he puts his arms around me.

I lean onto his chest and listen to his heart steadily beating. "R2," I say shakily.

"R2," he agrees. "We need details. Cal can get some. So can Carisa." He kisses my hair and says after a moment, "But I'll bet you can get some great details from DeLeon, and as I understand it, you have access, General."

I had almost forgotten DeLeon. I feel the smile start as I pull back and look at the man I love. "That is an excellent idea, Major."

"Thank you." He smiles back. "Now how about you and I tuck back in and discuss your interview agenda for tomorrow."

∼

Friday, July 1, 2366. Outside Bosch Hall. Seven and a half bells.

I have dismissed the guards who offered to walk DeLeon "to my office" and escort him myself. He is taller than I am, though not as tall as Matty, and fit enough. He is dark-haired with handsome features and a swarthy complexion as well as a debonair manner. He still wears a suit made of fine fabric in the latest style. Granted, it's a bit wrinkled and dirty from his time in the cell, but spiffy, nonetheless.

If I saw him in a crowd, I'd figure he was part of the upper class of his country, perhaps a royal or a banker. I wouldn't guess he was responsible for the selling of thousands upon thousands of vulnerable people into a nightmare of forced labor and abuse. Just considering that makes me want to hit him. Hard.

On his legs, he wears a fairly long ankle shackle, and his arms are bound with his hands in front of him. He can easily attempt escape if he dares. I hope he does.

I did opt to put a couple of layers of tape over his mouth. Whether that was to avoid any annoying table talk as I drove or to give me the early pleasure of ripping it off at the cave, I am unsure. As we arrive at my vehicle, he pauses at the back door and looks expectantly at me as if I am his hired chauffeur. I give a snorting laugh and grab his arm to walk him to the front passenger seat. Like hell will I leave a man with full use of his shoulders in my back seat. I pull the security belt across his shoulders and chest, pinning his arms close. Then I give a little slap to the retractor, causing the belt to tighten and keep his arms firmly against his chest.

I slide into the driver's seat and look at this trafficker who not only has become extravagantly wealthy on the backs of the enslaved but also ordered my children kidnapped earlier in the year. I regard him with a grin. "I'm in a really shitty mood,

Alejandro. So your job today is to talk until I am adequately cheered up."

And with that, we drive off of the base to the cave where Teddy first taught me how to interview the enemy.

~

Friday, July 1, 2366. Bosch, my house. Fourteen bells.

I push open the blue door to my little white house. The drive is full of my friends' vehicles, so I know that the audience I requested is here.

My front room is silent and empty, which I find disquieting. Chatter comes in through the back kitchen window. I walk into the kitchen and can see onto the patio. The unit—plus Demery, Gia, and Cal—all are present. They talk mostly in low tones, but there's the occasional laugh that attracts everyone's attention. I give a sigh. These are really good people, and I really don't want them in harm's way.

I open the back door and step down to the stonework I installed myself, years earlier, and am met with several rousing rounds of "Hey" and "There she is," as well as several quiet hand greetings. Matty stands from the chair he is sitting on and walks over to wrap me in his arms, then he gives me a long kiss as he lifts me and swings me in a semicircle before setting my feet on the ground. The move is met with a few whistles and hoots. I whisper to him, "You are ruining my credibility as a leader."

He looks at me, and his eyes are sparkling as he kisses my nose and wipes a smear of blood from my chin as he scrutinizes the growing bruise on my cheek. "The hell you say. I know I'll follow you anywhere."

I grin at my Matty, and then turn to my friends. "So…" I

point to the spatters of DeLeon blood on my clothes and face. "I was able to extract the count of guards and soldiers stationed and ready outside the Karuk Estate in Haida." The patio is quiet, waiting. "Two hundred." The number falls heavily in the room, and my people look at each other. I am loathe to ask the next thing, but I know I have to. I close my eyes and feel a self-deprecating smile start on my face. "I know I said I was going in alone." I open my eyes and look at my friends, my comrades-in-arms. "Two hundred is a bit much even for me, and so…" I take a deep breath. "I need your help. Hell, I'm going to need a hell of a lot of help. But I can't—well, I won't—order you to do this. I can only ask: Will you help me to get my kids home?"

My people all look at Gia, which I guess makes sense; she is ranking. Gia walks up, puts her hand on my cheek, and smiles the smile of an old friend. "Of course, Troop. You have to know we wouldn't have stayed away no matter what. Now let's hear the intel you got so we can plan our attack."

I nod and look from Gia to all the faces of these friends whom I have come to rely on so much. It used to terrify me to feel that need; now I guess it completes me. Thanks, RTT. So, I sit down and pull my chair close to the group as I tell them almost everything Alejandro DeLeon, the Southern Central Continent human trafficking cartel boss, had to say as he attempted, unsuccessfully, to cheer me up. It did not bother me that he failed to survive my interview.

Friday, July 1, 2366. Bosch, my house. Fifteen and a half bells.

The unit, heavy with Demery and Gia, is deep in discussion on the patio about the offensive they have planned. They have clearly been developing strategies well before today, and while I wanted to be annoyed, what I feel is gratitude for so many. Carisa found and sent over a decent, but somewhat dated, map of the close to eighty square kilometers of rugged land the Karuk Estate sits on, giving us an idea of topography and where Abernathy's army will likely be posted. Cal's people will use glider drones to collect images of the area as well as use local contacts to get us inside information. Miles has reiterated his offer of more troops and has had the BPF begin mobilization, saying that this is about striking a blow to human trafficking as well as rescuing my children.

I gently touch Matty's shoulder and then Cal's and walk into the house, pulling a glass of water and washing my hands for the fourth time since the interview. The men come in, and we look at each other. Then I turn silently and walk up the stairs. I stand for a moment at the head of the stairs and then decide on Grey's room to talk. The three of us walk in, with Matty closing the door behind us. He looks at me expectantly while Cal peers at the walls and the desk of my pre-teen daughter, his eyes undoubtedly missing nothing.

"You know how we've talked about an Abernathy escape route?" I begin.

Both men nod. Abernathy had slipped away via a tunnel slide behind a bookcase in New Detroit. Anyone willing to go to those lengths will certainly not leave egress to chance in the current situation.

"So, Karuk Estate: He is there now with the children and, we assume, Yumiko Shima. And there are two centuria stationed around it to draw our attention and our fire. Thanks to Carisa's research, we know Abernathy has issues with too many armed guards in his home or on the actual grounds of the estate. He only allows half a dozen soldiers to function as sentries and guards.

Actual troops aren't allowed any closer than five kilometers. But even so, based on some of the last things DeLeon mumbled, I believe that he's going to move out early in the onslaught. He is no soldier and will want to be far from danger. Also, when it comes to the kids, it's clear he doesn't intend for me to ever get them back. Once he has me, they are disposable." I put my hand to my brow and feel Matty's presence near me.

I reach out, grasp his hand, and squeeze for a moment before dropping it and turning to look at the model vessel Grey made for a science project. Matty had helped her because she was uninterested in my help. "DeLeon got a bit mouthy mid-interview," I say. "He looked at me and spat blood onto me. Then he said he didn't understand Abernathy's obsession. Specifics involved my lack of womanly behavior and that, in his view, I wasn't much to look at."

"I disagree," Matt says calmly.

I peer into the mirror on Grey's wall and wipe a smear of bloody mud or muddy blood off my face and chuckle just a bit. "He said, if it was him, he'd just get rid of the kids and not go to the trouble of taking them through the chinkana." I turn and look meaningfully at Cal. "I didn't know the word, but turns out, it refers to some ancient Incan tunnels. So, here's what I need to know: Is there an actual tunnel running from the Kurak Estate? And if so, where's the exit?" I trail off and turn my arms over.

Cal looks off into space for a moment and then nods. "I think we can get some of the new detection devices on that if we can get close enough. I'll contact the agents out there and have them start to pull data."

"Excellent. I knew you'd have a plan. They don't have much time, though." I turn to Matty. "The land holding is huge and will require quite a few units to secure it, but the home and grounds, while quite large, are far more manageable for a small team with only six sentries to contend with. Once we know if a tunnel exists and, if so, where this chinkana opens up, you and I can take it to go in after the kids."

I see a grin start on his face, and I hold up a hand and look at him. "So, a quick history review, Major, even though we have talked about it quite a bit. Will McCloud was not killed in a battle, nor for any tactical reason. He was targeted by Abernathy to cause me pain because it was apparent that I loved him." I feel my hand fold into a tight fist as I say this. "And it is apparent to everyone that I love you, Matty Warner." I smile at this man who has opened my heart. "So that makes you a walking target.

"Part of me still screams to keep you out of this mission. But as well as I can do on my own, I know things go better and smoother and there is more chance for success when I am working a mission with you."

Matty sensibly says nothing but nods his agreement.

Now I point at Matty. "We go in together. With both of us knowing that there is a target on your back. Abernathy will shoot you without a second thought. So, there is just one rule —you cannot get killed. I won't trade one part of my heart for another, so you better be well-outfitted, Major Warner."

Matty has quietly listened to me say my piece and now looks at me, eyes soft and loving. "Understood, General. No dying. Lots of anti-ammo wear." He pauses. "Just a point of order—are injuries acceptable?" His eyes are twinkling now.

"Asshole," I say under my breath with a smile. "Only minor ones, Major. And be sure…" I use my finger to repeat the large squiggle I made when we first met and wink. "…you return with all essential parts intact."

Matty laughs, and Cal says, "You two love birds need me to step out?"

All three of us chuckle a bit as we wrap up our private meeting. Matty starts to open the door, and I say, "Let's keep this plan among the three of us. You know the unit would want to follow us in as backup, but it's a job for just us."

Matty stops at these words, exhales, and closes the door. He turns and looks intently at me. "General…" There is BPF seriousness to his tone. "These are your troops, and they will do as you order. As will we." He gestures between Cal and him. "We all intend to meet the mission specs: Bring the children home. And we all want to come safely home ourselves. But seeing our general—our future MC—home safe is also part of our commitment to the force."

I see Cal nod. I consider the premise. "Okay." I nod as well. "I hear you. Yes, mission completion and all of us, including me, safely home. But, still, just for now, let's keep it quiet. We will inform the rest of the company of the plan on a need-to-know basis."

I see Matty sigh, and he and Cal look at each other. Then Matty shrugs and throws his arm around me. "Well, I guess that's the best I'll get today." He grins and gives me a kiss on my hair, and my heart feels full as we head back to the makeshift situation room on my back patio.

∽

Friday, July 1, 2366. Bosch, my house. Nineteen bells, Bosch time / Saturday, July 2, 2366. Kiharu. 9 a.m., Edo time.

"Why can't you just tell me what you are thinking?" Matty asks.

"Because I want to say it to you both. At the same time."

He sits at the table across from me, and as I say this, a crease develops in the middle of his forehead, then extends to his brows and trickles down his cheeks to his chin as I put the video call through to Edo. I am filled with admiration for this man who puts up with sharing my emotional energy with my annoying ex with whom I am determined to get along.

On the second buzz, Takai picks up, and his face is stiff. We have been texting for the past hour, and he, too, has insisted that I simply tell him what I want to say and not subject him to a call with "that man you seem to be living with." There was a time when I would have taken great joy in rubbing my new relationship in Takai's face, but that time, apparently, has passed.

Now he sits in front of the camera wearing a sleeveless knit shirt and loose linen pants—the clothes he likes to sleep in. He looks tired, and I know he is—since he mentioned it several times in his texts. *That's what you get for having a baby when you are the age you are, Takai.* He is only five years older than me, but when I think about getting up with an infant now, exhaustion overtakes me.

"Okay, I'm here, Kat. Now what is so important you had to make this a video call?" he grouses.

I glance at Matty and see him tip his head. I know he is struggling with the idea of agreeing with Takai.

I take a breath and think of how crucial it is that this conversation goes right.... "Okay, Takai, Matty—I do have something to say, and I need to say it face-to-face, without interruption, because I won't argue this with either of you."

I shift myself and the device to Matty's side of the table so both men are visible to each other on the screens, which are located almost ten thousand kilometers apart. They each nod, but both look as if they'd prefer to be somewhere else.

I begin. "First, the mission: Tomorrow, we go in to get the children. That is the goal of this mission. That is the only mission spec: to get the hostage Shima children out and to safety." I see Takai start to speak, but he stops as my index finger comes up, and I continue, "Yumiko Shima is secondary. If she can be rescued without endangering the primary objective, then she will be. But she is there of her own volition, and she had to know the danger that she was embracing, so she is secondary. Is that clear, Major?" I look over to my right.

Matty nods without hesitation.

"Takai, do you understand?" There is a long pause, and I prompt, "A simple 'yes' will do."

Takai's jaw works as it does when he is struggling with emotion, but he says, "Yes."

I turn to Matty. "Major…" I look at his face and those eyes that are so tender and know me so well. I soften, "Matty…" I know the scenario I am about to postulate will be unwelcome, but I push on. "The hostages, the children, are the primary objective of the mission specs, correct?"

Matty narrows his eyes as I repeat this. He knows something more is coming, and he is cautious. "Yes, General, the rescue of the children is the primary objective."

"Takai, the major and I will be conducting the extraction." The annoyed expression disappears from Takai's face, replaced with concern.

Now the hard part. "This grotesque dance Abernathy and I have been locked in for almost twenty years has colored so much of my life." I take a moment to look at these two men who have had to deal with that bastard's hold on me. "Now he has my children. I will no longer live this way." I turn to face Matty. "I need you to guarantee me that you will do whatever it takes to meet the mission specs. No matter what." I make a fist and say what I need to say. "Because this ends here. Either I will kill Abernathy tomorrow or he will kill me."

Matty answers first as Major Warner. "Yes, General, mission specs will be met, no matter what." Then he reaches out to caress my cheek. "And you see to it that only the first option is implemented, Kat Wallace."

I reach out and place my hand on his face and nod. "I'll do my best."

Takai is in full protest. "Don't be reckless, Kat. Get the children and get out. Let the FA deal with Abernathy."

In our marriage, the admonition of "Kat, don't be reckless" would often preface our more heated arguments. But now, it doesn't anger me. I even smile. The whole statement is so very much a Takai thing to say. "Ah, Takai, you are so much a diplomat and a man of peace. Abernathy, however, is a monster whose behavior is even worse than you know. There were things I could not even bring myself to relate to Phil back in the trial. Horrible, painful things. Now this monster has taken our children, and we don't know what he has done to them." Now I see Takai recoil at the thought.

I continue, "Believe me, I don't intend to die. I fully plan to kill him."

Both men give a small smile at this statement.

"However…" I take a deep breath. "I have been wrong before, and if I am wrong tomorrow, I need the two of you to work together to raise my children." I watch as the smiles fade, but I push on. "Takai, you are their beloved papa, but you belong in Edo, and while they love Edo, it's not their home. They can never fully belong there the way they do in Bosch." Takai nods at this; we both know I am speaking the truth.

I push on. "They also love Matthieu, much like they love Hayami." I look at my love. "And I dare say, Matty, you feel the same." His smile returns, though it is a sad one, and he nods in agreement. I finish my request. "So, I need a promise from you both that you will work together to give the children what they need. Matty?"

He looks at me, and I see tears accumulate in his eyes. He

takes two breaths and says, "Absolutely. I will build whatever bridges are needed for the good of the kids."

Under the table, I reach and squeeze his hand in gratitude. Then I look at the screen. "Takai?"

"But, Kat, you said nothing was going to happen to you, so why…?" Takai begins.

"I said I didn't intend to die. But I can't know what will happen. I need you to promise me, Takai." I look him in the eyes. "A real promise."

He looks away from the camera for a moment, then stands up and leaves the screen entirely. A moment later, he is back, and his eyes seem to be red, though that might just be a trick of the camera. Now he looks at me, and I see in his deep brown eyes the man I first fell in love with, open and vulnerable and trustworthy. He nods.

I smile and push a bit further. "Out loud, Takai."

He gives a short, sad bark of a laugh. "Yes, Kat. I will. I will be sure that our children remain…" He smiles. "…Bosch-doan."

SIXTEEN

The Request

Saturday, July 2, 2366. Sapporo City-Ship. 10:00 a.m., Edo time.

"What does he want? I'm a busy man, and I have no need to be scolded by the likes of him." Kenichi Tsukasa, head of the Koshijiya-rengo family gestured with his pruning shears as he carefully surveyed the small juniper bonsai that sat on the desk in front of him in a forest-green, rectangular pot.

The young Edoan man gave a bow of respect. "He says he wishes to ask a favor of you, Tsukasa-san."

At this, Tsukasa looked up. "How interesting." He looked out his window from his fourth-floor office on the city-ship that cruised slowly in the ocean near the large, northern island of Edo. The window overlooked the treetops and shorter buildings, and he could easily see the ocean beyond the ship's perimeter. "Fine. Show him in."

His secretary bowed again, then stepped out and returned in a moment with another man. This new man was fairly tall and lean. His dark hair carried just a few specks of gray, unlike the large, white swaths now part of Tsukasa's appearance. Tsukasa could see he was handsome, and his clothes were tasteful and stylish but not overdone. He watched as the man gave a bow and stood patiently to be acknowledged. But he could also sense a tension in the man's body, and his eyes were red-rimmed and held deep, dark circles as if the man had not slept well for some time.

"My secretary tells me you have a request, which I find a bit presumptuous, Shima, given your attitude toward me over the years."

Takai Shima nodded. "Please, accept my sincere apologies for any disrespect, Tsukasa-san. I understand that my wishes may not be of interest to you. However, my request is one that will assist mototsuma Kat as she seeks to retrieve our children."

At this, Tsukasa gestured to the chair. "Sit down. I am interested in anything that will help my friend. Though I have done much already."

Tsukasa had immediately sent men to investigate the disappearance of Kat's children after Riki had notified him that Yumiko Shima had taken them. After staying in close contact with Kat-san in Bosch as her people also tracked possible locations, he had called several underground contacts outside of Edo once it became apparent Abernathy was involved. As he and Kat-san pinpointed the likely location, he sent emissaries with several crates of arms to meet with the Bosch once they arrived outside of the city of Haida. And, of course, Riki had embarked on his own mission. Tsukasa smiled, thinking of Riki's arrival at his office when he had called him in to share that Abernathy had taken possession of the children.

Riki was a man typically slow to anger, but Tsukasa had watched as the big man's face had gone tense, and he began to open and close his fists. He stood without the formal permission typically expected and walked to Tsukasa's window.

"Tsukasa-san, you asked me to look after the safety of the children and of Kat-san. I have failed in this endeavor. I must be allowed to remedy this."

At this, Tsukasa nodded and said, "Riki, you have been my loyal heyazumi and a valued wakaishu for some time. But you now have your own path. You have my respect. I will do what I can to help."

He had agreed to Riki's request and informed Riki immediately of the children's location outside of Haida after Kat had relayed the information.

Takai sat in the chair, but his body did not relax. "Tsukasa-san, while Kat and I are no longer husband and wife, we are still parents of our children together." He paused and closed his eyes, taking a deep breath in. "Kat is Bosch, and as such, will take the path of attack to rescue the children."

Tsukasa raised his eyebrows. "I am not sure there is any other option, given their captor."

Takai nodded. "Agreed. However, I cannot take that path. While I have been trained as an FA officer with weapons, I am no soldier." Now this man leaned toward Tsukasa. "I am, however, a skilled diplomat and negotiator. The people of Haida are known to be independent and war-like. They are also suspicious of outsiders and uninterested in participating in FA or any other outside ventures. However, they are strong fighters, well-armed, and the battle is in their homeland. They could be excellent allies in this mission."

Tsukasa tipped his head to one side, considering the request. He had made some inroads in Haida and nurtured a handful of well-placed connections. But Shima was correct, the Haidas were suspicious of outsiders trying to impose their ways on them. "As I recall, the last time the FA sent a diplomat to negotiate with the Haida, he returned without either ear and a message that stated something like, 'You people obviously are not listening to our demand to be left alone, so we assume this man has no use for his ears.'" Tsukasa looked inquiringly at Takai.

Takai took a deep breath. "Yes. You are correct."

"So, are you tired of having your own ears or your own life?"

Now Takai leaned even farther forward, and his voice held an edge of heavy emotion. "Tsukasa-san, these are my children as well as Kat's. She will literally offer her life in battle for them. And I would do the same in my own way. I believe a good word from you would open many doors. And with your assistance and recommendation of contacts, I could be more successful than previous envoys. And that success could aid the Bosch Force and Kat in the rescue of our family." Takai Shima looked directly at Tsukasa. "Please, Tsukasa-sama, I need your help, for Kat and the children."

SEVENTEEN

It was Only a Matter of Time

Friday, July 1, 2366. Haida, Kurak Estate. 6:30 p.m., Haida time.

Yumiko Shima carefully arranged her obi bow so the ends were hidden and tidy on the front of her kimono. She had seen that some of the younger diplomats were turning their bows to the back, but she felt the traditional way it had been done for the past hundred years or more was much better. Her fingers fumbled a bit now, but she could still tie a neat knot. She checked her appearance in the looking glass and smoothed her hair, peering to see if any gray hairs had appeared. Mollified by the mirror's response, she readied herself for her final dinner in the vice president's exquisitely appointed home.

She tapped on the door to her grandsons' room. "Boys, are you ready?" The door opened and Yumiko was surprised to see Aika Grey, nicely turned out in the blue flowered dress Yumiko had bought for this trip. Her granddaughter had been quiet and withdrawn all day. When Yumiko had inquired what the matter was, Aika simply shrugged and said, "I don't know. I guess I'm just tired."

So, like a good obaachan, Yumiko had sent her granddaughter up to her room to have a rest before dinner. But even now, her eyes were a little red and her face drawn. She was not smiling her usual smile. Yumiko saw her granddaughter glance behind her to where her brothers stood and give a little nod.

When she turned her face back to Yumiko, a very small and seemingly forced smile appeared on Aika Grey's face as she said politely, "Good evening, Obaachan. Your kimono is lovely. The yellow obi looks so nice."

The trip is likely wearing on her, Yumiko thought. She, too, was ready to return to her beloved Edo. "Thank you, my dear. But why are you not in your room? I thought you had napped." Yumiko was glad she had only had one child to raise. It was very difficult to keep track of the comings and goings of these three. She was unsure if it was due to them simply being a mass of children or because they were being raised by a pirate.

"I did. A little. But, umm, the boys needed help with their neckwear. The last time they wore any was at Papa and Hayami's wedding."

Yumiko peered over her granddaughter at her grandsons. "I see. Well, you did quite a good job. They both look very nice." The two boys were standing with what she was delighted to see were very formal faces, shoulder to shoulder. Kita Keaton looked so much like her Takai when he was the same age that it made her heart jump. Except the long hair, but that could be remedied. Both boys wore black pants, one with a pale blue shirt and one with a pale yellow one. Their neckwear was in the style of the Central Continent but sported Edoan prints that made her quite proud. Then she looked at their feet and saw that both wore white socks. "No slippers?"

Tano Macrae spoke up, "Umm, no, ma'am. I think we left them by the back door."

Yumiko smiled and nodded. She supposed children were the same, generation to generation. "Well, get them before you come to the dining room. We must make our best impression on the vice president this evening as we will be returning to Edo tomorrow."

The boys looked at each other, and Tano Macrae looked as if he was about to say something else, but then he glanced at his sister and simply said, "Yes, ma'am."

"Remember, it is an honor to be here, children. The vice president's son will be joining us for dinner tonight. Knowing someone like him can be very advantageous. Be sure to use your best manners." The old woman touched her granddaughter's shoulder. "Aika Grey, please walk with me. Boys, get your slippers and join us."

Aika Grey nodded and stepped out, closing the door behind her, though before she did, she whispered something that Yumiko could not hear to her brothers.

Friday, July 1, 2366. Haida, Karuk Estate. 7:15 p.m. Haida time.

Susan and another thrall moved around the table, filling wine and water glasses, then each departed from a different door in the opulent, oval dining room. Rob Abernathy took another forkful of the pastry-wrapped, rosy-red beef, and as he chewed, a small smile began.

He was enjoying his meal quite a bit. The meat was cooked just right, and the wine he had selected was a perfect pairing. His son had brought him some excellent business news, which meant he had more markers to put toward his goals. And the three little brats were markedly quieter tonight than they had been at past meals. He imagined that his little talk with them the previous night had made the appropriate impression on them, though it really didn't matter. The boys would be gone soon enough, the girl would be taught some manners, and his threefold plan would be put into action.

He smiled at the children and lifted his glass of wine toward them. They each stared back sullenly. This evoked a chuckle from him. Things were unfolding exactly on schedule.

Yes, soon he would have everything he deserved. Mary would be back under his whip, the FA would be in crisis, and its beloved President Russell, her annoyingly nosy husband, and several other outspoken detractors of his, all sadly assassinated, and the murders pinned on the pirates. It was perfect. Bosch would be blamed for the attempted coup, and he would be the hero for destroying Bosch. And, finally, the presidency would be his.

He could hardly wait to have Mary watch his little drama play out. He had instructed his inside people to take a video of the demolition of her home. He wanted to watch her face as her little island burned to the ground and as its people were slaughtered and the survivors sold off to return to their status as the thralls they had been and were meant to be. After the island was essentially razed, Abernathy Enterprises, headed by his son, would take over the Glitter industry. It would be a win all around.

Yumiko Shima raised her glass to make a toast. "Mr. Vice President," she said in her annoyingly whiny voice, "thank you for hosting me and my grandchildren. We all appreciate the hospitality and will always remember this trip. It will be quite difficult to leave tomorrow morning."

Rob was so tired of listening to this old woman prattle on about Edo and fawn over everything he said and did. He was done with the pretense. He looked at her and raised an eyebrow. "You are such a fool, Ambassador. It will be far more than difficult. It is out of the question. This was always going to be a one-way trip for all of you as the children and I discussed last evening." He looked over at the three, who sat wide-eyed but silent, and then reached out and ran a finger over a lock of the girl's hair. He smiled when she jerked back from him.

"I appreciate you bringing me the children. They are the ultimate bait and will pull not only their mother but most of the other pirates from their island. Actually, Ambassador, I imagine you will enjoy watching the destruction of the Bosch as much as me, though you won't get to for terribly long as you will likely join your dead husband quite soon."

He pushed back from the table. "Now, if you'll excuse me, I have a war to start." He touched his son's sleeve and made a small jerk of his head, and Ashton immediately stood and walked to the farthest of the four dining room doorways to call in the guards they had stationed in the hallway.

Rob rather liked watching Yumiko Shima's face move from surprised to offended to scared. He enjoyed how fear looked on people's faces. She stared at him as if trying to understand some foreign language. "What do you mean, sir?"

Ashton appeared with four fully outfitted guards, all in black save the blue sash of the vice president's office. He gave one guard direction, pointing at Yumiko. "Take her back to her room and be sure she stays there."

"No!" The ambassador from Edo actually raised her voice. "What are you talking about? Take your hands off me." She slapped at the guard as he tried to move her from her seat. "I invoke my diplomatic privilege!" Ashton walked over, sneered, and slapped her.

Friday, July 1, 2366. Haida, Karuk Estate. 7:28 p.m., Haida time.

Grey, Kik, and Mac had sat still, afraid to move as Mr. A. was talking and the guards came in. But when Grey saw Ashton Abernathy's hand come up against her obaachan, she shot out of her chair. As he turned around after slapping the old woman, grinning at his father, she kicked him hard on the knee. And not just a kid kick but one of the kicks Riki and Matthieu had taught her. She was pretty sure she heard a crunch, and she watched the handsome young man collapse to the floor with a yell.

Suddenly, the room was in chaos: Mr. A. was yelling; Ashton was moaning; the guards were all talking at once. Her grandmother was practically screaming as she grasped at the tablecloth, trying to hold her position against the guard dragging her toward the door, causing plates of food, glasses of red wine, and heavy silverware to crash to the floor. Grey looked wildly around and yelled, "Split!" to her brothers, and all three headed for a different door as fast as they could.

EIGHTEEN

Wait One Minute

Saturday, July 2, 2366. Bosch, my house. Two bells and twelve —no, thirteen—no, now fourteen minutes.

I stare at the ceiling and can hear the clock tick. I review the FP: final prep.

The West Coast Battalion, made up of twenty-five battle units and the entire Burn the Ship company, is due to fly out to the west coast of the Central Continent a bit past dawn. Butler unit will be notified just before take-off that Captain Aaron Morton will take the pilot position and Master Sergeant Demery Ludlow will serve as navigator for the trip across the continent while Matty and I fly in the *Coupe*. During the trip, I will appoint Gia to serve as the field tactician while Major Warner and I take care of our business. Next to me, Matty's breathing tells me he is not even close to sleep. I turn my head and find we are looking at each other.

"There's something more, isn't there?" he asks in a low tone, though there is no one to wake in our house.

I nod. "There is. Something we are missing. I almost see it, but I just can't quite grasp it."

We slide our feet under the light blanket until they are touching, and our hands clasp. Matty sighs. "While it *seems* to all be focused on gaining your return, there's clearly more than *you* at play."

"Clearly." I return to staring straight up, watching the shifting of the moonlight and the shadows the curtain makes. "What exactly was it he said about Bosch?" My brow is wrinkled tightly as if tightening my face will make the thoughts come to the surface. Matty grabs his comm from his side of the bed and cues up the recording he made of my conversation with Rob Abernathy. The creepy voice reverberates around the room.

> *"You kept me from what was due me before, but I will have it now. Remember, Mary. This is all because of you. Everything that will happen to your children, your lover, the pirates who you call family, even Bosch itself, is your fault. You should never have run from me, but now, perhaps you should run from Bosch to me."*

"Wait," Matty says and re-cues the recording,

> *"...even Bosch itself, is your fault. You should never have run from me, but now, perhaps you should run from Bosch to me."*

"Oh, fuck." I sit up and turn on the electric light.

Matty is already pulling on his clothes. "*Oh, fuck* is right. We need to call the MC."

"And Gia. And Cal." I slip on my uniform, not bothering to search for my underclothes.

We race down the stairs, comms pasted to our ears as we work to rouse our compatriots.

As we hop about to pull on our shoes and throw the front door open on a peaceful July night, bright moonlight streaming down, making a path for us, the crickets around the door go silent as we both are saying urgently into our devices: "He's going to attack Bosch. Meet us at Bosch Hall."

∾

Saturday, July 2, 2366. Bosch Hall. About three bells.

"Listen again," I say urgently as I grab Matty's comm and push play. "He says *should*, not *will*."

Matty adds, "He may be a sick fuck, but he clearly is obsessed with and wants to be sure that Kat gets away from Bosch before whatever attack he is planning takes place. I think that's why he went big and stole the kids to guarantee she gets drawn away."

Miles nods, his brow creased. "And naturally, we'll send almost all of the Force with her."

Matty gives a rueful grin. "Well, she is Teddy's scion, after all."

"Enough out of you." I scowl at Matty's comment but nod at his logic.

Gia frowns. "So how do we balance our forces? We sure as hell aren't just sending Kat into the estate alone."

The room is quiet as we all consider options. Matty and I glance at each other, and Cal studiously stares at the floor.

It is Miles' voice that speaks first, and there is a faraway sound to it. "'All warfare is based on deception. Hence, when we are able to attack, we must seem unable; when using our forces, we must appear inactive; when we are near, we must make the enemy believe we are far away; when far away, we must make him believe we are near.'"

"Sun Tzu," Matty and I say almost at once and then meet

each other's eyes with a look that wavers between pride and disgust before we both give a laugh.

Gia grins. "Of course. The original strategist. He should have been a pirate."

"Twenty-eight hundred years and the basics still work," Miles says. "We will send, quite publicly, almost our entire force to Haida." I nod along with everyone else whose brows are all knit like mine. He continues, "And at the same time, quite privately, we will keep our entire forces here to defend Bosch." Four grins develop in the room.

Cal says, "That's brilliant, MC. How shall we manage that?"

Miles blinks, looks at Cal, and then pulls his head back. "How the fuck do I know? I just philosophize and give you the goal. You underlings figure out 'the details' as Teddy always liked to reference. I think you have about four bells."

The tension in the room breaks with laughter that fades into the thrum of work, as the five of us discuss options in planning the defense of Bosch while we also attack Karuk Estate near Haida.

Saturday, July 1, 2366. Bosch Hall and green. Five bells.

Miles gets up, stretches, and says, "I'm going to go for a walk outside, let the morning air refresh me."

Four people give a grunt of acknowledgment: Cal, Gia, Matty, and General Philip Patel, the general in charge of defense and tactical work. We called General Phil in at around four bells, and it was good to have a refreshed view of things. I watch Miles go out the door. After waiting a couple of minutes, I say to the team, "I'll be right back."

I catch up with Miles on the green. "MC, got a sec?" He turns, and in the morning light, his deep brown, beardless face with its high cheekbones looks far older than I have seen it before.

Then he smiles and the years fall away. "Always, for you, Kat."

"I'll be flying out soon," I say as we stand next to each other, looking out at the base we both love.

"With several units," Miles adds.

"Yeah." I nod my agreement. "I'd like Gia to stay behind and work with Phil on the defense of Bosch. She's one of the best tacticians I've seen."

Now Miles nods. "That's a good call. But it will take some convincing. She's going to want to be with you."

"I'll take care of it," I say.

"Okay."

A few moments of comfortable silence pass between us.

"So," I say in a steady voice that belies the strain of what I am about to say. "I also would like to advise you to choose an alternate for the master commander position."

Now Miles turns his head to look at me. I glance up at him, then look back to the green. "While I have every intent on returning to Bosch, there is a reasonable chance I could be captured or killed." Now that I have said it, I find I can grin. "I guess that's why you told me that officers make plans. They don't implement them. Losing those taller chess pieces makes the game a bit more challenging."

The voice that answers me is soft and kind. "I will consider an alternate. But yes, if this were any other mission, I'd be down your throat about going in. But those are your children. No force on heaven or earth could keep you from them. I just ask that you take the assists when they are offered and avoid unnecessary risks."

I consider the phrase "unnecessary risks" and know that Miles and I have very different interpretations of it. But I am touched by his concern and compassion. I stand a little straighter and clap my right fist to my chest in the Bosch salute. "Yes, sir, Master Commander."

Miles gives a small laugh and puts his arm over my shoulder. "Finally perfecting that salute," he says.

∽

July 2, 2366. Bosh Hall, MC office. Five bells.

Matt stood with Gia on the small balcony that overlooked the green, breathing in the fresh morning air. He could tell by the wispy white clouds that the day would be clear, and that meant hot later in the day.

"What do you suppose those two are talking about?" Gia asked, nodding toward the small figures of Kat and the master commander standing on the green, deep in conversation.

Matt looked and he suspected he knew the topic, but he said, "Who knows? Some secret MC topic, maybe?" He couldn't help but smile as he gazed down and looked at Kat. He let out a sigh.

Gia laughed quietly. "Still in the sighing stage of your relationship, are you?"

"I guess." Matt grinned but then the grin faded. "I am just eager to get the children back, and…" He paused.

She looked at him and raised her eyebrows. "And?"

"And I want Abernathy dead. For all the right reasons, certainly. But I have a selfish reason that just eats at me." Matt shook his head and set his foot on the lower rung of the balcony railing, leaning his elbows on the top.

Gia echoed his posture. "So, let's hear it."

Matt looked over at the tall, strong woman with her thick, dark hair fastened to the top of her head. They had become friends over the past year as they both had worked to get Kat elected and to support her in her generalship. He knew Gia had been suspicious of his intentions toward Kat earlier in the spring, and he couldn't blame her, given his track record. He looked out at the green. "That bastard occupies so much real estate in Kat's mind and in her life. And I fucking resent it. I mean, sure, we both have our past relationships. And I'm even okay ceding a bit of current space to Will—he was a good man, and I can certainly understand him loving her and her loving him.

"And even though I think he's a world-class prick, I know Takai is the father of Kat's children, and he deserves, I don't know, to maybe continue to breathe?"

Gia snorted a laugh at this comment.

Matt went on, "But Abernathy, he is like a cloud bank that is constantly present, sometimes thin…" Matt pointed to the July sky above them. "…but sometimes thick and dark, shutting out all the sunlight.

"I want him to be obliterated from the planet and from Kat's life." He hit the railing with his fist, and it gave a small shake. "Hell, here's the selfish part: *I* want to occupy all that space. *I* want to be the man that she thinks of when she wakes in the morning and falls asleep at night. *I* want to take all the hurt and pain and fear and anger that he brought her and turn it into love—for me." The fingers of Matt's right hand pointed at his chest, and he shook his head. "I'm such a selfish ass."

Gia now stepped off the railing and turned her body toward him. "Well, sure you are, Warner. What pilot isn't?" They both nodded at the truth in the statement. Then Gia went on, "But we should all be so lucky to have someone love us as completely as you clearly love Kat. And that goes a long way."

She smiled one of her infrequent smiles. "I think you may find you have already taken over the spaces that he used to occupy. I can see it in Kat's smile." She slapped Matt's shoulder. "Besides, Abernathy is going down. And you and Kat have your whole lives ahead of you."

Part IV

NINETEEN

Incursion

Saturday, July 2, 2366. A tunnel leading to Karuk Estate—hopefully. Eight and a quarter bells, Haida time.

We slip, crouched and fox-walking, through the smooth tunnel with weapons drawn. The sides are slightly damp, and there are places low enough that we must duck our heads. Ahead of us is nothing but a close blackness. I glance back and see the entrance as a pinprick of light. We stripped off our rain gear there and dropped it after we got under cover.

Cal's contact had directed us where to find the tunnel entrance, but it was an additional challenge as a summer storm had blown in, bringing with it copious amounts of rain. In here, though, there is no storm, only a long expanse of darkness between the entrance and us. The dark is pushed back around Matty and me as our headlamps illuminate the immediate vicinity. We are communicating with signs and moving as silently as possible because any talk or noise will likely be heard far down the borehole-like tunnel. We have six kilometers to cover as quickly and soundlessly as we can.

Eventually, we reach a long stretch of just dark where there is no visible entrance or exit. While I am not claustrophobic, it still gives me the creeps, and I am eager to get done with this portion of the mission. At the same time, I am hoping we don't have to move the kids back this way as they would find staying silent for an entire bell-plus almost impossible.

Matty gently taps my shoulder. I glance at him, keeping my head angled so I don't blind him with my headlamp. His lips are pressed together, and his face is tense with a sheen of sweat. He points forward. Clicking off my headlamp, I see the tiniest bit of light ahead. With a thumbs-up, we resume our hushed movement. Every few minutes, we each click off our lamps and glance up at the light that is growing larger. I power down my lamp entirely, remove it, and pocket it. Matty does the same shortly after, and we head for what appears to be a wooden door with metal braces.

We give it a push once we are upon it, and it swings gently open several centimeters to what must be a dim basement. Boxes of root vegetables are stacked in front, and I can make out an open wooden staircase that runs up to a landing off to the left. We shove the door a bit and push the vegetable boxes forward enough to slide each one out. We shut it and try to return the boxes to their original places, though it is clear from the marks on the dusty floor that we disturbed the door. Hopefully, that won't become an issue.

We make our way to the staircase, passing a small, rough room, its hatch slightly ajar. We peer in. It's a brick-walled room stained with black, sooty covering. Matty looks perplexed, and I whisper the first words we have said since entering the tunnel a good three-quarters of a bell earlier. "Coal room. We had 'em in the North." He shrugs. Bosch never used coal, only wood and peat in the settlement days, then biodiesel, and finally, our clean electricity powered by solar and fusion. But we sure used coal in the North Country. I had to shovel it when I was a kid. I remember recently reading that in the resettlement of Ohlone Bay, coal was rediscovered and used for a good 150 years afterward.

We start to mount the stairs and get to the top, only hitting one significantly creaky step. I am in front so I listen closely at the door and hear nothing. We nod to each other, and our eyes linger with words that can't be said. I ever-so-slowly turn the knob and push, letting my rifle barrel lead the way bit by bit.

I am about to shift from my squatted position to head out to the main house when I feel my gun barrel grabbed and I am pulled forward to tumble out, landing on my back on a soft rug, looking up at a crystal light fixture that practically blinds me. Four dark figures appear above me, the barrels of their four rifles trained on me. My weapon is jerked from my hands, and I let it go. *Well, that was fast. Captured.*

The door I had been so careful with is thrown open, and feet stomp on the steps, running to the basement. I lift my head a tiny bit to listen better. They are back within minutes. "All clear," a voice says. "She's alone." I let my head rest back on the rug and think gratefully, *Well done, Matty. Just as planned.*

Saturday, July 2, 2366. Karuk Estate basement. Nine bells and a bit, Haida time.

Matt sat plastered against the wall in the coal room, trying to control his breathing, feeling the damp chill from his sweat and the tightness in his chest that had plagued him since the moment they'd set foot in the tunnel. With its hatchway shut, the cramped room was almost as dark as that closed-off shaft had been.

He'd hated small, dark spaces ever since he was about four, when his brother Paul had locked him into one of the partially collapsed, old wine caves in the vineyard for several hours until his mother had shown up and rescued him, drying his tears and murmuring reassurances while taking him out into the amazing, wide-open night with a very guilty, tear-streaked Paul silently trailing her. Now the only small space he was comfortable in was the cockpit of a vessel, and that was because he was the pilot. The one in control. But for this mission to be successful, he couldn't just stay in the cockpit, and he had to stuff that fear far, far down.

He had rolled backward off the side of the steps when Kat had been pulled forward. It was one of the hardest things he had ever done. Not because he landed on his hip or because he was now shoved into a tiny space that seemed to get tinier by the moment. But because he and Kat had made an agreement. Hell, they had made a plan.

To keep the fear that the walls surrounding him would crush him at bay, he decided to actively remember how he got here. They had made love passionately, even fiercely, the previous night, wanting to shelve the thousands of thoughts that occupied their minds and hoping that the exhaustion and peace that followed would lead to sleep. It hadn't.

A tiny part of Matt took a moment to delight in how Kat had embraced their sexual life. She had said before they had ever made love that she was worried she would disappoint him, but now, he would whisper to her after each time, "Nope, still not disappointed," and she would laugh. "Maybe next time." And next time happened often. Last night, they talked afterward, holding each other, Matt on his back with Kat's head resting on his chest, her body curled against his.

"So, we go in tomorrow," she had said.

"Mm-hmm." His hand ran along her naked back down to her wonderful, round, firm rump.

She murmured, "And while we go in as a team, we are two separate troopers, and we have to focus on the mission specs."

He paused his fingers for a moment—not typical pillow talk, but with Kat, all of life was delightfully far from typical. He considered the myriad paths this conversation might take. "That's correct."

She traced her fingers along his chest, pausing to play with the smattering of curly hair she found near his nipples. "So, if one of us is taken out in whatever fashion, the other has to carry out the plan and make sure the extraction is successful."

His brightwork girl had taken to discussing the rescue of her children as *the mission* and *the extraction*. Matt knew distancing herself was her way of maintaining focus and controlling her emotions. "That's a two-way road, Kat. You don't endanger the mission if you think I have been taken out."

Now she sat up on her elbow and looked at him. He saw her eyes and gave a laugh. "Kat Wallace, you are scheming up yet another plan. It's written all over your face."

She had smiled at him and winked and then, starting with a lovely kiss, proceeded to share her plan as she made love to him again. While there were parts of the plan he would normally have protested fiercely, the manner in which they were proposed was delightful. He had never enjoyed a work meeting more.

But now, here he was. Hiding in a cell-like… What had she called it? A coal room. He took a breath and held his arms out, pressing on the walls to be certain they wouldn't collapse on him. *Focus on what's happening outside of here, Matt.* He heard the searchers do a cursory check of the basement and thought that at least their tramping about had eradicated any evidence of his and Kat's prints. He listened until the steps faded upstairs and then waited a few more minutes.

Then, with relief, he moved out to meet the mission specs.

∾

Saturday, July 2, 2366. Karuk Estate study. Nine and a quarter bells Haida time.

"Oh, you have surely lost your touch, Mary. I truly did not expect it would be this easy." Rob Abernathy sits in a comfortable, wingback chair, a small lamp burning next to him, sipping on his morning coffee, his right foot resting casually on his left knee. He takes a breath and regards me, tipping his head very slowly from one side to the next as I kneel in front of him, hands bound behind my back.

Two guards with newer Chinese Zips stand a distance away on either side. My Rus KORD 9R70, my pair of Glock-147s, my helmet, and my bone-handled knife are piled on the table next to the vice president of the Federal Alliance. Outside, the rain makes a constant thrum, broken occasionally by a gust of wind eddying around a corner of the mansion. He motions to one of the guards. "Turn on some more light in here. I want to see her face better."

The guard follows the command and walks about the room, clicking switches. The room becomes fairly bright, with one light focused directly on me, causing me to squint. Now Abernathy drops both feet on the ground and leans forward, his elbows on his knees as he studies me. He shakes his head. "Well, Mary, while you are still lovely, you have clearly aged. But I suppose pirating is a difficult life. And your hair…" He clicks his tongue in dismay. "A woman really shouldn't have hair so short. Your hair was so lovely and long." I roll my eyes.

I'd comment, but the piece of tape the guard slapped on my mouth is forcing me to keep all my statements, of which I have come up with many, to myself.

"So, you are here to trade yourself for your children, correct?" He looks at me expectantly.

"Mmm-hmm." I nod. My brain murmurs silently, *And to kill you and cut you into tiny pieces, you loathsome piece of fucking trash.*

He laughs. "How delightful and so inspiring. Such is a mother's love." He looks over to the other side of the room, where a handsome young man, who bears a striking resemblance to this fucker in front of me, sits with one leg heavily bandaged around the knee and elevated on a footstool. "Isn't that marvelous, Ashton? Do you think your mother would do the same for you?"

Ashton looks uncomfortable. "Well…"

"Oh, please, you know perfectly well that she couldn't care less about you and your whereabouts, no more than either of us do about that worthless sister of yours. Now, if we were talking about her rescuing a bottle of expensive Rus vodka…" Rob laughs and I watch as the young man's face crumples slightly at the comment and then shifts to a laugh.

Abernathy looks at me. "My wife enjoys her drink." A look of contempt crosses his face. I think, *Can't say I blame her,* as he refocuses on me. "But let's return to your predicament. You wish to make a trade—yourself for three other people. Now, that hardly seems fair on my end. I would ordinarily require minimally the same number in exchange. But you are in luck. It so happens you've come on the heels of what I'd call, well, a fortunate accident. Because I now possess only one of your children." A vile smile spreads across his face.

Thoughts race through me. *Has he sold them? Sweet Earth, did he hurt them?* A loud buzzing starts in my head, and I feel dizzy. I have maintained my upright position on my knees for the length of this monologue, but now, with a moan that dies at my sealed lips, I sit back, collapsing onto my heels, my shoulders sagging forward. The polished, wooden floor comes up toward me quickly, and I miss having my face land hard on it when a guard catches one of my arms and roughly jerks me back to a vertical position.

I try to shrug this hand off me, and I hear laughter from both sides of the room. Showing emotion plays into his hands, and while I know I should shut it down, I cannot help myself. Anger creeps across my vision, taking the shock and pain of Abernathy's statement with it and leaving a trail of red miasma. I sit up straight and raise my head, looking directly, at first, at Abernathy, and then at his son. All the murderous thoughts in my mind are now sharpened, and they flash from my eyes.

Rob looks undisturbed. "Now, now, Mary, dear. I did nothing to them. They did it themselves. All three children were ill-behaved last night at dinner and took off running. We caught your girl, but those boys of yours slipped outside. After a search of the gardens, we found their prints near the bluff and saw evidence of a fall. They were really quite stupid to run out there in the dark. I had warned them of the danger of the cliffs early on in their visit." He gives a sigh and creases his brows. "It spoiled my plans to sell them."

My heart is starting its own free fall, but something holds it from fully plummeting. Something Akio said years ago whispers to me, *Those boys are little goats. Definitely born of the mountain.* Indeed, my boys spent their earliest years toddling on the footpaths and trails that zigzag the sides of Mizueyama, the mountain near Kiharu where they were born. *They wouldn't just run off a bluff.* I grab my heart back and let Caution, Relief, and Hope hold it. I will investigate. After I take care of the situation at hand.

But I know I have a part to play, so I shake my head and widen my eyes in horror. I cannot let tears come because that would lose the hold I now have on my emotions. But no matter. I never cried in Bellcoast, and he was gone before my tears started as I held Will's bloody, lifeless body, so it is unlikely he will expect me to cry.

A satisfied smile crosses his face. He stands and slowly comes toward me. He looks at me and it seems he is smelling something bad. He glances up at the guard on my left. "Get Susan to come and get her prepared. One of you will stay with them at all times." The sentry nods, then immediately turns and walks out the door. Abernathy turns his attention back to me. He reaches down and rips the tape from my cheeks and mouth in a single, sudden movement that hurts but is initially more surprising than painful.

"There. Anything to say?" he asks levelly.

I suck at my lips and roll them to get feeling back in them. "You are going to suffer as you die, you son of a bitch." My voice is equally as calm.

"Delightful. It will be so very…" He leans down and breathes out the next word into my ear in a way that makes my skin crawl. "…satisfying…when I break you."

He runs two of his fingers along my jawbone, and I jerk my head back to avoid the touch. "Fuck you," I practically spit.

He raises an eyebrow. "Oh, most definitely, but there are steps to be taken first." He walks past me, and I twist my head and body to keep him in my sights. A distance behind me, there is a large desk set with its work side framed by heavy blue velvet drapes. Rob Abernathy pauses and pulls a cord to reveal three floor-to-ceiling panels that create a bay window.

Outside, the light is dull and gray, and I can see sheets of rain coming down and being swirled about as the wind surges.

"What a miserable day," he says as he stands and gazes out the window.

His son speaks up. "It's the Chinese. I saw on the Obi that they have machines, and they are controlling the weather. It even said that's likely what started the shift three hundred years ago."

Abernathy turns and looks blankly at his son and then at me. "Are the young people on Bosch this stupid? That they'll believe anything they hear on an Obi?"

I shrug and stay silent. Naturally, he continues, "Now, don't get me wrong. I am delighted to have the masses believe what they are told. It works to the advantage of those of us in control. But really, Ashton, I would have hoped you might have been a bit more... Wait, what's the pirate word?" He looks at me again.

"Savvy?" I volunteer.

He smiles. "Yes, you need to be more…savvy, Ashton." He gives a small laugh. "Listen to me, sounding like a pirate. Of course, there won't be any pirates soon. I will see to that. But that's a topic for later. Now, what was I looking for?" He looks down at the desk. "Oh, yes. A small memento that will improve your appearance."

He opens the desk drawer and rummages just a bit. After a moment, he draws out what looks like a piece of coiled rope. The rope looks frayed, and there is a green ribbon twisted down its center. I recognize it with a chill that passes through me. It's hair. *Oh, fuck, it's my hair.* In a move that nauseates me, he puts it to his nose, takes a long inhale, and then smiles while staring at me.

I turn as the door opens and catch my breath, afraid that

Matty may have been captured as well. But instead, it's a young woman, not terribly tall but sturdy in her shoulders and round in her hips. She is hustled in by the guard holding her arm. Though she's not resisting, he keeps his hand on her, nonetheless. She is tanned but not fully brown and wears a faded blue pinafore that hits just past her knees, with a lightweight long-sleeved white blouse under it. Her sleeves are pushed up, and her hands are wet. There is a thrall brand on the inside of her left arm, and her dark blonde hair is worn in a thick braid.

Abernathy strides to her, and I see her automatically cringe as he moves to face her. He thrusts the coil of hair forward. "Here. You were trained in attaching hair. Put this on her. Make sure it holds well."

She glances at the hair and takes it, then walks over to me, pulling her arm from the guard who looks as if he is going to re-grab her, but stops as Mr. Vice President's hand comes up. She runs her hands through my hair, a move that still makes me cringe after all these years. But I will myself to stay still. So far, only two adults can do that without me overreacting: Mama and Matty. She walks behind me and picks at my curls. "Yes, sir. It will take a few hours. The hair isn't thick, so I can't guarantee that the added hair will stay for the usual six weeks." Her voice as she says this has taken on a different tone. She is matter-of-fact and professional. She doesn't sound like the thrall I know she is.

"Oh, not to worry. She's unlikely to be alive in six weeks," my enslaver says smoothly.

I sneer. "One of us surely won't be."

"Oh…" The word comes out of her in a long, shaky breath. She thinks I'm going to die. I expect she has seen it happen before, just as I had. But this time, I think she'll be pleasantly surprised with the outcome. Now she clears her throat just a bit. "I mean…yes, sir, I'll do my best, sir." There is the obsequious tone.

He nods, obviously pleased at the reaction he drew from us both. "Fine. See to it. Then get her bathed and ready by 1 p.m. I'll have suitable attire delivered. She's an old friend and will be my special guest for, well, let's call it a private luncheon."

Susan-the-Thrall, who I am guessing was a hair designer in a past life, walks in front of me, and her face reflects her sadness and regret. "Yes, sir."

TWENTY

Restoration

Saturday, July 2, 2366. Karuk Estate kitchen. Ten bells, Haida time.

The kitchen is even bigger than the one back in Bellcoast where Old Dorothy would cook for the house. It was also where she'd make her special teas for us women thralls, to make sure we bled no matter what had been done to us. It was her way of caring for us, but it was also her own little rebellion. Thrall owners love to have babies born into enslavement as it saves them markers and gives them power over the mother. I remember Abernathy's annoyance after he started with me that I never fell pregnant. Nor would I, not as long as Old Dorothy made tea. Fortunately, before they murdered her, she passed the recipe to Carisa and me, though I already had Grandma Rina's similar one in my head.

A guard stands nearby, looking bored. I glance at him—not quite Matty-tall, probably mid-twenties, black hair, lightly tanned skin with a mole the size of a raisin on his right cheek. I dub him mole-guard in my head. Susan sets up her hair shop next to a large, wooden table in the center of the kitchen as I sit tied into a straight-backed chair. My arms are restrained at my sides to the elbows, but my hands are free, and Susan hands me a large, round mirror to hold.

As she prepares to restore my braid to its past home, I look around the room. The corner farthest from me has a large, silvery cook stove and oven, and the interior walls are lined with white cupboards and counters. There is a spacious window on one wall, and I can see the rain blowing about. Underneath is the sink, with counters stretching on either side and large cupboards below them. It looks like there is even one of those auto-dishwashers near the sink. Very fancy. At the end of the counter is an enormous icebox, and just past that, a door that seems to lead outside. Interesting. It could be a future egress.

"Drop your chin, please." Susan's voice brings me back to my present.

I dutifully drop it. "I hate having people touch my hair." I figure I should give this woman fair warning.

She gives a soft laugh. "I don't doubt it. I used to love having my hair done by the women I worked with. You know, before. Now, I'm not sure I could tolerate it." She glances into the mirror that I am holding, and I see her raise her eyebrows.

For reasons I can't explain, I hold the mirror still with my right hand and push my left forearm against my body, shoving up the sleeve slightly. I roll my left arm over, exposing both my thrall brand and part of my original BPF tattoo. I glance at it and then into the mirror at her face behind my shoulder. She nods ever so slightly. And then she begins to chat.

"Well, we have had quite the spring and summer here. The rains came as usual in March and April, but they lasted so very long this year. It's no wonder that the gardens are so lush and wild with all that." She rattles on and on about the weather, the gardens, and the storms that came in June.

For a good bell, I patiently half-listen, adding in an occasional "Uh-huh" and "You don't say," as she begins to meticulously fasten seventeen-year-old strands of long hair to my current curls. My thoughts drift to the Bosch defense plan the team came up with yesterday.

Gia had only tried one "But, Kat, I want to help *you*," and then relented when I told her she was the best one to stay and implement the defense. I also extracted a promise from her to take care of Mama in case I don't make it back. That evoked a whole stream of Commander Ka'ne cautions and recommendations, which made me smile and say, "See? This is why you are the best one to defend Bosch. You think of every contingency."

"Turn your head to the right, please, sugar," Susan says, and I do. As she continues to talk, I shift over the next half-bell to reviewing the mission in my head.

Matty should be out and about from the basement by now, certainly. I try to picture him moving through the hallways, setting up the three small explosives, peeking and pushing into all the rooms until he finds the kids. I am warmed inwardly by both the idea of their safety and the vision of Matty. He is definitely in the house somewhere. I have heard no hullabaloo that would indicate his capture. While I know he didn't particularly like this plan since, well, since he loves me, he capitulated because he knew it was a good one.

Matty has a target on his back with Abernathy, but I don't. For whatever reason, I'm pretty sure Rob won't kill me, at least not right away. Even all those years ago, there were moments when I was sure he was about to and then something stayed his hand. I'm banking on that still being true, which is why I actively sought to be captured. I am the distraction.

Matt had protested as we flew in, "Kat, I'm not sure I can

just let you put yourself back in his hands. He may not kill you, but he'll hurt you."

He is not wrong. I could only respond, "Not having you and the kids safe would be far more painful. Besides, you know I can take care of myself. Let's stick to the plan."

His agreement was less than enthusiastic.

My role in this mission is to keep the enemy's focus on me. That will allow Matty to perform the extraction.

Once the actual mission specs are met, and the hostages, the children—*my children*… *Shhhhh*, I hush my brain. I can't think of them as mine until the mission is completed. Too much risk of responding with emotion… But once they are safe, then I will undertake my own personal mission to take my pirate's revenge and kill Rob Abernathy. Doubt and Fear peer at me. *What if he was telling the truth, and there's just one child to save?* I give an involuntary gasp.

"Did I pull too hard? Sorry, sugar," Susan says as if she has said the same thing dozens of times.

I give a tiny shake of my head. "No. No, you are fine."

"Good. You let me know if I pull too hard."

I take a deep breath and order Fear and Doubt to step back. "Okay," I respond to my involuntary hairdresser.

She nods and returns to her detailed review of what seems to be each week of the past dozen. "The place was pretty quiet through the end of May. Then all those fighting men came. I tell you it was more cooking than one woman could keep up with. It was a good thing those soldiers came equipped with their own cooks and such." Susan keeps up the continuous useless prattle as she tugs and pulls at my hair, and I shift in the chair and lick my lips.

"Oh, for pity's sake." Susan turns to the sentry. "I'm getting this girl some water." Out of the corner of my eye, I see him idly wave his hand in permission. She walks over to a cabinet and gets a glass and fills it at the sink, bringing it to me and putting it to my lips. My bound arms are of no help, so she patiently tips it while I thirstily gulp.

She pulls it away after only allowing me half the glass. "You can have the rest later when I get you bathed. I don't want you to need to pee in the middle of your attachment and have to have him…" She jerks her head over at mole-guard. "…be staring at you while you go."

"Reasonable thinking. Thanks," I say and smile.

"Sure, sugar." She shrugs. "Now back to work." She picks up where she left off, discussing the presence of a larger number of guards and then their disappearance about ten days previous. I start to shift back to mission planning.

"…and then we had some children arrive, and my goodness, are they lovely." Suddenly, my focus is entirely on her. I look into the mirror and see her looking back at me. She has talked with my babies. I feel my armor start to drop, and I quickly pull it back up. I begin to speak and see her eyes flick toward mole-guard, and she shakes her head a little.

She continues reattaching my despised past to my head. "They have been a joy to have in the house. I mean, they have added so much life to the old place. And energy… My goodness. Up with the sun and running about in and out of every door all the blessed day. But don't get me wrong, all three of them are polite and helpful and just a joy to be around."

I am listening carefully because I know she is telling me something. Then I hear it: *She's talking about them in the present. If the boys had fallen…*

"Now that girl is just as sweet as pie, but those boys, well, they keep me laughing every day with their twin antics." She looks intently in the mirror, and I see it in her eyes. They are alive—all of them. Abernathy is lying. No surprise there. I can't help it now; tears of relief flood out of my eyes. She gives another small nod and a smile, then puts a hand on my shoulder and squeezes. "There, there. I'll be done soon, and you'll be back to your old self. Won't that be nice?" I look in the mirror and see her pull a face and roll her eyes, and now I want to laugh. I really like this Susan woman. I will do what I can for her.

I glance at mole-guard, who has now pulled up a chair and is leaning forward, dully staring at his feet with his rifle across his lap. Now there's dedication to a job. I begin my own chatter. I talk about the weather in Bosch and how some of the plants are different here while some are the same. I describe Mama and the family. I talk about how hard it is sometimes to get certain fruits in the stores, all useless information. Then I talk about my love life with a giggle. I look into the mirror at Susan's intent face and describe Matty's looks—skin color, height, hair, and then say, "He cares about those three children and would go anywhere and do anything to see them safely home."

Susan nods her understanding. We have an ally on the inside now. I wish I could tell her to let Matty know to take her along, but I don't dare say anything like that with Moley, his new pet name, present, however dull and bored he is.

Susan returns to idle talk for another three-quarters of a bell before announcing, "Done." She runs her hands through my now long hair.

"It falls practically to your waist," she murmurs, and I hear admiration in her tone.

I give a little laugh as I remember how I used to love the attention to my hair when I was in the North Country. And then I remember it was my hair that got me caught, and that meant my Sean was killed. With that memory, the loathing for it flows back, and I scowl. "It used to be longer, practically down to my bottom, but when I hacked it off, there were a few inches left that Mama took care of for me later."

Susan nods placidly as she braids the now-thick strands. I hear the sound of satin rubbing on hair and know there is a green ribbon being braided in. "I see," she says. "When was that?"

"When I escaped from Rob 'The Monster' Abernathy the first time." Moley's head comes up as I say this, and he stands. I decide to have a little fun at his expense. "I bested my guard then, and he wasn't nearly as stupid as this one." I give Moley my patented I'm-going-to-kill-you look as I say this, and I am delighted to see him initially take a step back. Then he recovers himself and likely remembers I am tied to a chair. He sneers and comes at me, turning his rifle to deliver a butt-stroke.

Susan calmly steps between the two of us, half-braided hair in her hand. "I was instructed to prepare her for a private luncheon at 1 p.m. Do you think that her face will be healed by then? Or perhaps you'd like to be the one to deliver him damaged goods." I smile to myself as I hear her stand her ground.

There is a clear pause in the action. "Whatever. I can always teach her some manners later. If she's alive." He laughs at his own jest as he moves back to his seat.

I look back to the center of the kitchen. *Oh, I'll be alive. And it's not me who'll be dealt a lesson, Moley.*

Susan turns and calmly finishes the braid without another word as I sit with my chin up, my resolve renewed by this small confrontation. She puts a clip on the bottom and then says, "Now, let's get these restraints off you and get you bathed and fed before you have to go." She trails off.

I feel a tiny falter in my confidence regarding my role as distractor. I call up Teddy's voice in my head: *"You may have to do some shit you don't much like, girl. But if the mission specs are worthy, you'll be okay."* I blink and swallow back the old fears, which would soon be revisited. The mission specs. The hostages. The children. My children. I bring my chin up. "Yep. Let's get this done."

TWENTY-ONE

Which Way?

Saturday, July 2, 2366. Karuk Estate, Nine and a quarter bells. Haida time.

Matt's bare feet moved quietly down the hall. He had abandoned his boots and even his socks after his stay in the coal room. They were beyond filthy. He'd opened a vegetable box and peeled off several cabbage leaves, using them to wipe the majority of soot off his clothes, face, and hands. He was not about to leave an easily followed trail of black smears on the walls as he searched for the children.

Avoiding the guards patrolling the house meant he had to duck into two different rooms downstairs and wait for them to pass. Thankfully, the rooms were both unoccupied and spacious. He liked the feel of being able to take a deep breath, knowing the walls were sturdy and stable, even as the wind and rain lashed at them outside. The remnants of the fear were fading as he was up in open areas. Here, he had enough room to operate.

Since he was waiting on guards, he went ahead and placed a small signal explosive in an unobtrusive corner of each room and verified both were connected to the remote he carried. That was two of the three he needed to set. The signals to Kat that the mission specs were met and the children were safe.

Close to a half-bell had passed by the time he came out of the second room and looked back and forth down the long, sumptuously appointed hallway. There were two opulent stairways in either direction. He had heard the patrols' voices fade off to his right and decided to start with the stairs to his left that led to the second floor. He systematically checked each door, finding seven sumptuous bedrooms and an equal number of closets and washrooms on this floor. But to his dismay, he found no children, no children's flotsam, and no Yumiko Shima.

He frowned as he thought of that woman, then rolled his neck, trying to release some of the fury he felt toward her. *Be reasonable, Matt, she's an old woman, and you've never even met her.* Nope, he still felt murderous toward her. Another small stab of self-recrimination pricked him, but now he pushed it away. The old woman had not only tried to sell Kat back as a thrall but also hired someone to try to kill her. And now, there were the children. Children he was coming to love, whose safety and well-being he was committed to. So, this was how fathers felt. She had put those children in danger. She deserved every bit of his fury and more.

So, where the hell are they? He looked up and down the hall as he closed the last door. *Not here.* He stopped to think, then sighed. The other stairway. "It's always in the last place you look, Matt, my boy," Matt heard his dad intone in his mind. He remembered, at age twelve, finally retorting to his father, exasperated at his foolishness, "Well, of course, it is because then you've found it." His dad had laughed and laughed. "Good point, Son. Thanks for letting me know." Matt grinned at the memory as he made his way back to the stairs. He paused and waited for any patrol, keeping all his senses on alert.

He didn't like tight spaces, but he also didn't like being as exposed as he was on the stairway. So, once assured that the hallway below was empty, he got low and crept down the elegantly carpeted steps as fast as he could while still keeping a clear view all around himself. He moved toward the far staircase, but a pair of sentries posted up in front of a set of elaborate double doors, not far from the stairwell, sent him ducking into a closet. He peered out, his Scorp at the ready. He had to get to the steps. He could simply shoot the guards, but it wasn't subtle. And there were four other armed guards somewhere. He didn't relish the idea of a gun battle with children in the house and Kat somewhere, captured.

So, he stood among the several fashionable overcoats in the remarkably roomy closet, set the last signal explosive, and began to review his options. He could make his way outside and go up the wall to the second floor, though this storm made slipping more likely. Or he could wait. Hopefully, no one was getting their coats and going out.

A few moments later, a clicking sound caught his attention, and he peered out. The double doors opened, and he saw Kat, hands bound behind her, being walked by a guard with another woman on her other side. Anger bubbled up inside of him, and his fingers ran along his Scorp as he thought about putting a bullet into the head of the sentry who roughly marched her along. *That's what Kat calls your "caveman self," Warner.* He took a deep breath as he watched her move down the hall. She seemed uninjured. *She damn well better stay that way*, he thought, though he and Kat both knew that was unlikely. He kept his eyes on her until she disappeared into a room.

Now a tall, blond, handsome man appeared at the doorway

and spoke to the two other sentries. Abernathy. Matt felt himself go icy cold inside. All the things Kat had told him and all that he had read echoed in his mind. *Kill him.* The impulse was strong and real. *Kill him. Take out the sentries with your weapon and then kill him.* He started to open the door and raise his gun.

Then another voice whispered inside him. *Remember the plan.* The plan. The children. Killing Abernathy now could just as easily result in their execution before he could free them. He closed his eyes and let the barrel of his gun drop. He pushed the urge to tear the man's head off with his bare hands deep down, hoping there would be time for that later, and let his own head fall back against the wall of the closet. *Remember the plan: Get the children to safety. Detonate the three signal explosions so Kat knows when the mission specs are complete. Wait for her at the rendezvous point.*

Like hell, I'll just wait for you at some rendezvous, Kat. I'll be back and clear your way out with hellfire. He looked out again as the Monster disappeared back into the room, pulling the doors shut. The soldiers posted at the doors turned and walked away to another part of the house, leaving the stairwell unguarded. He took a breath and surveyed the scene, then swiftly walked to the stairs to search the other wing and find the children. *Mission specs, Gen. I'm following them, dammit.*

Saturday, July 2, 2366. Haida, Karuk Estate. Ten-plus bells, Haida time.

This level was much like the one he had just been on, a long hallway lined with doors. But this side also had an additional staircase going up to a third story. Matt hesitated, trying to decide where to start. He would check this floor first. As he started down the hall, his bare feet appreciative of the thick carpet runner decorated with some intricate design, he began to systematically evaluate each door. Three rooms were easily entered but were empty. The fourth door he came to, though, was locked.

He softly rattled the door and wished Kat was here with her pick set. He could jimmy a latch, but it took him a bit, and he admired the small, rolled kit that Kat carried, with so many different tools. With a sigh, Matt began to pull off his backpack to remove his own equipment.

As he started to insert the pick, a voice murmured through the door, "Who is it?" His heart leaped as he recognized Grey's voice.

He leaned in and said in a loud whisper, "Grey. It's me, Matt. Open up."

There was whispering in the room he could not hear, and he looked up and down the hallway. *Where are the sentries if the hostages are here?* Then he heard the lock manipulated, and the door opened.

"Get in here." Grey reached and pulled him with her slender arm. "Matthieu! You are here. Where's Mama?" Grey's face was at once that of a scared little girl and a hopeful young woman. Matt looked around. This was definitely not a child's room. It was tidy, and on the dresser top sat a travel case filled with, as his mother always said, lotions and potions. In a chair by the window, he saw an old Edonese woman sitting looking out at the rain, her face slack but with a bruise on one side of it. She had a shawl on her shoulders and a light blanket tucked around her lap.

He watched as Grey went to her. "Obaachan, Matthieu is here to rescue us. I need you to stand up." The old woman just murmured something Matt could not understand and made no move, not even turning her head toward her granddaughter.

Yumiko Shima. He wanted to rant at her, but she seemed so frail, and Grey was so obliging and gentle that he held his tongue. Instead, he asked, "Which room are the boys in?"

Grey's eyes filled with tears. "They… Mr. A., the vice president—he says they fell off the bluff and are dead, but…they wouldn't—they can't be… I… I…don't…. Well, I don't want to believe him."

Matt was stunned. The boys, dead? He went to Grey and squatted down so he could look up into her anguished brown eyes. This news cut into his heart in a way he couldn't explain, but he knew it was up to him to keep hope alive until they both knew the truth and were safely away from here. "Listen, Grey. Abernathy is a very, very bad person. And he's a known liar. I'll find out the truth for us."

She snuffled and nodded. "I know. He gave me the creeps almost from the start. I think he wants to hurt Mama. Where is she? She shouldn't stay here. Oh, Matt…I can't tell her about Kik and Mac." The little girl fell onto Matt's shoulder, crying.

He held her as she sobbed, rubbing her back, and her pain added to the fuel he was accumulating for the fire he would set to burn this place to the ground in his fury.

After her crying subsided some, he said, "Your mama is the strongest person I know, and she can not only take care of you and the boys…" He choked a little as he said this but knew he could never exclude them, no matter the harshness of the truth. "…but she also can take care of herself. Abernathy is no match for your mama." In his heart, he told Kat, *You hear me, love? Fight that bastard. I'm getting the kids. Mission specs.*

Grey wiped at her eyes and her nose with the back of her hand, and Matt almost smiled because it was such a Kat-like gesture. "Mama is amazing. But where is she?"

Matt refused to lie but decided to be vague. "She's in the house, but she is keeping Abernathy distracted for us."

"And she'll catch up with us soon?" she asked.

Matt nodded. "Absolutely." He followed up with, *That better not be a lie*, to himself. It was time to focus on getting out. "Let's move from here to somewhere safer and we'll make an escape plan. Then I'll go and look for the boys."

∽

Saturday, July 2, 2366. Haida, Karuk Estate. Eleven and a half bells, Haida time.

Deciding where to go was the easy part. Grey had told him about a back staircase that would lead to the servants' quarters. Getting Yumiko Shima to come with them was another issue altogether.

Matt approached her and she turned her head and focused on him. He watched as she surveyed him. Her eyes settled on the tattoos on his arms where he had pushed up his sleeves. In that moment, she had transformed from a frail, old woman to an imperious ambassador. And not a particularly nice one. "I will go nowhere with a pirate. You people are nothing but thieves and scoundrels. My embassy will send someone for me. Get out of my room!" Her voice began to rise, and Grey rushed to hush her. She stubbornly refused to stand up.

Matt couldn't help but snap back, "Listen, old woman, you deliberately brought three children here to danger, and you told no one where you were going. Now maybe you didn't want to let their scoundrel pirate mother know, but you didn't even tell your precious Takai. No one in Edo will be coming for you. It's pirate or nothing. Take it or leave it."

"I'll leave it, thank you very much." She turned to Grey.

"Send him away." Then she turned back to watch the rain, and the ambassador melted away, leaving the frail shell.

Matt sighed. "Grey, we need to move, now. Leave her here. I'll come back for her when we don't care how much noise she makes."

Grey nodded. "I'll go get my backpack." She paused. "And Kik's and Mac's—they might want them." Matt started to object but remembered there were no guards up here. He walked with her to the door and peered out. The hallway was still empty, so he nodded to her, and she slipped out of Yumiko's room.

Grey would only be gone a moment, so Matt walked over to Yumiko. "Listen, old woman, you can stay here and die for all I care, but I'm getting the children out." He leaned down and rotated Yumiko's face to his. There was shock in her eyes and perhaps a touch of fear, which was good for what he was about to say. "You will not say a word about me or about Kat being here to *anyone*. Are we clear? If you do, I'll be sure to return for you, and you won't like it." Her eyes widened and Matt released her face. He glanced up through the window to see the flashes of vessel fire in the distance: The Bosch were engaged. He sent them his wishes: *Fair winds, my friends. Stay safe.* Then he went out the door to wait for Grey.

Matt and Grey made their way to the servants' quarters. A quick room check found one small, rough room that appeared unoccupied. They sat down together on the floor in the dim room lit by a single bulb on the ceiling. Grey sat, looking sad and defeated. She held her brothers' backpacks in her lap, her fingers toying with the zippers and straps. "We had packed them before dinner last night. Before Mr. A. told us we couldn't leave and that awful Ashton slapped Obaachan," Grey solemnly told Matt.

"What happened then?" Matt asked. He needed to know

exactly what had transpired if he was to determine where the boys were—and if they were alive, or dead as Abernathy had said.

"I got mad and kicked Ashton in the knee and then everything went crazy. Kik and Mac and I all ran in different directions. I was headed out the front door, but Mr. A. caught me and dragged me up to Obaachan's room. She was on her bed, and she was just staring." Grey wrinkled her face. "Matthieu, it's really strange. It's like she doesn't realize what awful things happened at that dinner. She just keeps saying that the embassy will come." She looked at the closed door that Matt had braced with a chair.

"She's likely in shock, but she'll be okay upstairs," Matt said, though he had no idea if it was true, and he frankly didn't care.

Grey nodded. "Mr. A. said I was to stay there, and when I yelled that I was going to run away, he started to laugh. He said, 'Fine. Run, just like your mother.'" Grey took a breath. "Matt..." Her dark eyes looked seriously at him. "...he said Mama used to be a thrall. I think she used to be his thrall."

Matt pressed his lips together. He knew Kat had been very careful not to let the children know about her past enslavement. She had told him, "When they are older and can make sense of it, I'll tell them. But for now, I just want to let them be children." *Sorry, love, looks like the time is now.* He looked at Kat's dark-eyed daughter. "Yes, Grey. Your mama was once enslaved, and Abernathy hurt her. But she was strong and smart. And she escaped. And that's when she met your Papa T and became Bosch."

"Is that why Mama hates traffickers so much?" Grey asked.

"Mmm-hmm. She doesn't want anybody to be enslaved." Matt hoped to hell he was handling this right. "Did he say anything else when he put you in Yumiko's room?"

Grey's face was serious. "He said I could run one direction for hundreds of kilometers and that I'd get lost in the woods, and there were mountain lions and I'd get killed. Or I could run in another direction and then I'd fall off the cliffs and get killed. He said he'd rather I stay in the room, but if I wanted to die, that was fine with him."

Matt nodded and thought, *No wonder there were no sentries. The bastard doesn't give a fuck what happens to the children.*

"Around midnight, he came in and turned on the light and woke us up. He said Kik and Mac had decided to run the wrong way and went off the cliffs and were dead. He had even smiled at me then and said, 'Bad choice, don't you think?' Then he turned the light off and closed the door."

Grey looked like she was about to start crying again. Matt felt like crying too, but instead, he looked into her eyes and said, "Listen, I will find them, Grey. No matter what. I will find out the truth. You stay in here and don't let anyone but me in. I'm going to get you some food and water and then go hunting." He stood and reached out a hand to help her to her feet.

They agreed on a special knock for the door, the one Grey said that she and her brothers used when they played mission. Matt wanted to smile at the image, but he was too heartsick. Then he showed her how to position the chair under the knob and stepped out. The door closed, and he heard the chair slip into place against it. After he took several steps down the hallway, he paused and leaned onto the wall. He wanted to weep and rage. The boys gone? But he couldn't take the word of Abernathy. No, he had work to do. Provide for Grey and then search the bluff. He gathered himself and pushed on.

∼

Blow the Man Down

Saturday, July 2, 2366. Haida, Karuk Estate. Twelve and a half bells, Haida time.

Matt moved back down the servants' quarters hallway and carefully re-checked each room, most of which had signs of occupation but no current occupants. He had done a cursory check while collecting sparse food and supplies for Grey but was heartsick and distracted. Now, he was determined to be more thorough. He had found no boys so far. In fact, there was no one coming or going. *Well, of course, thralls are kept working constantly. That's the point. It's not like they get to pop down and have a break. They likely aren't allowed to return to their quarter until late.* With this thought, he dropped his guard and simply peered into the last room in the hall.

"Excuse me? What do you want?" a voice asked very near his back.

He spun and brought his weapon up—and found himself staring at a capable-looking young woman in a blue pinafore who looked rightfully terrified over the gun pointed at her.

"Um, who are you?" Matt asked, lowering his weapon slightly. Just because she was a woman—*and a thrall*, he thought as he noted the brand on her arm—did not mean she wasn't a threat.

The young woman seemed to study him. "I'm Susan." She narrowed her eyes and looked him up and down as if checking off some kind of mental list. "And you're Matty."

Matt frowned, "How…?"

"Your partner told me you'd come." Then she leaned in and whispered, "She said her name was Kat. And I am supposed to tell you about the boys."

Matt widened his eyes and felt the first real drop of hope since Grey had told him the boys were gone. He dropped the point of his gun and stepped back from the door and motioned Susan inside.

∼

Saturday, July 2, 2366. Haida, Karuk Estate grounds. Thirteen and a quarter bells, Haida time.

"Ahh! Fuck!" Matt exclaimed in a quiet voice as his bare foot caught on yet another root. The rain had turned the ground muddy in parts and almost a slurry in others, easily disguising sharp sticks, rocks, and now, this damn root. The path was so dim with the thick clouds and ongoing rain, and so narrow from the trees and underscrub's lush summer growth, that he could barely see enough to trust his steps. Hell, he could barely see at all.

In the servants' quarters, Susan disclosed that she had snuck the boys out of the house the previous night. Then, leaving him nervously waiting, she'd headed off to the kitchen, returning moments later with a bag of food and bottles filled with water. She stuffed two blankets in the bag and handed it to Matt.

"It's too dangerous for me to try to find paper and actually make you a map, but here…" She took a handful of flour out of her apron pocket and moved to a small table, over which she sifted the flour. With her finger, she drew a crude map on the flour-coated surface of the table, indicating where she had left the boys. Matt stared at it, talked through every line of the map with Susan, and then erased and redrew it to commit it to memory.

Before he left, he looked back at her, frowning. "Why did Abernathy tell Grey they were dead?"

Susan shrugged. "I don't know. Maybe because he's a

horrible man?"

Matt trusted the woman somewhat...perhaps 60, maybe 65 percent at that point. She could have been instructed to send him on some futile errand, ending in his doom. His instincts told him otherwise, but still, he did not tell her about Grey, nor about the Force that at that moment was engaging Abernathy's army. But she seemed kind, and she wasn't wrong about Abernathy. That counted for quite a bit.

The first step on the map he'd "drawn" in his mind: Head straight up the path from the house until it clearly branched. Check. He had hiked, slogged, and climbed the steadily increasing incline until it finally leveled off, leading into the deep forest. He could no longer distinguish between the thunder that rolled through and what he was sure were the sounds of heated battle between his people and the vice president's personal army. He longed to join that fight, but at the same time, wished his unit was here with him. He considered the mountain lions Grey had mentioned but decided that, unlike him, they were far too savvy to be out in this weather.

He'd veered left when the road branched, per the map's instructions. Step two: Continue to a footbridge, then take the next right branch once over it. The ground sucked at his feet as he moved toward where the footbridge was supposed to be. He paused. A heavy thrum had begun, with crescendos and crashes ringing through the trees. The closer he got, the louder it grew, elevating from a thrum to thunder.

He squinted, craning his neck forward. The stream that he assumed the footbridge would cross was gone. In its place, thanks to the deluge of rain, a deep, roaring river now spilled from the rocky banks, eddying through the surrounding trees and then racing downhill to the bluffs and finally pouring into the ocean, where the water would finally take its ease. The closest bridge post jutted up as waves swirled and foamed around it.

Traveling downstream was not an option, so he continued upstream, scouting to find a space where he could cross safely. Susan had given him a poncho, and although she could find no boots to fit him, he was glad for that little extra protection from the rain. He walked head down, only looking up occasionally under the brim of his helmet to avoid colliding with a tree—pretty much the only other living thing visible at that point since he figured every fucking animal and bug in the surrounding five kilometers had either gotten to higher ground or drowned.

So, it came as a significant surprise when he felt two bullets hit him full in the chest.

∼

Saturday, July 2, 2366. Haida, Karuk Estate grounds. Thirteen and three-quarters bells, Haida time.

What the fuck was that...? Matt lay flat on his back in the mud and struggled to suck a breath in. *I've been shot.* His trust meter for Susan dropped to the low teens. He felt as if someone had taken a sledgehammer to his chest. Twice. Finally, he pulled in a shallow breath and then another. Under his poncho, he automatically shifted his Scorpion to point between his feet and tried to scan his surroundings, using as little movement as possible. At first, all he could see was rain and trees. He scanned again. There, at the ten-bell position, a shadow. It moved like a soldier and soon drew near.

"I got him!" a voice called.

"Great," another voice responded. "You shot a fucking

pirate. Make sure he's dead, pull his weapon, and let's keep patrolling. I want to get out of this rain."

Two of the estate guards out on patrol, Matt realized. He considered his options. If he shot the one hovering nearby at close range, the fucker would likely fall on top of him, and then the far one would shoot him. Not a good plan, especially since he wasn't sure whether his body armor could take a third shot. *No... Hand-to-hand and then shoot*, he decided. He took a long, painful breath in and held still. The shadow shooter walked up and poked at Matt with his rifle.

Matt knocked the barrel toward the sky and wrapped his left leg around the soldier's right knee, folding his own right ankle over his left. Then he rapidly bent his knees, pulling the man forward, which, unfortunately, resulted in the butt end of the gun crashing into Matt's nose and cheek, but he ignored the pain and pushed his legs straight up, causing the soldier to go face-down over Matt's head, the rifle landing to the side in the muck. Matt punched upward and felt his knuckles make painful contact with the man's face. Immediately, still flat on his back, he lifted his Scorp and began firing into the trees toward where he had heard the other voice.

There was no answering fire, so he rolled to his feet and turned his weapon on the man he'd downed, who now lay face down in the mud. Matt rolled him over and groaned. A kid, no older than nineteen. He barely had any hair on his face yet. A trickle of blood ran from his mouth. Matt patted him down and stripped him of his weapons, adding them to his inventory as the kid began to moan softly.

You and me both, kid, Matt thought as he re-set his nose with his bruised hands, wincing from the pain that lanced through him. He didn't think his cheekbone was fractured, but it sure was bloody. He took a wipe from his first aid kit, cleared the blood from his face, and then blindly fastened a couple of butterfly-shaped bandages on it to hold the edges together. He was certainly no doctor, but at least the bleeding slowed.

After securing the kid's hands behind him and dragging him to higher ground, he tracked into the trees and quickly found the second soldier, not much older, dead with two bullet wounds in him. *Fuck, I hate soldiering. Give me a Glitter run or extraction. Even a damned trafficking raze.* Anything was better than shooting random people—kids—who had been hired to shoot at him. He rubbed the uninjured side of his face and took the second soldier's weapons. He paused, arranged the body in what might be a comfortable position, and set the unfortunate young man's helmet over his face. He gave a Bosch salute and then returned to the task of crossing the creek and getting to Kik and Mac.

Saturday, July 2, 2366. Haida, Karuk Estate grounds. Fourteen bells, Haida time.

He looked up at the sheer rock layers that extended as far as he could see. This was the "steep incline" Susan had indicated on the map. Hell, it wasn't an incline; it was the damned foot of a mountain range.

He had stood in the rain several minutes after his encounter with the patrol. Was there any point in going on? Maybe the boys actually were dead, and Susan had sent him to be killed. But he reminded himself, he didn't run into the sentries until he left the directions Susan had given him. And he had zero other leads. So, he decided to push on.

It had taken him a good quarter-bell of stealthy creeping to find a crossable section of the creek-now-river. Then he had figured he would have to backtrack until he found the far side of the footbridge. But as he hiked, he saw the next landmark from the map: a true giant of a tree cracked in two, creating a canopy across the path. He walked under the tree, marveling at its size, and then veered off the trail to the left. And there was the "incline," within which should be several caves if he followed it to the left. Susan said she had left the boys in the third cave.

He walked along, keeping the mountain on his right shoulder. After a few minutes, he spied a hollow in the rocks. A few meters farther, and then he saw another. He had seen no other patrols, so he started to call, "Kik? Mac? Boys?"

Within a few minutes of hiking to the left, he heard what had to be the sweetest sounds ever. "Matt? We're over here!" And indeed, they were. Two very wet, very dirty seven-and-a-half-year-old boys stood at the entrance to a cave. Matt laughed. "Of course, you'd hide out in a cave—you're your mother's sons!" he said as he hugged them each individually and then the two of them together. Elated, his body warmed, his heart overflowing as he listened to them chatter in their twin way about the adventures that had befallen them.

It took him a moment of watching and listening to realize that neither of them had shoes on, and Mac wore a t-shirt with no overshirt.

"Susan took them last night," explained Mac when Matt asked about the missing items as he distributed the food, water, and dry blankets that Susan had sent with him.

Matt frowned. "What do you mean?" This did not sound like the woman he had just met, who, despite Matt's wavering trustometer, had definitely not sent him on a fool's errand.

"Well, we both ran into the kitchen, first Mac, then me," Kik said. "When I ran in, Susan was doing dishes, and she opened the cupboard at her knees and pointed at it. Mac was in there and waved me in."

Mac picked up the tale. "And, like, two seconds later…"

"It was longer than that," Kik corrected.

"Not by much," Mac retorted. "Anyhow, one of the guards came in, and Susan said, 'I think they ran outside.' So, then the guard went out. And Susan opened the cupboard and said, 'I need your shoes and one shirt.' So, we gave them to her."

"Yeah," Kik said. "Cuz she rescued us from the bad guys."

Mac nodded in vigorous agreement. "When she walked us to this cave later last night, she said she had stuffed my shirt with the goose carcass from the icebox and the big beef bones and threw it off the bluff and used our shoes to make prints that look like we ran and slid."

"And then she threw our shoes down the bluff too," Kik finished.

They sat quietly for the briefest moment, all three considering the story. Then Mac said, "I think she was pretty brave. I want to rescue her back."

Matt nodded, then gave both boys another hug around their shoulders. "Yeah. You are right. I think we should rescue her back as well."

TWENTY-TWO

A Lousy Trip Down Memory Lane

Saturday, July 2, 2366. Haida, Karuk Estate, Abernathy private quarters, third floor. 13 bells, Haida time

The rain is still coming down hard outside the windows, which curve around the turret that contains my room. I look up. The ceiling is a circle, made of what I can only imagine to be rare woods cut into triangles, their peaks meeting at the center. An elaborate crystal chandelier with electric bulbs hangs from the center, lighting the room below with sparkles and even little rainbows on the splendidly wallpapered walls.

I sit on a comfortable stool, my back to the door, dressed in a blue silk dress that accentuates my curves and is revealing in all…well, in any other situation, I'd say the right places, but in this case, it's the wrong places. I have dainty, blue, satin slippers on my feet, and my braid lies attractively over my shoulder, its tail with its green ribbon woven through it passing over my decolletage. I even have a bit of makeup on, done by Susan who apologized as she applied it. No matter.

My hands have been re-bound behind me. My ankles have also been rendered immobile, but in a nod to style, my wrists and ankles are both tied with an elegant blue rope, just the shade of my shoes. It seems more suitable for a curtain tieback, but it is sturdy enough, and the guard put the backs of my hands together, making it almost impossible to remove the ties without a cutting tool.

I am still alone, so I take in the room. Across from me, behind a small, cherry wood coffee table, there is a sofa with a curved back and embroidered upholstery in a deep red. Two electric lamps jut up behind it, probably set up on some antique console table. A matching wingback chair sits nearby, with a small drink table off to the side. The walls contain beautiful art, most of it quite valuable, and I play with the idea of how I might pull a heist.

I turn my head and see a large, four-poster bed, piled high with pillows. Beyond the bed, an ornately carved dresser sits near a door, which I imagine must lead to a walk-in closet or perhaps a washroom. A full-length cheval mirror stands nearby. Directly next to the bed on either side are tables. The one I can see also has ornately carved legs. I squint and try to make out the figures. I think one is of a lion.

A medium-sized black box sits on this table, and I sigh. I know what kinds of things are in there. I am also privy to the psychological game Abernathy is playing here. Letting me sit here and think about what's to come. Fucker. I really hate that it's working.

I'm tired of looking at the room, so I decide to think about the defensive strategies the Bosch had planned. Gia and General Phil Patel were brilliant in their tactics, placing a medium-sized force in each district to patrol the coasts while our pilots take some of the newest vessels up to heights that the rest of the planet doesn't know we can reach. They will wait there and swoop down to fire as needed. The districts will call up past BPF members and create militias to put off any invaders that push beyond the beach or make it through alive from the skies.

Cal provided the names of troopers and citizens sympathetic to Howard Archer who might behave treacherously. We agreed not to round them up, but we quietly placed two armed watchers near each one, so that if treason tried to grow, it could be cut off before it blossomed.

The door behind me opens. There's no creak, but I can feel the air change. Ugly Terror tries to slip into my mind, but I shove it into a dark room in my mind and lock that door. *Your job is to keep him distracted, Kat. Mission specs.*

"Well, here's my little Mary." His voice makes my skin crawl.

I can't help it. I automatically say, "My name's not Mary, you fuck."

He walks up and looks at me. "You look much better with long hair, Mary."

I don't answer.

"Mary, it's impolite to ignore your host," he chastens.

I sigh, "My name. Is not. Mary." I look directly into his dead eyes.

He smiles and says quietly, "Ah, I see." Then he backhands me hard with his fist, knocking me off my stool and onto the floor where I land on my face. His foot lands in my ribs over and over. Let the games begin.

Saturday, July 2, 2366. Haida, Karuk Estate, Abernathy private quarters, third floor. Fourteen bells, Haida time.

I awake and try to open my eyes, but they seem to be stuck shut with something. Finally, after some effort, the first one comes open and then the other, and I see the grain of the wood floor very closely. I try to roll over, moaning slightly with pain from the effort, but find I can't fully turn. Now I realize why. There is a weight on top of me.

As my consciousness increases, I realize my hands and feet are bound, and I remember where I am and what is happening. I feel Anger pop up and say, *Didn't Teddy say you'd never be hurt like that again? What a liar.* Fuck off, Anger. I put myself here. As long as he is occupied with me, Matty has a chance to get the hostages free. Get my babies free and away. I have heard no trio of explosions. Unless they went off while I was out. That'd be okay. I try to shift the weight off my back, and I hear that voice.

"Awake and ready for round two, Mary? How delightful." His feet move from where they were pressed on my back and land on either side of me. He pulls me up, standing behind me, gripping my upper arms and squeezing, digging his fingers painfully into my biceps. I struggle automatically, but he pulls me back close to him and whispers in my ear, "My hands are a bit sore from round one. Let's use the whip this time, shall we?"

He tosses me on the bed face first, and I use its softness to roll to my back. I bring my knees up and land a kick straight into his chest, knocking him backward. Shit. Probably shouldn't have done that. I'm not exactly playing from a position of strength. I hear him scrabble up. He comes at me across the bed from over my head and punches me hard in the belly, causing me to gag and struggle to catch my breath. He pushes his face next to mine. "You cunt. You'll pay for that with blood. And if your own blood won't make you behave, remember, there's always sweet, precious Grey."

At my daughter's name, I release all my fighting tension.

Clearly, no explosions happened when I was unconscious. "Fine. No more kicking. We keep this just between us," I say.

"What's your name, cunt?" He twists my ear hard.

I don't even hesitate. "Mary. It's Mary." *For now.*

"Oh, very good. But you still owe me some blood." I hear the box open, and the whip cracks in the air once, twice, and then it cuts into me, from my cheek to my breast, and I cry out, just a little. And then it comes down, again and again and again.

Saturday, July 2, 2366. Haida, Karuk Estate, Abernathy private quarters, third floor. Fifteen and a-half bells, Haida time.

This time, when I regain consciousness, I know my eyes are sticky with blood. I am naked and on the floor next to the bed. Every part of me hurts. *I'm too fucking old for this shit*, I think. I am not the girl I was nineteen years ago, for better and for worse. I start to consider that perhaps Rob Abernathy has changed in that time too. Maybe I've misjudged him. Maybe he will go ahead and kill me. I feel like I should discuss this with Ruth, but the odds of me making it to Tuesday's appointment seem remote.

I gotta hand it to whoever tied the restraints on my hands and feet. They are good. I try to not make a sound as I look around. I remember being thrown against the dresser; things got a bit fuzzy after that. Something sparkles on the floor, and the light above me is strange and flickering.

"I need you to clean up that mess. And have you had any word when the power will be back on?" Abernathy's voice is calm, almost happy.

"No, sir. When I went out to the road, a worker there said

there were several lightning strikes. But it could also have been weapon fire as well. Either way, the power is out, and the devices don't work. I brought more candles." Susan's voice is small, and there is definite fear in it.

"Well, dammit. How are Mary and I to watch the destruction of Bosch and the crisis in Truevale?"

"I... I don't know, sir," Susan says.

Abernathy is clearly annoyed now. "Well, of course, you don't. You are stupid. Just sweep up that mess."

Footsteps come toward the bed, and the dresser and Susan's feet appear in my line of vision. She gasps a little at the sight of me, which I imagine is pretty grisly.

"Oh, don't worry about her. Get the glass cleaned up," Abernathy calls.

I slowly turn my head to look at her, and our eyes meet. I wink. Her face does not change. She begins to sweep, and I hear the tinkle of what must be broken glass. She leans down and begins to pick up shards of the mirror that I now recall knocking over on my way to the dresser. Susan brings a bin over, then carefully lifts the larger shards and drops them in, sweeping the smaller ones into a dustpan.

She says nothing to me and nothing to Abernathy. She simply does as instructed. Her feet move past me as she gathers some of the farthest scattered bits of the looking glass. Then I feel it—pressed into my hand—a long, sharp shard of mirror. I don't hesitate. I roll onto my right side as silently as possible so my back, with my bound hands holding my prize, is hidden under the bed's edge.

"Well, that should do it, sir," she says briskly and I watch as she carries the bin and her broom out of my sight line. Her footsteps fade and the door closes.

~

Saturday, July 2, 2366. Haida, Karuk Estate, Abernathy private quarters, third floor. Fifteen and three-quarters bells, Haida Time

Here I am again, sawing at something with a shard of glass. This time, it's not my hair, though. My hand that grips the shard is cut and bleeding, but I keep sawing away as silently as I can.

A knock on the door. Perfect. Abernathy's footsteps and then the door opens.

"Ashton. What do you want? I'm busy." Abernathy's voice holds that touch of constant impatience I have noticed he uses with his son.

"Father, there have been reports of deep incursions along the borders. With this rain, the commanders say the soldiers can't see, but there have been some heavy casualties on our side—one even only a few kilometers from here."

I keep sawing, but I smile. *Go, team.*

Abernathy is quick to answer. "That is why we have soldiers and commanders, son. Leave the fighting to them."

Ashton's voice whines, "Still, I think we need to leave and get to safety."

My hands suddenly come apart. I roll my wrists for a moment and then wrap part of the rope around one end of the shard.

"Nonsense. We are perfectly safe here. We should welcome the incursions. It makes our position that much more tenable. The Bosch will appear to have assassinated President Russell and that Reston lout, as well as General Hanna and those three annoying congresswomen, and they will be seen clearly trying to assassinate me and will send an attack force to Bosch." Abernathy's voice is calm.

My eyes widen as I curl my body down to cut the rope

holding my ankles. I shake my head inwardly. Well, it's not like Cal and I hadn't predicted something like this.

My feet come apart, and I lay still. Revenge is going to taste fucking sweet. Signal explosions or not. I'm about to finish this dysfunctional little affair we have shared over the past almost two decades. *If I live, RTT is going to be able to afford that guest house now because this shit is going to take years to unpack.*

"I suppose that's true, Father. But just in case, I'm going to check the tunnel." Ashton's hobbling footsteps fade away. He sounds worried, as well he should be. My company is a force to be reckoned with. A Bosch Pirate Force, as a matter of fact.

"Suit yourself." The door closes, and I hear Abernathy walk over and pour a drink.

I barely breathe. The ice tinkles as he takes a drink. He sets the glass down with a clink. Now his footsteps approach the side of the bed, where I lie on the floor. I press my ankles together, a drape of rope on them and on my hands, held convincingly behind me, and let my head rest down and my eyes close.

He stands over me in his dressing gown and nudges me with his foot. "Wake up." I lie still. A second nudge and I give a small moan. "I'm ready for more. Come on."

My hand holding the shard is quick, but it catches the knot of his robe and only skims the surface of his chest. The second stroke comes down and slices his cheek. He yells in pain and kicks at me. I jump out of the way and land in a crouch. "You know what, Rob? I think I'm ready for a bit more too. Let's trade places, though."

He dodges around the end of the bed and grabs for the whip. I leap up to stand on the bed as the whip comes at me. Keeping constant eye contact with my prey, I lean my head and shoulders back to avoid the bite, but I reach my hand up to grab the tip of the fall. It cuts into my hand, but I don't notice. With a quick twist of my wrist, I wrap a length of it in my fist. I lean forward, creating slack, and quickly jerk it back, pulling the entire whip from his astonished hand. I toss it into the air, grabbing the handle as it comes down. In less than a second, I send the end of the whip, the fall, out, which cuts a red streak down Vice President Abernathy's bare chest.

My eyes are wild as I stand naked and blood-covered on the bed, whip in one hand and shard of mirror in the other. "I need to aim a bit lower next time," I say with a growl and pull my arm back. And just like that, Rob Abernathy, vice president of the Federal Alliance of Nations, turns and runs for the door, throwing it open and scuttling through it. He slams it shut behind him, and I hear the key locking it from the outside.

I yell at the top of my lungs, "You coward! Fucking Bellcoast couldn't hold me, Rob. Do you think that little door will? I'm coming for you!"

TWENTY-THREE

We Gather Together

Saturday, July 2, 2366. Haida, Karuk Estate. Fifteen and a quarter bells, Haida time.

Matt had been gone for almost three bells when Grey smelled smoke. She had eaten the apple and hard bread Matt had found for her. She drank the water and even used the pot under the bed that Matt had said was for "relieving yourself." She had thought it was funny that he seemed uncomfortable saying that when she heard him and Mama and their friends saying way cruder things when she listened through the vent.

The ceiling light had gone off, and though she clicked the switch back and forth several times, it stayed off. The windowless room was dark, so Grey opted to nap a bit on the hard mattress. Now, however, she was sure she was smelling smoke. And she had been taught that smoke means fire and to get out of the house if she smelled it.

Matt had told her to stay put. But he hadn't known there was going to be a fire. She made up her mind and moved the chair. She felt the door; it wasn't hot, so she opened it. There were no billows of smoke, but she could still smell it. Though the light in the hall was very dim, it felt bright to her after being in the pitch-black room. She started toward the kitchen and the door outside when she remembered: Obaachan.

Saturday, July 2, 2366, Haida, Karuk Estate. Fifteen and a half bells, Haida time.

Grey pounded up the stairs to Obaachan's room. She knew she had to get out of the house before it really started burning, but she couldn't leave her grandmother to die. She rushed into the room. Obaachan still sat at the window, though she turned her head at the sound of the door flying open. Grey was taken aback by the look of disdain on her grandmother's face.

"C'mon, Obaachan. We need to leave," she urged, tugging at the old woman's sleeve.

"I told you. The embassy will send a transport for me. You have chosen the pirates. I hope you are happy with your choice. I was always afraid you'd be like your mother. If only you'd had a different one." Yumiko Shima's voice carried a chill.

Grey felt all the emotions she had been wrestling with over the past twenty-four hours come tumbling out her mouth in a yell. "Stop it, Obaachan! What are you talking about? Of course, I am like my mama. I am her daughter. And I don't want any other mama. You are just being mean. And, and… dumb. There is no transport coming. But the house *is* on fire, and we need to leave." She was now pulling on her grandmother's arm.

Her obaachan did not seem concerned with Grey's tirade. Instead, she looked toward the door, finally stood up, and said, "Well, here is a young man of substance."

Grey was initially thrilled as her obaachan stood, but when she turned around to see Ashton Abernathy grinning at the door, all her anger returned. "What do you want?" She hated this man.

"The old bat says I have substance. Sounds like she likes me more than she likes you. Also, I owe you something for this knee, you little brat." He walked over and slapped Grey so hard she practically lost her footing.

Ashton began to laugh.

Grey was stunned into silence, holding her cheek. Her obaachan looked at her. "You really shouldn't have kicked him. A lady doesn't do things like that. You'll never become a diplomat like your father and grandfather, behaving like a pirate. You should apologize."

Grey felt tears of pain and anger squeeze out of her eyes. Her obaachan was acting like it was her fault. "I'm glad I kicked him. I'll do it again!" She ran at Ashton to deliver another kick.

But her obaachan grabbed her arm and held her back. "You'll do nothing of the sort."

"He slapped you last night." Grey pointed at the awful young man who stood grinning and leaning on the door jamb.

"I don't recall that happening. I just remember you children acting poorly and creating a disruption. Not the diplomatic way at all."

Grey knew that her obaachan was acting strangely, but she had enough of being treated like this. She shook her arm loose from the woman's grasp and yelled, "You don't remember? Fine! I don't want to be a diplomat. I'm going to be a pirate!"

Her obaachan was about to respond when they all heard a loud cry from the third floor.

Ashton turned. "That's Father!"

Grey darted out the door, shoving at Ashton, who regained

his balance and hobbled quickly after her. Within moments, they heard the door slam and feet thumping down the steps. Mr. A. appeared, wearing only a dressing gown that now hung open, blood on his face and chest.

During that same moment, a voice screamed from the room above them. "You coward! Fucking Bellcoast couldn't hold me, Rob. Do you think that little door will? I'm coming for you!"

Grey looked up; her eyes widened, and she smiled. She yelled, "Mama!" Then Mr. A. grabbed her around the waist and dragged her with him down the stairs, shoving his son backward and into her obaachan.

Saturday, July 2, 2366. Haida, Karuk Estate. Fifteen and three-quarters bells-plus, Haida time.

Grey squirmed and kicked all the way down the steps. At the bottom, Mr. A. shoved her up against the wall and held her there with his hand tight around her throat. "Listen to me, you little bitch, you come quietly and you might live. Otherwise, I'll throw you down to the same rocks that killed your brothers."

Grey knew he would do it. So, she did what her mama had taught her when they played mission. *Wait for the opportunity.* She nodded and managed to squeak out, "Okay." The hand relaxed and moved to her upper arm, and he dragged her to the door that went to the basement. He threw it open, and smoke came billowing out. He slammed it. "Well, shit." Turning, he steered her for the kitchen door. A loud crashing sound came from far above them. Grey heard Mr. A. murmur, "Crazy cunt. Gotta get away from her."

Grey had not heard that word before, but she could tell it

was a swear—and about her mama. She decided it meant, *Strong woman who is coming after me.* Because that was what Mama had said, so she was pretty sure it was going to happen.

As they entered the kitchen, Susan turned from the window, where both lightning flashes and weapon fire were visible. "Sir, what…?" She looked at them both in horror.

"It's none of your business," Mr. A., barked.

Susan stepped in front of him. "Let the child go, sir."

"This is what happens to nosey bitches." Mr. A. spat and punched Susan hard in the head. The woman fell to the floor.

Mr. A. pulled Grey with him outside, into the rain. The wind whipped it into their faces, drenching them thoroughly. Even though it was July, a chill sank into Grey.

"C'mon," Mr. A. said and stumbled along the path toward the west side of the house.

Grey pulled at him in the direction of the gardens. "No, not that way. This way."

He batted at her, landing a slap on the side of her head, then jerked her toward him until their faces were close. "No!" He looked around and yelled into the wind, "I decide." Grey went silent and let him drag her toward the west side of the house and the bluff.

Saturday, July 2, 2366. Haida, Karuk Estate. Almost sixteen bells, Haida time.

"Grey?" Matty tramped wet, muddy prints along the servants' hallway as he called. "Grey?" He raised his voice a little. It still hurt to take a deep breath. He wanted to set off the three explosives he had planted in the house. To signal Kat that the children were out of harm's way and then get them all away from this place. His thoughts had turned quite dark on the hike back as he imagined Kat coping with… He had forced his brain to stop there because he felt his anger growing stronger and far more difficult to manage at that point.

The children. He had found the boys and left them safe, dry, and fed in the cave. And he had made sure Grey was settled and safe not three bells earlier. *Dammit, these children never stay put.* No wonder all his old friends who were parents looked tired. He thought about Aaron and wondered if he knew about this part of having children.

He had found the room he had left her in dark, with the bed slept in, an apple core on the floor and pee in the pot. But no actual Grey. A whiff of smoke coming through the floorboards made him wrinkle his brow, so he moved quickly into the hall to call for her. He glanced at the stairway that they had come down. Yumiko. Smoke. Grey may have gone to get her obaachan.

He ran up the stairs and opened the unobtrusive door, peering down the hallway they had come from. Someone's legs were on the floor, extending from Yumiko's room. "Grey!" he gasped and ran to the doorway. Yumiko lay on her back, half in and half out of her room, eyes closed. She was breathing but barely. Matt lifted her. She weighed almost nothing.

He saw a smear of blood on the floor, and as he gently laid her on the bed, he saw where she had hit her head on the corner of the bedstead when she…fell? Was pushed? He didn't know. He settled her in bed so that she looked comfortable and covered her with the light blanket from the chair. It was the best he could do. He had to get Grey. Mission specs. He started to leave and then hesitated. "If you die, old woman, I hope you know it was a pirate who gave you comfort at the end."

> Saturday, July 2, 2366. Haida, Karuk Estate. Fifteen and three-quarters bells-plus, Haida time.

I am no longer thinking. I am simply acting. I will not be kept from the prey I have hunted all this time. I pull at the door and shake it to no avail. I turn to the windows. Third story. A dozen meters. The bed is filthy with my blood and even nastier fluids. I pull the sheets and light blankets off, then roll and twist four of them and tie them into a long rope.

I pile the coiled sheet rope onto the couch and push it over to the windows. They don't open, but who really gives a fuck, right? I allow myself a tremendous and satisfying roar as I launch the cherry wood table through the window, which shatters spectacularly, sending a few glass slivers onto my skin and into my hair.

I tie one end of my makeshift rope to the couch leg; the other, I secure to one of the lamps that had sat artistically behind it. Then I fling the lamp through the window and watch the sheet rope arc out with it. It gets caught on the jagged fragments of glass that still cling to the window frame a time or two, but I shake it loose. And then, taking the whip in one hand and my glass shard blade in my teeth, I swing out into the storm to take the revenge that has been so long delayed, calling my prey to me.

Saturday, July 2, 2366. Haida, Karuk Estate, bluff side. Sixteen bells, Haida time.

Matt stood at the top of the stairs and thought. *Susan.* She had known where the boys were; maybe she'd know about Grey now. He went down the back stairs, and as he came to the first floor, he noticed the smoky smell was growing stronger. *Where is that coming from?* He scanned the hallway for any of the remaining estate guards and then slipped down the hall, following the smell. He saw a wisp of smoke slip from under the basement door.

His hand on the closed door assured him no flames loomed behind it, so he opened it just a bit. More smoke drifted out, but he felt no heat. Taking a deep breath of fresh air, he went partway down the stairs, where the smoke was only a bit thicker. He could make out two guards piled on each other, clearly having been dispatched. *By whom?* Matt wondered. The vegetable boxes were shoved clear from the closed tunnel door, and copious smoke leaked out from around the perimeter of the rough wood. *Fire in the tunnel? But why?* Finding more questions than answers, he focused on tracking down Grey. At least he knew the house was safe.

He made his way to the kitchen to find Susan and get her help. He found her sitting on the floor, holding a towel to her eye. There was dried blood on her cheek and chin.

Matt was next to her in a moment, helping her into a chair. "What happened? Have you seen Grey?"

"Outside. He took her outside." She pointed at the partially open kitchen door. "Go!"

Without a pause, Matt ran into the rain. *Which way?* Then he heard a loud…something. Not a scream. Not a yell. No, it was a fucking battle cry that pierced through the howling storm, and it came from the west side of the house. Kat's voice

—he was sure of it. As he moved toward the sound, he felt someone near him.

Susan was at his elbow. She glanced at him through the deluge. "I need to see that little girl safe as well."

Matt shrugged and nodded.

They came around the corner of the house and took in the sight. Susan cried, "Aiya! Look at that!" Matt already was staring. For a moment, he was confused since her hair was long and braided, but he knew it was the woman whom he would follow to the gates of hell, General Kat Wallace. She was swaying several feet above the ground holding onto a white rope that extended from the high turret window. She was naked, the rain washing blood from her body. She held a stock whip in one hand and something that sparkled between her teeth. Her eyes were wild and seemed focused in front of him.

He turned his head to see what she saw. There, by the firepit, was Grey, and she was holding a gun on Rob Abernathy. Matt raised his weapon, blinking away the blinding effects of the storm, as the rain and wind buffeted him from outside, and his anger raged from within.

Saturday, July 2, 2366. Haida, Karuk Estate. Sixteen bells, Haida time.

Mr. A. dragged Grey toward the bluff. *Where Kik and Mac died*, she thought. And all at once, she knew what had really happened. *I know he is going to throw me off, too.* From over to the left came a wild, yelling sound. Mr. A. stopped and his grip relaxed, and she heard him say, "What in the name of God?"

This is it. My opportunity. She screamed at him, "Stop it!"

and then pulled her arm up to her mouth, taking a hard bite of his hand. He swore, "Bitch!" but released her. She broke for the firepit and, shoving the lid to the wood box aside, reached in and grabbed the gun she and her brothers had hidden there a few days earlier.

"I am not going to let you kill me. Not like you did to Kik and Mac," she yelled.

Mr. A. regarded her. She knew he would be afraid now. Guns could really hurt people. But his expression changed from brief panic to smugness, his lips twisting up into a slowly growing smile. "You are a stupid child, Grey Shima. But you can be trained. Do you think I'd be foolish enough to leave a gun with live ammo in it where you children could get it?"

Grey, standing drenched and shaking, paused, confused, and turned the gun slightly, looking at it.

He was in front of her so quickly, his hands pulling the pistol from hers, she had no time to act. He turned it and pushed it under her chin, pointing it upward, then whispered, "Actually, I did leave it loaded." She felt herself scooped up, then pulled back against Mr. A's chest. Her head was even with his as he hissed into her ear, "You are my ticket away from that insane woman up there."

Grey looked at the mansion and saw her mama, naked, holding onto a rope coming from the turret window. She didn't think she looked insane. She thought she looked beautiful.

The gun was pressed hard under Grey's chin. She couldn't even swallow, and she felt spit accumulate in the corner of her mouth. She held very still. Mr. A. began to shout, and it hurt her ear that was pressed close to his cheek. "I am leaving with her, Mary. There will be no trade. I keep her and I'll make her into what you should have been."

He gave a barking kind of laugh. "I win, Mary. You have

lost all your children. Again." Now his voice shifted, and it sounded to Grey like it was something sharp, meant to cause pain. "You know, that long-ago first one was killed on my orders. I told that group of traders not to bring me any cowbirds. You could have had another. I certainly did my part. But you failed me there." He squeezed his arm around Grey's middle and rubbed his cheek on the side of her head. His breath felt hot. "This one won't, though."

Grey looked and saw her mother leap to the ground, glance to either side, and then move toward where Mr. A. held her. A guard came running toward her mama from the left. Grey tried to yell to warn her, but the gun pressed painfully, and she couldn't open her mouth. She was sure Mama would be knocked over. But instead, her mama simply grabbed the barrel of the rifle the man pointed at her, said something Grey couldn't hear, and then shoved the butt end of the weapon into the man, causing him to double over. Grey saw Mama's knee come up hard in the man's face, and he collapsed in a heap on the wet ground.

Mama had barely broken her stride toward her and Mr. A., getting closer by the moment. Grey looked to the other side and saw Susan and Matthieu, his gun up and pointed toward her and Mr. A. The rain kept coming, but Grey could hear a roaring behind her, getting louder and louder. It was the sea. They were standing on the edge of the bluff.

Saturday, July 2, 2366. Haida, Karuk Estate. Sixteen bells and seven minutes, Haida time.

After vanquishing mole-guard, which was fun, I walk steadily toward the pair until I am but a few meters away. My prey and the girl, as she can only be *the girl* for now as I hunt this monster. He stands on the rocky crag, holding the girl tightly to him with one arm, a pistol pushed hard under her chin. "Stay where you are, Mary. Or I'll shoot her and throw her body to the rocks. I swear, I will."

The girl with her bedraggled brown waves and deep-brown, frightened eyes, and her young girl's body that just is standing on the precipice of womanhood, looks at me and says with a plea, "Mama."

In a flash, I remember all the things that happened to me in the years I was her age and a bit older. Things that I swore my child would be safe from. And here we are. Not safe at all. Despair starts to pull at me. I hear a low whistle and glance to the edge of this immense, beautiful, horrible house, and there is Matty, gun trained on the pair, but his shot held back by good judgment. Susan-from-the-Kitchen stands a bit behind him, her hand at her mouth.

There has been so much pain in my life, but standing here, Despair is now pushed away. All I feel from this beautiful girl who came from me and the beautiful man who came to me is complete love: Papa's, Mama's, the sibs, my circle of friends who extend around the New Earth—we have tried to make it a better place. My children and their children will make it even better. I hope they all know how much I love them.

I hear running footsteps behind me and see the girl's eyes get big as the Monster starts to smile. Then I hear the loud report of Matty's Scorp and a small grunt and thud behind me. *Opportunity.*

I make it all happen in an instant. As Abernathy's body shifts to take in what happened behind me, I throw the glass shard with all my might from my left hand and draw the whip back with my right. The whip flashes forward as the shard slashes the knuckles of Abernathy's gun hand. The gun drops to the earth as both his hands rise in pain, and the girl drops to her feet on the ground. His mouth opens; he must be yelling something, but I hear nothing. The whip's end wraps securely around his left wrist. I feel a tug as I see him start to lean precariously and flail his arms, trying to stay balanced. I take two quick steps forward and place a hand on the girl's—*my* girl's—shoulder. I squeeze it as I pull her forward away from the bluff.

"I love you, Grey. Run to Matty," I order and push the Monster backward away from my child and my life. I release the whip handle, but it doesn't drop: my own wrist is tangled in the thong. It is oddly unexpected and yet, I feel no panic, only a bit of sadness that I couldn't say goodbye. Then Rob Abernathy tips backward in what looks like slow motion, reaching out and grasping at me and catching my braid in his fist, pulling on me as he tumbles off the bluff into the wet July afternoon, dragging me with him to the rough and rocky coast of the Ohlone Bay.

Saturday, July 2, 2366. Haida, Karuk Estate. Sixteen bells and nine minutes, Haida time.

Matt watched the tableau unfold and his life collapse. He wanted to take the shot at Abernathy, but Grey's head and body covered him. The monster held her so close to the cliff's edge, Matt was afraid if he had taken his shot, Abernathy would have dragged Grey with him.

Then the remaining guard came running at Kat. That was a clear shot, and he took it, the guard crumpling to the ground. It freed Kat to pull Grey away. He hoped she would step back, clearing his field to take the shot. But then Grey came running toward him, and his shot spun uselessly into the sky as he watched his brightwork girl, his motorcycle warrior, his best friend, and the woman he had planned a life with disappear over the bluff. The universe punched him hard as he yelled out in shock and agony, "No!" and then hopelessly, "Kat…"

"Matthieu!" Grey yelled as she flung herself into his arms, which immediately surrounded her. She turned, and, realizing there was no Kat behind her, she began to shriek and wail. "Mama! Mama! Where's Mama, Matthieu?" All Matt could do was hold her close and stare at the empty air where once love had been.

∽

Saturday, July 2, 2366. Haida, Karuk Estate. Sixteen bells and nine minutes, Haida time.

So, this is how it ends. No last words, no meaning. I feel a quick jerk in my body and a low snap, followed by a loose sensation. A heaviness drags on my right arm and pulls my head to the left. My left arm feels disconnected. I suppose that's to be expected. The fall is taking so long. I look down and see Abernathy looking up at me with the sharp rocks and the pounding surf spread in a magnificent background, but still, so far below.

His eyes are no longer dead. Now, they are filled with terror. He grips the whip and my braid as if they could save him. I find I have time to smile as I rotate my right wrist out of the thong and feel the whip give way. As his left arm drops, terror grows in his eyes. The pull on my hair is tremendous as the wind bumps at my head, but the pain is abating.

It turns out there is time for last words, so I take the opportunity. "You lose, Rob. You never got what you wanted in life. I did. I was happy. So, I win."

He looks confused now, and he seems to be looking above me and mouthing something, but the wind and the pounding surf take it away. I feel my old hair pull away from my scalp, taking some of the new with it. And just like that, the Monster is gone, dropping away from me. I expect to follow, but I feel as if I am moving slightly upward. Maybe it's like that ancient story of the Little Mermaid, and I am being lifted into the clouds as seafoam. Maybe I'll see Papa there.

I feel a jerk in my upper body and then a sharp blow at my temple, and things go black.

∽

Saturday, July 2, 2366. Haida, Karuk Estate. Sixteen bells and ten, Haida time.

Matt wanted to lash out at the world that had taken everything from him, but here, in his arms, was someone who was also broken and needed him to be strong. So, he held Grey tightly as she screamed, and the wind whipped and howled. "Let me go! Matthieu! I have to get Mama!" There was no way he was letting her look over that edge. But he knew *he* had to.

"Grey." It was Susan's voice, and she reached over and stroked Grey's hair. "Let's get you inside." Matt looked at the woman who was both brave and kind and saw tears running from her eyes. Her left eye held an ugly gash in the upper lid that was still oozing blood.

"No. Please, let me stay." Grey was becoming frantic. "Mama can't be gone. Matt, then I will have lost them all."

"Oh, Sweet Earth. No, baby." Matt heard himself use Kat's

pet name for her children. "No, you haven't lost them all. The boys are safe."

Grey paused in her struggles to get to the cliff and looked at him, stunned and unbelieving. "What?"

"Susan hid them from Abernathy." He pointed to the woman in the blue pinafore. Before he could explain more, a man's scream of terror came bubbling up from beyond the bluff, and all three turned. "Stay here," Matt said firmly and pushed Grey into Susan's arms.

He ran for the cliff, not wanting to look but knowing he must. As he got closer, he heard another sound. It was also a man's voice but one he thought he recognized. It was not the awful voice of Abernathy from the comm the other night but familiar, nonetheless. It came again. "Help, I need help." Now he rushed to the edge, knowing he would see the broken form of his Kat at the bottom, waiting for the sea to claim it. He swallowed and peered over. He had to blink twice to take it in. Then he said in a low voice filled with awe, "Holy shit, Riki."

"Matt-san, some help, please." There was a strained tone of understandable urgency in his strong Edoan friend's voice.

Riki was crammed on a narrow ledge, back against the headland wall. His legs were tightly wrapped around a scrub pine that had sprouted out from the cliff, his face rigid with effort. His hands grasped tightly onto an arm that hung at an odd angle. The arm was attached to a limp Kat Wallace.

Matt called down, "Hold on, buddy." He sprang up, then turned and ran to the turret window, where he jerked down the sheet rope that Kat had made. Now, as he gathered it up and raced back to the cliff, he said over and over in what felt like one of his mother's devotions, "Hold on, my love."

TWENTY-FOUR

The Afterlife

Monday, July 4, 2366. Haida, Bay Street Hospital. Daytime, probably.

The light is very diffuse, but it feels bright to me. I cautiously blink my eyes, but don't fully open them, trying to slowly acclimate. I have two thoughts: 1) I didn't realize the afterlife would have crisp, clean sheets, but it does, and I approve. 2) I thought all pain would be gone once I died, but Sweet Fucking New Earth, it isn't. My head hurts like hell. I feel like my body is one big bruise. And I can't seem to move my left arm.

I turn my head ever so slowly on the sweet-smelling pillow. *Pillows in the afterlife! Shiny!* Each millimeter feels like someone is banging on it from the inside with a sledgehammer. I shift my eyes down to see what's up with my arm. There is some kind of brown strap on it. That's weird. My thoughts are moving through some kind of thick, dense fog. I look beyond my body and see Bailey across from me in a bed with rails around it. I notice my bed has some as well.

"Bailey? Did you die, too? I'm sorry. But I'm glad to see you." My voice is hoarse and comes out in a low whisper. I guess Bailey couldn't hear me because there is no response. I look around a bit more and see no one else. Maybe that means the kids and Matty are alive. I feel tears spring to my eyes as I think of them. I let out a breath that I didn't know I was holding. *Why am I breathing?*

"Kat, you're awake?" Bailey's voice is a whisper, but it draws my eyes back to them.

I wrinkle my brow. "Why would we sleep if we are dead?"

I hear them give a quiet laugh. "Shit, Kat, I feel too lousy to be dead. We are in a hospital in Haida." They start to fumble in their white sheets.

Hospital?

∽

Monday, July 4, 2366. New Caribbean, Camaguey. 9:00 a.m. sharp.

Ashton Abernathy sat in his new suit, sweating in the small, well-furnished office. The floors were covered with a sisal rug, and a fan slowly moved the steaming air around. He tapped his foot impatiently and began to drum his fingers. His knee was throbbing. Where was that woman?

Several minutes later, she returned, accompanied by a stylishly dressed man. "Mr. Abernathy?" The man extended his hand.

Ashton looked at the dark hand and then at the man. "Yes." His own pale hands remained on the chair arms.

"Ah." The man pursed his lips and gave a small nod. "You wanted to make a withdrawal from this account, correct?"

"Yes." The younger man's voice conveyed his impatience. "My father's accounts through Abernathy Enterprises are locked up pending the investigation into his untimely death.

The family needs funds, and this account is intended to provide that."

The man frowned slightly. "Please accept my condolences on your father's passing. Unfortunately, the last of the funds were transferred from here last Friday into the accounts designated."

Ashton paused. "What do you mean, transferred?"

"Transferred, as in moved as instructed. All funds were equally distributed among the six foundations your father requested, along with the arrangement that any incoming funds will automatically be dispensed to those foundations in perpetuity."

"What foundations? My father would never authorize such a move." Ashton was becoming angry. "I want to see the request." He punctuated his last statement by hitting his forefinger on the chair arm as his father had always done when trying to drive a point home with him.

The dark man nodded and then said with what Ashton felt was a touch of frustration. "Yes, sir. Madam Alonso and I will collect the documents. Please wait here." Both camagueyanos stepped quickly out of the office, pulling the door shut as they went.

Ashton stood up and paced a bit. He was so angry when his father had chosen that little bitch who had broken his kneecap to escape with instead of him, his own son, that he had left the estate. The tunnel had been on fire, and then he'd spied that large man in the basement who had attacked the two guards Ashton had ordered to travel with him. He had turned and ran until he was at the road, then paid some workman returning to Haida to take him to the public airfield, where he immediately chartered a flight and charged it to the family account.

Ashton realized his father's poor choice had doomed him

when the news came that the vice president had gone over the cliff on the west side of the house. Rob Abernathy, dead. Ashton felt no sadness, just a sense of relief. But also, he felt anger at that girl bubbling and stewing inside of him.

It was his father's own fault that he fell. He had been far too obsessed with that pirate woman—that was why those stupid children had taken his father's focus. That girl's defiant face as she hobbled him appeared in Ashton's head. Now there was a score he'd like to settle, kid or not. Now all the personal and business funds were frozen, thanks to an ongoing investigation headed by the FA attorney general. But his father had disclosed to Ashton the details of his JourneysAbroad accounts, and Ashton did not intend to go without the things that made life comfortable.

He frowned, pulled out his comm, and punched in the numbers for the Sarapion bank. As he spoke to the bank manager, he began to feel the blood drain from his face. Dizziness overwhelmed him, so he sat back in the chair. He said little, not bothering to respond when the bank manager on the other end asked if he had any questions. He simply hung up and sat staring at his feet.

The markers were gone.

The dark man returned without the woman. He held papers in his hands. "As you can see, Mr. Abernathy, the funds were distributed to the six branches of the Bureau for Persons newly Freed. I looked into it, of course, before making the first transfer. It is an organization specifically set up to support people who have survived human trafficking. An elegant solution to a nasty business, if you ask me."

"I didn't ask you," Ashton snapped. The manager in Sarapion had told the same story.

The manager, face neutral, held out a small booklet. "This is their prospectus if you'd like to read it."

Ashton was about to slap it from the man's hand, but he froze as he looked at the logo. Inside a circle were two crossed daggers and the initials "BPF." "Oh, fuck me. It's the goddamn pirates." Ashton stood and stormed from the room.

The bank manager looked at the logo, then at the angry man storming out of his bank…and smiled.

Thursday, July 7, 2366. Haida Airfield. Ten bells.

I'm going home.

Matty has insisted I travel on the hospital vessel so I can rest, so Mama will fly the Coupe back with Riki and the children. I have discovered that Matty is quite the persnickety nurse, fussing over me, only allowing two visitors at a time, and usually, only one child at a time. So, I have only seen the children altogether once and for about ten minutes. They were glowing but quiet as I am sure they had been instructed, and we just held each other and smiled.

Matty says that according to the Haida doctors, I need a quiet and dim room after all the blows my head received. I asked him where he was back in my recruit days, and he just looked at me, rolled his eyes, and gave me a piece of chocolate because he says I can't drink wine or bourbon until I'm healed. I might have killed him at that point, but several of the nursing staff told me a story that granted him a reprieve: Matty insisted that he be the one to wash the blood and filth from my hair and body after I was stabilized. They said he was so gentle, soaping and rinsing my wounds as he softly sang to me and murmured words of love. Both the male and female nurses sighed and smiled as they described it.

I addressed the subject on my first walk in the hospital hall.

"I don't remember that bath happening, so I am owed a singing sponge bath by the man I love."

"Is that so? You still love me with this?" He pointed at his face, which now sports a slightly crooked nose and ten centimeters of stitches across his left cheek.

I grinned. "Well, you know how shallow I am. We'll have to see how it heals."

Matty gave a small laugh and glared at me. "Don't make me laugh, Kat Wallace. It hurts."

"We are quite the pair, Matthieu Warner," I say as my own laugh is cut short as pain shoots through my broken ribs.

Matty also said he and Aaron had taken a small boat to the rocks at the bottom of the bluff to see Abernathy's body. Matty's face had gone quite hard as he said, "It was there. It didn't deserve either ground or sea burial. We each took the opportunity to give it a few kicks and may have emptied a round or two into it. But then we left it to the seabirds and the tide." He also found my braid trapped between two rocks. "I loosened it and scattered it and let the waves carry it free. The ribbon got caught in a gust of wind and blew up into the sky." I liked that.

Riki visited and told me his part of the story. He had come onto Karuk Estate to find the children not long after Matty and I arrived. He had packed the tunnel with crates and set them on fire to keep Abernathy from escaping and disabled a couple of guards that walked in on him. He had heard the ruckus and rightfully assessed Grey might be in danger of falling.

He had said, "Kat-san, I knew you and Matt..." Here he paused because he has been trying to drop the honorifics with Matt and, hopefully, eventually, me. "...would manage above the bluff, so I took below the bluff and lowered myself to move until I could shift just below the torn fence section. I was going to crawl up and take him from behind, but then you both fell. I could not let you go. Please accept my apologies for your dislocated shoulder."

I just looked at him. I wanted to laugh, but Matty was in the corner and would have scolded me. So, I just leaned forward, kissed him on the cheek, and said, "You have always been my friend, and now you are my hero. Thank you." He blushed quite pink and hurried out after that.

Bailey had said that after the initial push, Abernathy's armies pushed back hard. It breaks my heart that we lost people. But then the Haida stepped in with some pretty impressive war machines and that turned the tide for us. The FA also sent some ground troops to lend a hand, though the battle was pretty wrapped up by then. Their medical vehicles, supplies, and attention were invaluable.

No one had known why the Haida showed up, but Riki had told me before he left, "Tsukasa-san divulged that Shima-san…"

"Takai?" I repeated with surprise.

"Yes, Takai-san requested Tsukasa-san's help and negotiated with the Haida to secure assistance." At this, he gave a very Boschian shrug of his large shoulders and a roll of his hands and his eyes, closing with, "I know, right?" This delighted me—he was becoming Bosch.

Interestingly, Takai has mentioned nothing about the negotiations. He only said, "I came to see the children as soon as the forces would allow." Matty said he arrived within one of the first Haida vehicles that rolled onto the estate, rushing inside to find us in the servants' quarters, where all three of my sweet babes sat with Matty, Riki, and Susan, tending me as I lay unconscious.

Takai returned to Edo with Yumiko, who has not regained consciousness and still hovers between life and death. Before he left, he came to see me while Matty was getting breakfast and said, "I'm glad you were able to follow through on your intention not to die, Kat."

"Apparently, it took some doing to make good on it this time," I quipped.

He went serious and took my hand. "Then try not to push your luck anymore. I don't really want to live in a world without a Kat Wallace in it." Then he gave me a forehead peck of a kiss and left.

I secretly spoke to Miles on the comm because, well, because Matty says no work. He told me that Gia was amazing, and the general's table is eager to have her be part of the club. Bosch suffered no deaths in its defense, a few injuries, and some loss of property.

Apparently, the FA had their own attempted coup that was handily put off in large part thanks to our 3-P people we had placed in offices of those known to be "problematic" for the vice president. Miles said Phil Reston had called and will be sending both of us and Cal several cases of bourbon as thanks for preserving both his life and the life of the FA president and his new wife, Alyssa Russell.

I guess it is no surprise the FA showed up to assist in the defense of Bosch, not to attack as Abernathy had intended. By the time they arrived, the BPF had the situation well in hand. It's good to have friends, though. The important thing is that my island and my people are safe. Now, Matty and I, and what he is quick to say is *our* family, are going home to Bosch.

Epilogue

Saturday, July 30, 2366. Bosch, BPF green. Nine bells fifty-five minutes.

The sky is a brilliant blue. The sun has been up for some time, and with only a smattering of small puffy clouds, the day promises to be hot by early afternoon. Birdsong pours from the trees that speckle the base grounds. When there is a breeze, it brings with it the hint of the sea and the faint, plaintive cries from the seabirds.

I feel the sweat drip under my damnable and omnipresent shoulder brace and under my curls that Mama worked to get just right, even though I lost a bit of hair when Riki cut at my braid, and it tore away. I even let Mama, Carisa, and Gia fuss with me and make me up, though I did attempt to wipe much of it away a bit later in the washroom near my office. Betsy came in, saw me rubbing at my face, and then smiled.

"What's the matter, dear?" she asked. "Don't you like it?" She had taken the handkerchief from me and carefully dabbed where I had smeared.

This woman had made me feel at home from my first day

on Bosch, and she was about to become my right hand. I shrugged, looking in the glass at the two of us standing together. "I do like the look. But it's not really me, and I think the troops and guests should know what they are getting into."

Betsy had laughed. "Oh, my sweet friend, after all these years, I surely think they know."

I take my seat on the officer end of the dais at the right side of my master commander, with the four seasoned generals and Gia on the left. On the far side of the grandstand, sitting still and solemn, are the forty-eight recruits including Flossie Porter. Most are likely in various stages of hangovers, but they wait, eager to graduate and become part of the Bosch Pirate Force.

I look out at the sea of faces that fill the seats assembled across the green in front of the dais and extend far back. The Force side is a sea of black and red, with every trooper in their best uniform and wearing a three-cornered hat as a sign of respect. I see my comrades from each recruitment class, the units that have worked under my command, and the friends and compatriots I have had the honor to serve with. There are also almost a dozen empty seats in the center, left open to honor those who gave their lives in the battle of Haida as well as the ambushed Awilda. I will name each one aloud soon.

The civilian side is packed with citizens from every district in Bosch. So many familiar faces, and so many new, encouraging ones. There is even a special section for international guests, which include the president of the FA, with whom I cannot wait to chat; her husband, my friend Phil; and representatives from New Caribbean, Ruthenian, Tabonne, and even Mynia. Edo is unofficially represented by a distinguished older man (who is rumored to have involvement with Edo's infamous yakuza). He escorts a tiny, ancient priestess of The Way.

And then there is the family section. Mama wears a black tunic and Papa's second-best vest, the best one having accompanied him to the beyond. Carisa sits on one side of her, and Mama's beau, Jace Richmond, sits on the other. Next to him are Takai, Hayami, and little Sumiko. Then my three beautiful babies, safe and whole, sit in a line. Grey is wearing my general's vest. She has been talking with Ruth since we returned and with me. She had to learn some hard things, but she seems like she is healing. The boys argued about what they should wear and were thrilled when I offered them my three-cornered hat from graduation. I just happen to have two.

Next to the boys, Riki sits, proudly wearing the Citizen medallion Miles gave him for heroism and service to Bosch. And much to my delight, the next seat is occupied by Susan, who returned with us to Bosch and also sports the same medallion for all she did to keep me and my family safe. Riki has taken quite a shine to her, and I think the feeling is mutual.

Behind them are Peter and Sharon, Paul and Elise, and Mimi and Ryann, and their children sit, the children unusually calm and patient as if they know the day calls for patience. I'm guessing appropriate pirate bribes were involved. I know they were for me.

My eyes drift to Matty, who sits on the aisle of the Force side, one long leg extended casually as he leans back in his seat and smiles at me. He whispered to me last week that while he thought three children was an excellent number, four might be better. That had brought me to a sitting position in bed, where I gave him a quick run-down of some of the details of what a pregnancy and an infant would do to our lives. After I had finished and curled my back to his front, he had wrapped me in his strong arms and replied, "It's your body, so it's your call, but I think it sounds like hella fun."

And he wonders why I call him summer child.

The ceremony begins, and Miles gives his farewell speech that I have helped him edit and revise about six times. It's lovely and there is not a dry eye on the green when he finishes. Then all the generals but me come forward, and each says far too many words about Miles. This results in the audience—me included—rising to our feet and clapping for several minutes until Miles takes center stage again, quieting and seating us with a small hand gesture. He then simply says, "It is my pleasure to pass the office of master commander to a person who has shown through word and action her commitment to Bosch. General Wallace, please come forward."

I rise, hearing renewed applause and cheers, and walk to Miles, who looks as relaxed and delighted as I have ever seen him. He helps me don my elegant master commander vest, draping the left side over my bandaged shoulder, then kisses me on the forehead, peers down at me, and whispers, "I am so proud of you, Kat, and I know Teddy is as well." Then he steps back and salutes. We have practiced the transition ceremony, but his words catch at my heart, causing me to press my hand to my heart and smile at my friend and mentor before I return the salute as crisply as any trooper would. I turn once more to look upon the people who took me in so long ago and gave me a home.

I step aside from the podium, but decide, for decorum's sake, not to plop down at the front of the dais. "I don't think there is any way for me to truly express how absolutely astonished and profoundly honored I am to be here. Yes, for the receipt of the position MC Baldwin-Bosch, the council, and the general's table have granted me, but really, I mean I am honored to be *here*." I point to the earth below me with both index fingers and then open and spread my palms to encompass all the people I see. "It is because of all of you and your warmth, your generosity, your teaching, your friendships, and your challenges that I can say: This is my home. I am Bosch. I have the honor to serve as the master commander of Bosch. My name is Kat. Kat Wallace."

Notes

6. Diamonds, Kisses, and Tea—Just Your Usual Week

1. Edoan for intruder

10. Clue #2

1. *The Pirate-Ship* by William Bingham Tappan circa 1830

About the Author

Sarah Branson is the award-winning author of the four-book *Pirates of New Earth* series. Kat's presence in her life required her to learn to fly, fight and shoot. She looks forward to exploring what the next character has in store for her.

Sarah started conjuring stories of pirates at seven years old when her family hopped a freighter to Australia. Since then, she has grown up, traveling the globe, teaching middle and high school students, raising a family, and working as a receptionist, retail clerk, writing tutor, and certified nurse midwife.

She has lived in the US, Australia, Japan and Brazil and

traveled elsewhere extensively. Through these myriad experiences, she has developed a deep appreciation for people's strength and endurance and believes that badass women will inherit the earth.

Sarah now works full-time as a writer and an author creating stories of action, adventure, revenge and romance with characters you'll never forget. She lives with her husband in Connecticut.

For more information and updates:
www.sarahbranson.com

Acknowledgments

I am amazed at and grateful for the community that has grown and developed through the inspiration, creation, and writing of *Pirates of New Earth*. Some members arrived through friends and friends-of-friends, some appeared through my own searchings, and so many arose through the books themselves.

People seem to be drawn to Kat, her antics and adventures, her messiness, and her resiliency. While her time is three hundred years in the future and her career as a pirate is not one many of us can lay claim to, her story still resonates with us. She wants to make the world a better place for herself, her family, her nation, and those who are at risk. She works hard, screws up, tries again, and learns who she can depend upon and who she cannot. There is a bit of Kat in all of us and lots of all of us in Kat.

Because I opted to release the series rapidly, I have written and thanked folks several times over the past eleven months. But gratitude knows no bounds so I want to thank first and foremost every reader who has taken the time to get to know Kat and cheer at her successes, weep at her losses, and be furious with her enemies. You are each the reason she exists.

I was fortunate early on to find Martha Bullen who has advised and guided me, keeping me on my calendar, making suggestions for improvement, commiserating as necessary, and cheering with me at each success. While she is still the book coach I rely on, she has also become a cherished friend.

David Aretha and Andrea Vanryken are both skilled and

insightful editors and their combined knowledge and expertise have made my writing stronger and infinitely more readable.

Alan Hebel and Ian Koviak of The Book Designers have produced exquisite covers for each book in the series. Each new cover reveal has thrilled me and hit the mark for readers.

Maggie McLaughlin has negotiated the tangled web of uploading this book and the earlier ones to both Amazon and Ingram. She graciously accomplishes this even while hunkering down through a hurricane and patiently fixes errors (usually my own!) when I text her in a panic. Her good humor and calm demeanor are perfect for her position.

And my early readers–Brittany, Iris, Steve, Drew, Chris, Anna, Sally, Melissa, Cassie, Kate, Jacqueline, and Carey–willingness to read and review is such a support and an amazing gift of time and talent. They are each a treasure and as a group are everything an author could ask for.

Then there is the family. My children and their spouses, David and Jana, Megan and Josh, and Daniel and Jansu, have been steadfast in their support and enthusiasm of this venture their mother has taken up. I couldn't ask for more. The five grandboys are delightfully supportive, though they are a bit dismayed they cannot read the books yet. Don't worry guys, a more age-appropriate book is in the works.

And Rick, who makes this crazy voyage seem like the best adventure yet. I wouldn't want to take the trip with anyone else.

Also by Sarah Branson

Pirates of New Earth Series

Book One: A Merry Life

Book Two: Navigating the Storm

Book Three: Burn the Ship

Anthology

A Million Ways: Stories of Motherhood

Made in the USA
Monee, IL
13 March 2023